Rebeccah wasted no time now.

She got to her feet, watching her assailant trying to fight back nausea through clenched teeth. She ran to the car, making little high-pitched noises, but not thinking about them, not caring about them, all that mattered was getting—into—the—car. And then she was there, pulling the door shut, locking it.

She turned the car around and trained the headlights on him. She saw his eyes go wide and watched him lurch away lamely, as if he were in a potato-sack race for his life, and she steered the car toward him. She braked, not wanting to kill him, just hurt him enough to keep him from getting away, because she'd decided it was up to her to put a stop to this evil . . . .

*St. Martin's Press books
by Eugene Izzi*

THE TAKE
THE EIGHTH VICTIM
BAD GUYS *(coming in April 1989)*

THE EIGHTH VICTIM

EUGENE IZZI

ST. MARTIN'S PRESS/NEW YORK

THE EIGHTH VICTIM

ISBN: 0-312-91218-8   Can. ISBN: 0-312-91219-6

Printed in the United States of America

First St. Martin's Press mass market edition/October 1988

10 9 8 7 6 5 4 3 2 1

The Eighth Victim *is dedicated to Chris and Jan Heaney with love and gratitude*

Acknowledgments

I would like to give my deepest thanks to Philip Spitzer, the best agent in the world, Jared Kieling, the best editor I've ever known, Chris Heaney, the best friend you could ever have, and Bill and the Doc.

Without these five men this book would never have been published.

E.I.

Chapter One

Victor Perry was awakened from a much-needed and well-deserved sleep by the ringing of his telephone. He looked at the digital display on his bedside clock: 3:45. Goddamn. Not again. Why couldn't folks wait to die until daylight? He fumbled the receiver to his ear, croaked a hoarse noise into it, then cleared his throat noisily, cursing cigarettes, before trying again. "Hello? Lieutenant Perry here."

It was his wife.

"Vic?" she slurred. "Vic, izzatyou?"

Victor held the phone to his chest for a moment, took a deep breath, then put it back to his ear, exhaling carefully through his nose. "Yes," he said with patient effort, "it's me." Who the hell else would be answering my phone at 3:45 in the Christless morning. But he kept that to himself. About the only thing she hadn't accused

1

him of recently was being gay, and he saw no reason to present her with an excuse to do it now.

He said, "I thought we discussed your calling me when you've been drinking, Claire."

He got an amazed and drunken snort. "I have *not* been drinking," she said with a drunk's dignity. "I'm lonely, that's why I called." She began to sob.

Victor fought to stay detached. He couldn't help her, that he knew. . . . But it didn't keep the guilt away, that knowledge.

He tried to concentrate on decoding her drunken speech.

"IjezwannacomhomVicbabyohGodImissyouandI'll-quitdrinkin'."

He got it this time, by God, after all these months of practice. He had heard it all before.

"Good-bye, Claire," he said softly, and hung up the phone.

He rolled over onto his side, bunching the pillows up under his head the way he liked them, feeling them bend to the pressure of his head and forming around it, and tried to fight, once again, guilt that was never at all rightly his.

He thought of all the years he had come home drunk, staggering drunk, vomit on his pant cuffs and shoes, and he remembered Claire giving him alcohol baths and helping him to bed and making his coffee the morning after and coddling him, *enabling* him, he knew now, but being a good, loving wife, he had thought then. And he remembered her starting to drink with him, to be a companion, she had told him, a wife, a buddy, and then they both got hooked too far. He got off the merry-go-round and she had stayed on, and on and on all these years. And he remembered finally letting her go, asking her for a divorce, and her begging, telling him the one-night stands meant nothing to her, she would never have even thought of cheating on him if she hadn't been drunk, and she had never had any kind of answer for him when he asked, "Then why do you still drink?" She had only been able to look at him, knowing that he knew the answer to that one even better than she did.

And that was when he was finally able to admit to himself that it was over.

The phone rang again and he sighed, wishing just for a second that he was in a line of work where he didn't have to be on twenty-four-hour call. He took a breath, then answered again.

"You killed my baby," his wife whispered, getting all the venom she could into her voice, laying on the guilt as thick as she could, hitting him low, where she knew she could really hurt him.

"Claire . . ." But Vic's voice trailed off; he had no comeback. He gently put the phone back and bit back the bitter words he wanted to scream. Screaming would do no good now. There had been too many months and days and hours of that. Then, after the separation, when he felt he could see Claire unemotionally, with some detachment, there had been calm explanations, and she would sit across from him in the restaurant or the car or wherever they happened to be—but never home, he hadn't allowed her into the house since catching her there with another man—and slowly shake her head, looking down at her lap, and after several shakes she'd lift her head, for effect, and stab him right in the eyes with her deadly, accusing glare.

The calls would come shortly, any second now, he knew. He sighed and stared at the ceiling, hands behind his head, craving a smoke, thinking of a cancerous tumored lung to drive the aching away. It didn't want to work now, his simple little personal therapy. He wanted a smoke, and that was that. He thanked God that he had learned his lesson when he had stopped drinking. Get whatever it is you want to give up out of the house, or you'll grab it in a moment of weakness. He wasn't about to get up and get dressed now and run out to the 7-Eleven, or, worse yet, to a bar, to get a pack of smokes. He wasn't that bad yet. If he could give up alcohol, he could give up cigarettes. But, God, did his lungs ache.

He looked around the room at the good furniture in his bedroom, expensive stuff, stuff bought ten years ago and still holding up well. The two dressers, the leather chair he would sit and read in at night, before bed . . . shoulda put in a fireplace, give it a touch of class. King-size bed, which seemed way, way too big to sleep in alone.

No matter what he did, no matter how hard he tried to keep her from his mind, Claire kept popping back, he and Claire together when he would try to talk with her, like adults. Mature.

"SIDS, Claire," he would say, calmly, calmly, wanting to grab her by the shoulders and shake her and scream it into her face. "Sudden Infant Death Syndrome, Claire, crib death, that's what killed Elizabeth. Crib death. Not you, not me. If you'd only come to the classes with me, you'd learn that we have to get on with our lives, have to bury the guilt, rid ourselves—"

And it was here, always at this point, when getting help was mentioned, that Claire would begin her fascinating slow ascent, from staring down slowly, slowly, moving her head until her eyes were staring at his belly, then his tie, then his chin, and at last, the glare, right in the eyes, and the head would stop shaking and they'd stare at each other, frozen in a child's game, Vic foolishly trying not to blink or avert his eyes.

But he was powerless to stop the game. One day, he simply decided it wasn't worth the effort. If Claire wanted help understanding the death of their only child, if Claire wanted help coming to an understanding of her drinking, then Claire would by God in heaven have to ask for it.

And now the phone rang again and again, ten times each, then she'd stop to hang up and try again, and, as always, she would give up after sixteen times. Sixteen times. One hundred and sixty rings. As if it were all a game and she alone knew the rules.

Vic was tempted to unplug the phone, the hell with it. If he was really needed, he would be alerted by a plainclothes cop, or a nearby squad would be dispatched, right to the house. He had a busy day ahead of him, seven open files, seven bodies calling for justice to be done. Seven lives that once had been, and would be on his mind every waking minute. He would see their eyes open and vacant, staring off into an unknown and terrifying eternity, and he would remember, with clarity, each of them until the killer was brought to justice. Pinched, popped, put into the trick bag. Locked up and charged. Sometimes they got away, sometimes they were caught and did their time, and sometimes they died as violently as they had lived. But Vic remembered the victims, the rich and poor alike, until his end of the job was done.

It was one of the reasons he was a lieutenant so young. At thirty-six.

And it was also one of the reasons he hesitated to unplug the phone. If there was a late development in any of the seven open cases, he wanted to be the first to know.

In the end he let it ring, losing his count from time to time, thinking, trying to stay calm and in control, but getting misty-eyed remembering Elizabeth, those blue blue eyes sparkling with humor, her toothless grin upon spotting him, reaching for him, uttering unintelligible sounds which he took to be da-da and pa-pa, smacking wet sticky lips against his mouth and trying valiantly but with absolutely no success to hold her pudgy little legs straight on his lap while he held her.

Sleeping beside him, or on his chest, her baby breath sweet and milky on his face.

Smiling while his heart broke at her beauty, and his chest swelled with pride and love.

Gone now. Sweet Jesus Christ in heaven, all gone, never to return.

The phone stopped jangling, and the sudden silence shocked him from his reflections. He lay back and tried to relax, tried to empty his mind, but she was there, Elizabeth was, as if it were only yesterday.

Thom Geere's alarm went off at just about the time that Victor Perry was trying to ignore Claire's thirteenth call, and the buzzer dragged him blessedly up and out of a dream so real that each time he had it he would sit up screaming and would have to force his pillow into his mouth to keep him from waking up the other boarders in Mrs. Calloway's rooming house. Even after he knew it was a dream, *the* dream, he couldn't trust himself not to call out.

But this time the dream hadn't ended as usual, the kids hadn't caught him, they were still just calling names, screaming, maybe working up the nerve to attack, and so he could keep his hands away from the pillow, thank God. He sat up in bed and looked around him, his hangover pounding in his temples, thinking that the idea that had seemed so brilliant the night before seemed kind of dumb now, even scary. Could he do it; could he really do it? He popped two white crosses to get his eyes up and open all the way, then lit a joint. Cheap shit. He figured the next time he ran across Petey the Pear he'd kick his ass for him, selling him cheap shit probably cut with oregano, and as the speed began to course through his veins and the grass calmed his nerves he looked around him, thinking maybe his idea was a pretty good Halloween prank after all.

The room was big, as rented rooms go, and had its own bathroom and entrance, so Thom Geere always called it his "apartment," but Mrs. Calloway had no such airs about her and had very strict rules about no cooking, no loud music, no women upstairs, and he was bending the rules already, he knew, by hanging his pictures and his black light up on the ceiling, but he by God paid her thirty-five a week while the rummies holed up with their gin bottles down the hall got away with twenty, so she best not bitch too much, or he'd leave the fucking upside-down cross over the doorway the next time she came to change the sheets. That would show her.

As he dressed, looking at his handiwork completed in a delirious high the night before, the massive twelve-inch, three-inch thick phallus he had made out of modeling clay, he began to giggle. Yeah, it was one hell of an idea, and it was all a game anyway; it wasn't like he *believed* in any of the weird shit he hung on his walls and talked about with his friends over wine and dope and listened to at top volume on his Sony Walkman cassette player, it wasn't like he was a *real* goddamn devil worshiper. It was in fun. That's all. It was what all the kids were doing these days. Expressing themselves and shocking the old folks at the same time. It was a game.

The fact that Thom Geere still thought of himself as a kid at twenty-six was a good indicator of where his head was at these days, and as he dressed he plugged in the cassette, listening to the heavy metal group Iron Maiden, and the poster with the black light aimed at it made him shiver sometimes, until it seemed to *become* him, getting somehow inside him, and this was one of those times. He welcomed it, allowed himself to be taken over by the picture of a goat's head, with demonic, yellow-slit eyes, horned, with rotting teeth, a sick, evil grin on its half-human face.

He picked up his playthings, the false penis along with two putty breasts, and went silently out of the house, not wanting anyone to hear him leave on this Halloween morning.

Thom headed for the Church of Our Lady of Sorrows down the block from the boarding house, directly across the street from the house he had been born and raised in. He could have found the church blindfolded from anywhere in the city of Chicago, he believed. He had gone for eight terrible and cruel years to the school adjoining the church, had listened to all of the crap the nuns and the priests had told him, and had been terrified of hell and God since as long as he could remember. He had gone, every Sunday, with his mom and dad to Mass there, until much later, when his father had died, and when Mom had suddenly had a change of heart and joined up with that asshole spiritualist over on the East Side. That was where the *real* action would take place, tonight. He would start out here at this convenient rathole Catholic joint, see if he had what it took to desecrate a sacred building, a "House of Christ," and if he pulled it off—if he was man enough, as he liked to think of it—then he could wind the day up with a bang at the Church of the Spiritual Redeemer, and finally take his revenge on his mother and that stuck-up, pretty girl bitch, Rebeccah.

As he approached the church he paused, frightened. What if one of the little old ladies with the black dresses showed up early, as they always did? He sat on the curb before the church, lit another joint, and dropped four more white crosses. For courage. He smoked the joint and it came to him what he would do if one of those old bitches surprised him in the act. Oh yes, he'd give those religious hypocrites something to talk about.

He dropped the roach into the street, stood up, and walked to the side window that had been broken for years. He slipped into the church silently and began to work his magic.

He had the penis fastened to the figure of Christ on the cross, and the breasts he put on Christ's chest. He stepped back, admiring his work, panting from his efforts and from fear, sweating from the excitement. He had a cramp and doubled over, wondering if he would make it back to the boarding house before he shit himself, when a thought hit him, one even better than the first one about doing the deed to one of the old ladies in black. He strode forward, giggling now, and stood on the altar, then squatted down and began to defecate on it. It was then that the voice behind him called him, and he got so scared he jumped right off the altar with his pants down around his legs.

It was Sister Mary Bonaventure, principal of Our

Lady of Sorrows school, and she had been walking into the church, head down, solemnly praying as she did every morning at five minutes after four precisely, when she saw a figure atop the altar out of the corner of her eye. "Here, here!" she called out, "what in Heaven's name—" And she saw only his back, but that hair was indelibly etched in her memory, the wiry, uncombed, and uncombable bushy head of black hair that could only belong to—

"Thom Geere!" she called out. "What in God's name—" And she saw the crucifix now, and the unspeakable blasphemies performed upon it, and she was, for perhaps the first time in her life, struck dumb. In a split second she put it all together—Thom Geere, the desecration of the crucifix, his squatting on the altar doing, doing, dear God in Heaven, oh dear God in Heaven, he could not have been— And suddenly she was galvanized, forgetting her own safety, forgetting that she was giving up forty years and a hundred pounds to the young madman before her, and she raised her hand and rushed toward him, as if he were still an eighth grader smoking in the alley and needed to be punished for his sins, and Thom Geere pulled his pants up, collecting himself, and began to smile.

"Got a lady in black, after all, Mama," he said.

Vic was almost there now, on the ragged edge of sleep, when the phone rang again, shattering his peace. He leapt from the bed now, mad as hell, and grabbed the phone, shouting into it, "Claire, I swear I'll change the goddamn number—" when the male voice broke into his ear.

"Uh, Lieutenant Perry?" it asked.

"Yes," Vic said.

"Uh, sorry to bother you, sir, but, uh, we got a nasty one down in the Fourth, a bad one like we ain't never had."

"Who is this?"

"Oh, uh, sorry, sir. This is Patrolman Skelker. Fourth Precinct? Remember you met me at the—"

Vic cut him off, chastising himself at terrifying the young patrolman. The kid was young and full of ambition, like he himself had been once a while back.

"I remember you, Jim," Vic said, "And I'm sorry about the way I answered the phone. Working dispatch tonight?"

"No, sir," Skelker said, his confidence restored by the lieutenant's unexpected apology. "Detective Michaels just called in from Our Lady of Sorrows Church over in South Chicago, and asked me to call you and ask you to get there as soon as you can. I was first on the scene, and believe me, Lieutenant, you ain't never seen nothing like this."

Vic was fully awake now. Jim Skelker was no rookie; he had seen plenty of violence and death by now. Skelker wasn't given to exaggeration, either.

"You at the precinct house now, Jim?"

"Yes, sir." There was a pause, and Victor knew that Skelker had more to say but was embarrassed to say it. He waited patiently. That was one of his greatest character assets. He could wait with the best of them. Finally Skelker broke the silence.

"I had to get away, sir," he said, his voice nearly breaking. "I ain't never seen, never . . . words can't explain, sir." Victor liked Patrolman Skelker, and wanted to help him. He tried to now.

"You feel up to going back to the scene, Jim? If it's as

bad as you say, I'll need your opinions and impressions for my investigation."

He could almost feel a reassertion of control come over the wires from Skelker. Skelker said, "Yes, sir. I'm okay now." Then, acknowledging that this was not a social call, Skelker said, "I'll meet you at the scene, sir," and broke the connection.

Victor dressed hurriedly against the early-morning autumn chill, showering and shaving first, brushing his teeth, swirling a couple ounces of Listerine around in his mouth, wondering all the while what in the hell could make a veteran patrol cop like Jim Skelker so uneasy he would leave the scene of a major murder investigation. As he walked from the house and double-locked the door, he understood that the big day he had already planned on having had just gotten bigger. "Eight," he muttered, and, stuffing his hands into his coat pockets, trotted to the garage.

Chapter Two

The last mayoral election had been one for the books, even by Chicago's standards. The charges and counter-charges had been made and in most cases proved before the March primary had rolled around, with the kid gloves never even having been put on, let alone taken off. Racism, patronage, cronyism, straightforward crookedness, moneylending schemes, kickbacks, political favoritism, family favoritism, and even a hint of a murder charge pending had been mentioned between the candidates, all within the same political party. The Republicans had tried their best to take advantage of the Democrats' infighting and had gone all out to present an alternative, but theirs, once again, as at every election in the past thirty-five years, had been a token candidate. Chicago had been and in the foreseeable future would remain a Democrat's city. And when the smoke had cleared, the incumbent had gone the way of his two predecessors and been a one-term mayor. He jived and juked and talked trash for the cameras, but even after two recounts Edward P. Konrack remained victorious. His first official act as mayor was to beef up the Police Department, a convenient scapegoat of his immediate predecessors, and part of that beefing up was the creation of the Major Crimes Unit, or MCU, an elite task force of veteran officers, none below the rank of sergeant, who soon took on the name Major Murder Unit because that was the crime they investigated most often. Your spouse killings, your apparent motiveless random murder, these remained the domain of the homicide detectives in the precinct where the crime occurred. But the sensational murders, the serial killings, these were investigated and 85 percent of the time solved by the Major Murder Unit, and the unit was called out at the discretion of the commander of the precinct in which the murder had occurred.

On this Halloween morning, Detective Sergeant Lou Michaels had been the MCU Officer on Call, and he got the first impressions so valuable to a veteran homicide detective at the scene of a crime. In the five-man MCU team that Lieutenant Victor Perry commanded, Lou was the one the lieutenant was closest to, the one he spent most of his free time with, the one the lieutenant trusted the most, the one he had asked the captain for specifically when the mayor first assigned him to head one of the units. And because the MCU was an almost autonomous command, Perry, Michaels, and the rest of the team could easily and gratefully bypass the ass-kissing and game-playing that most detectives were forced to perform in order to be promoted or assigned. This was a godsend for both men, because the closest either of them ever came to political wheeling and dealing was exercising their right to vote in election years. And so the new mayor had their loyalty, respect, and, perhaps most importantly, their devotion, for now no politically connected suspect could make a call and have a detective reassigned, or even fired, as had been the case more than once in the past. The mayor had made it easier for them to do their jobs, and once the MCU team was on an investigation, it was on it until the thing was either solved or the suspects they came up with escaped through the legal loopholes available to them or until the detectives reluctantly had to leave them alone due to lack of evidence. And because of this power they carried, they walked softly, extremely softly, and made sure that every move they made was above suspicion. There were Old Guard members in the City Council just waiting for one of the MCU teams to abuse its power so they could cut off funding by making an example of the one unit involved. And so the units made no waves, made their arrests legally, and had the highest conviction rate of any MCU network in the nation. And it was this habit, this ingrained paranoia, the knowledge that certain party members were loyal to previous mayors in spite of the fact that the leader of the so-called Evil Cabal, the City Council Twenty-Nine, had turned the city around and made it a safe place to live in once again, that made Detective Sergeant Michaels call into the Fourth Precinct and ask that Vic, his friend and boss, be awakened and brought to the scene. He wanted to make good and sure that the unit's collective ass was covered, because he knew, instinctively, what a terrible panic this one was going to raise throughout the city.

* * *

When Perry arrived in his personal vehicle, a two-year-old Chrysler Imperial, he came to a stop two blocks from the police lines, and got out of the car and wondered, while locking it, how in the hell a couple of hundred people found out about a violent death, sudden and unexpected, well before dawn.

South Chicago, where he had been born and raised. Off the top of his head he could think of seven Catholic churches within a one-mile radius. The National Shrine to St. Jude was less than a block away from where he stood, leaning against his car, getting the feel again after all these years, looking at the brown and black faces smiling and laughing, most of them; some somber, some plain sad. He could barely make out Skelker and Michaels standing in the middle of the sidewalk, inside the orange police lines, heads together, waiting for him. Well, let them wait.

He was remembering when he could get anywhere in the city for a quarter and a nickel transfer. Wondering how long it had been since he'd been on a bus, how many years? He looked down the street, trying to make out the spire atop the Shrine to St. Jude.

Hell, it was housed now in a Mexican church, Our Lady of Guadalupe, where Hispanic priests said mass in their native tongue each day. Changes. Changes.

Changes scared the hell out of Vic Perry, and in his lifetime South Chicago had scared him many times.

A mile from where he stood, an enraged citizen named Richard Speck had slaughtered eight student nurses one drug-crazed night, taking his time, enjoying himself, changing South Chicago forever to its residents, making it a place to fear.

In his father's time it had been a mixture of Jews,

Italians, and Poles, a hodgepodge of working class and the elite, the consumer living right next door to the merchant, neither having reason to fear the other, as the businesses were run back then with pride and dignity and each customer was treated with respect. Vic could remember Tony's Standard Station on Commercial Avenue, where, for two bucks regular, you were entitled to a window washing and a courtesy check of the air in your tires, check the oil. Long gone, those days. Now it was all self-serve, and if you could get the attention of the goof behind the bullet-proof glass you might get a pack of smokes for under a buck-fifty, never mind a quart of oil, that's down the street in the K-Mart, for Chrissakes.

The sixties, when Vic was growing up, saw a stark change as the neighborhood began to turn, white middle class working stiffs running southeast a ways to Hegewisch, some even venturing as far as the suburbs, into Calumet City and Burnham, a stone's throw from the city proper but country living to the millworkers.

Republic Steel had become LTV and then had closed its doors, adding to the misery and depression of the area, where sons had once followed fathers and grandfathers into the mills, making a good buck, looking for a break, a better way for their families; some cracking under the frustration and humiliation of being jobless, losing homes and cars and families, seeing all their dreams go out the window when the unemployment benefits ran out, barely able to feed the children from the welfare money, watching their proud community go first black, then a mixture of Colombians and Puerto Ricans, right alongside the Mexicans who had *always* been there, but were such good neighbors they were tolerated and even liked.

Vic used to go into the city, down into the Loop, and stand under the El tracks, waiting, out of the way, far back from the curb where it seemed that any time of day there would be a crowd waiting to cross going in either direction, and wait for tourists. He could always tell them, for they were the ones who ducked down and cringed with fear as the trains passed overhead with a deafening roar of steel on steel and the rush of air as the metal bullet split the sky above them. He never said anything, but he'd smile. This was his city, it belonged to him, and he loved it, each and every street and neighborhood inside its boundaries. Tall, strong, and powerful as a teenager, Vic felt safe and secure, a part of any neighborhood he entered, and he was accepted. His dark good looks gave him some mystery and power, and his clean good clothes set him apart, separate but equal, from the rest. So he'd hear the blues on the South Side, eat ribs and shrimp and Polish Sausage at Mr. BeeBees', get back on the bus and head north, watch the queers strolling arm in arm, dressed to kill, watch the blue-haired old rich ladies walking their dyed poodles down Michigan Avenue, unaware that they could throw a stone with their shriveled old arms and it might well fall in the shadow of Cabrini-Green, one of the fiercest public housing projects in the nation. Even Vic never strolled into the Green. Hell, the cops stayed out of there if they could.

Changes. Chicago had seen many of them even in Vic's time. And they had all been scary.

But the change that frightened him the most was this seemingly sudden new attitude toward death, the increase in senseless violent crime—that scared the hell out of Vic Perry.

Vic pushed himself away from the car, lost in

thought, looking up at the facade of GayDay's Ice Cream Parlor where he used to blow his allowance for the week on a hot fudge sundae, staying in one of Papageorge's booths until dark, acting like a big kid, trying to be tough.

It seemed to Vic that it had all started, the terrible downhill slide of South Chicago, after the nurse murders. After Speck. Suddenly people were locking their doors. Men and women who had been neighbors for years suddenly argued and shouted about the senseless crime; doors started being locked at dusk and children were called in earlier than before. Suddenly the people seemed to know that it could happen here after all, and their idea of the American Dream changed. It was no longer owning your own home that mattered, nor having a good job in the mill. It was having the job and the home in an area where things like the murders of eight student nurses didn't *happen* that these people wanted, and the real estate signs started popping up. Those that could afford it, moved. The whites started drifting south a little ways to the East Side and Hegewisch, and the Hispanics and blacks came in bunches, forced by economic necessity into homes the middle-class whites no longer wanted. They did not turn South Chicago into a ghetto, not by any means. The lawns remained tended carefully, mown neatly. The hedges were trimmed. The problem was, after the whites moved out, the politicians seemed to think that South Chicago didn't exist any longer, and the funds that once were available suddenly dried up.

And the younger, bolder generation of gangbangers moved in.

There had always been gangs and knife fights and death, sometimes, not often, and sometimes, someone would even get shot. That was a part of life. But some-how, as far as Vic was concerned, it got all bollixed up and respect seemed to wither and blow away with the spring wind as the aimless took to the streets at night, preying upon the old and infirm, the weak and fright-ened. And they had no regard or respect for the law.

As a kid Vic used to play cards sometimes in the summertime with Bone and Bird and Ralphy and the Claw, and when the squad car would pull along the curb they would leave the cards, the money, beer, every-thing, and run like hell, for all they were worth, praying they would not be taken down to the Fourth Precinct house and forced to sit on the hard wooden bench until their fathers could come down and get them. They weren't afraid of the cops so much as they were afraid of the look in their parents' eyes when they picked them up, the disappointment, the shame. Back then it was not a badge of honor to have been arrested. You didn't brag about it to your friends. It was not a rite of manhood. And you stayed away from the guys who went to St. Charles and the Audy Home, not because they scared you, but because they were unworthy of respect, these bums. And you *respected*.

When the coppers pinched you, for, say, walking down the street in an unfamiliar neighborhood, you didn't con them or jive them, you didn't give them a ration of shit and scream about your rights or call them Nazis, you yes-sirred and no-sirred, and spoke only when spoken to and you stood straight and hoped your hair wasn't too long or they'd figure you for a hippy and run you in and search up your ass for drugs. You gave them respect because they were the man, the main, main man, and they had the gun and the badge and the power, and don't you ever forget it.

THE EIGHTH VICTIM

Vic didn't know if it was the breakdown of the family or the influence of the gangs or the changing of the neighborhoods or the civil rights riots of the sixties or if it was the fucking Supreme Court, but, son of a bitch, suddenly, there was no more respect to be found in the city of Chicago. Suddenly, they were no longer the man, but the pig. Today, even the lowest-level drug pusher and numbers runner made more than your average rookie cop, unless, of course, he was on the take, which was anyone's guess. Today, you stopped kids staggering down the street so wasted they can't see straight and you had to listen about their *rights*. And when you took them home—the precinct station cells were far too crowded—you caught hell from their mothers. "Picking on my baby, you bastard; why aren't you out there busting John Wayne Gacy or something, getting the rapists and murderers off the streets?"

Vic plowed through the corner crowd of onlookers, ignoring the questions, the shouted insults, pinning his badge to his coat so he would be let through by the uniforms facing the crowd at the barrier. When he reached Michaels and Skelker, Michaels was telling the story about a narcotics bust he had taken part in. Vic came and stood quietly next to them, acknowledged only by a brief nod from both cops. There would be no gossip outside the church, no speculation, no investigation begun into this case until they were inside, after the crime-scene guys were gone, and they were away from the crowds and the damn press, who were even now standing outside the police lines, jostling, shouting at the stone-faced officers in uniform about the Almighty First Amendment, and were ignored for their efforts.

"So we got this guy," Lou was saying, "this big black guy, make William Perry look like a pansy, dead to rights. Cold. He had four keys of coke in the trunk of his ride, which was impounded for evidence, and while he's sitting around, shooting the breeze with us, waiting for his boss to pop up with a lawyer and get him the fuck outta there, before he starts singing, he goes, 'C'mon, fellas, I can understand why youse gots to be nailin' me, but does you-all gots to take my bro-ham away from me?' Right away I get excited, see, on account of I think this asshole's bro is somehow in on the drug thing and he just accidentally ratted on him. We started on him heavy, and after five minutes it gets clear that he's talking about his Cadillac. He's got this Fleetwood Brougham, see, that we impounded? Christ, was I embarrassed, but I learned a lesson. I cornered this big black Gang Crime sergeant one night and he taught me the black slang I needed to know, so that I'd know what in the hell the ghetto boys was talking about." Skelker laughed politely and Vic smiled. He had heard the story before.

He was staring into the church, watching for the forensic boys to finish dusting, picture taking, and the such, and as soon as he saw the ME walk away from the corpse he began walking toward the double doors. Skelker and Michaels followed, silent, all business now. They had both been inside the church earlier, and knew that what was before them was no laughing matter.

The ME came toward them, his usually jovial face stern, white, chalk-white, shaking his head. He shook hands with Vic, nodded to Lou and Skelker, and said, "I guess it had to happen, Vic, goddammit." He looked around him at his surroundings. "Sorry," he near-whispered, then said, "Cause of death would appear at this time to be from severe trauma to the brain, in other words, Vic, she was beaten to death. Raped, too, while the beating was going down. We've got sperm samples, should have some pubic hairs and the blood type for you before lunch, if anyone's gonna eat lunch after seeing that." He pointed his thumb over his shoulder, at the church. "You got a search going in the area?"

Vic nodded. The precinct boys would have begun that before Michaels was even called into things.

"Tell them your perp has pants full of shit. There's fecal matter on the altar, some on the floor too; obviously the maniac was caught in the act by the victim. The stuff on the floor is smeared, so it's all over his shoes, probably down his leg and on his shorts.

"Now here's one for you. There's modeling clay stuck on the chest and the legs of the crucifix, just splotches of it, as if the perp had fastened some sort of shape to the body, then, after killing the victim, panicked and tore the things off. I'll have more for you in a couple hours, I guess."

He looked up at Perry now, seriously, all of their usual banter and joking a thing of the past as far as this case was concerned. "Did you know I was raised Catholic?" he asked.

Perry looked at him, said, "As was I, Doc," then watched as the ME walked from the building, followed by his crew and the rest of the forensic team. The building and its unholy bounty belonged to them now. Vic walked to the body, got on his knees, and studied it. There were bruises and marks and cuts all over the face, and the victim had died fighting. Her face still held the determination and terror she had been feeling at death. He took a deep breath, remembering her, his own sixth-grade teacher, twenty-some odd years back, her strict, no-nonsense approach to life and teaching, telling the boys they would all be hoods and riffraff, accusing the girls of hiding razor blades in their ratted-out hairdos, somehow inspiring them to double their efforts to get good grades, so they could win her approval and not grow up to be the animals she said they would certainly be if they did not study and go on to college—and if they were very, very good and never had sex or smoked or took a drink of alcohol, maybe, just maybe, they would make it to Purgatory for a couple of million years before being allowed into the Great Presence. He closed his eyes and shook his head to take away the memories, hoping the precinct boys would find this one strolling around the neighborhood, maybe watching from a distance, the way some of them did.

He was afraid of what he would do if and when he found him. He turned to Michaels. "Call the rest of the team, get them here. I want the priest, the altar boys, the old ladies who line up and wait for the doors to be unlocked, all of them, in the rectory in one hour. We gotta get this son of a bitch, Lou, now, today."

Lou Michaels was staring at him, almost shocked.

"Did you know, Lou, that I went to school here? Went to Mass here maybe a million times?"

Lou stirred, then said softly, "Maybe we oughta let another unit have this one, Vic."

Perry looked at him, level-eyed and steady. "No," he said, and waved to the meat-wagon boys that it was okay to take the body away.

He walked to the altar, his eyes drawn involuntarily to what lay in the center of it. This, he knew, did not necessarily have to be part of whatever desecration the killer had planned. He knew full well that a lot of small-time crooks and thieves couldn't control their bowels during a score, this was no big thing. But on the altar, for God's sake.

He studied the clay fragments between the legs of the wooden figure of Christ hanging on the cross, then let his eyes travel up to the chest. Okay, a long clay cock was probably attached, and maybe tits, women's tits, on the chest. Or else some sick words across the chest. Christ, it had been a long time since a murder scene had shocked him.

He was remembering Sister Mary Bonaventure, the naked, gray-skinned body now on its way to the ME's office for autopsy. Guilt again, remembering even farther back, kidding with the guys after school while sneaking smokes in the alley. "Think she's got any up there?" Trying to outdo each other, gross each other out. "Think she got any hair on her pussy?" Or, "Think the father's gettin' any of that?" Or, "Do they bleed?" The mystery of the women in the long flowing garments and vestments; the mystery of women in general magnified a thousand times in their immature minds by these chaste so-called "wives of the Lord." He took out his penknife and cut a sample of the clay out of the groove in the wood where it had been placed, put the clay, wrapped in his handkerchief, into his pocket, and turned to Skelker.

"Get somebody in here to clean this up."

He drew Lou aside. "Go pick up Ray and Mick. You can call Mick if you want, tell him we'll be working out of the Fourth Precinct on this one, but stop by Ray's, and knock lightly. His old lady's expecting any day now, we don't want to bother her." What he didn't want to add was the fact that he himself would not, if he could help it, go over to Tomczak's. For months now he had been worried that Ray Tomczak was crooked, and suspected that Ray was under investigation by the head-hunters down at the Office of Professional Standards.

Just what the MCU needed for a vote of confidence from the public. Dirty headlines.

"What about the office over at the Seventh?" Lou asked.

"I'll call, make sure it's held. Christ, you got any idea how many Catholics there are in this city? This'll take a definite priority." Sure it would, and the little girl with the dark eyes, the old lady burned to death in her sleep, the wife of the U.S. Steel executive raped and murdered behind the garage, in her own alley, and the four others, the four unavenged others, would have to wait. But he didn't tell Lou that. Instead he said, "I'll call Frank and Bobby soon as I get to the precinct, make sure they don't head north."

Lou turned to Skelker, who was coordinating the clean-up crew that had been waiting inside the meat wagon, smoking cigarettes and drinking coffee, cursing that this had to happen so close to the end of their shift. Lou ordered Skelker to get on the street as soon as he was through, searching the neighborhood, looking for witnesses, locating any possible evidence dropped or left behind by the suspect. Anybody who could do this could not be too damn smart. Maybe they'd get lucky. He prayed they'd get lucky. Not for the nun's sake, but for the unit's. They sure as shit didn't need eight fucking open cases.

The men in the unit were used to late-night calls. When a hot new one came in, they had to be told where to report, what precinct would be giving them space. On Halloween morning they had three reserved offices already, relating to their seven cases. Usually, one or two of the men would be working on a case in any given precinct, the others spread out around the city, gathering evidence, questioning witnesses, sending bluesuits out on the shitwork, commandeering them out of squad cars and away from desks, giving their lives some glamour and excitement. Not on this one, however. Everything would be put on hold for this case. The entire MCU team would be, as they rarely were, in one place at the same time, together, concentrating on getting their man.

Bobby Franchese was sleeping when the phone shattered the silence of his bedroom. His wife, used to the late-night intrusions his job forced upon them, didn't stir. Bobby came fully awake by the second ring, had the phone to his ear and was listening intently, without comment, to his boss, then hung up with only a soft "Okay" in reply. Bobby stretched twice, as hard as he could, then rolled from bed and headed for the bathroom to shower.

He was a light-skinned black man, the product of an Italian soccer star and a black South Side mother. He called himself, in moments of jest, the Chicago Franco Harris. He was six feet six inches tall, and weighed an even one-ninety. This naturally fooled a lot of people into thinking he was just another tall and skinny spade who couldn't make it in the NBA. Bobby's height and tailored suits masked the tight, ropy muscles of a long-jumper. He could chin himself a dozen times with one hand—either hand—and his speed was equaled in the unit only by Mick Muldoon, who worked long and hard in a South Side gym studying karate. But even Mick would think twice before going heads-up with Bobby. Bobby's easygoing, laid-back nature had fooled more than one murder suspect who decided to make his move, then lived to regret it.

Within an hour Bobby was showered, shaved,

dressed, and in his car on his way to the Fourth Precinct, drinking coffee from a White Hen insulated cup, his mind racing through his personal mental file of crazies. But he couldn't come up with a single name he could figure for this one.

Mickey Muldoon was awake when Lou Michaels knocked on his door. He was always up before dawn, every day, without fail. This habit gave him time to meditate, stretch, and do some yoga exercises before he began his workday.

He lowered himself, each morning, to the floor, crossed his legs and placed his heels well onto the opposite thigh, cleared his mind of all worldly preoccupations, everything—ex-wife, his kids, his cases, his financial problems—then imagined himself floating, on his back, out beyond the horizon of Lake Michigan, on a calm day, almost without waves, the sun gently kissing his exposed skin, clouds white and gentle above him, the call of gulls the only sound for hundreds of miles. Slowly, slowly, inch by inch, Mick would see himself begin to submerge—there, his calves and buttocks were completely under, the water just starting to lap at his chest, lightly stroking at his nipples in gentle waves. Now his ears filled with water, and the hollowness of deep water blocked out even the gulls' cries. He kept his eyes open as water filled them, blurred his vision, obscured the clouds. Now the whole world was blue, at peace, and he felt within himself a calmness he would never feel in the presence of any other human being. Totally adrift, his heart slowed, his breathing coming in far-apart, long breaths, Mick, relaxed and off somewhere beyond reality, meditated.

He thought a fish of some kind was disturbing him

and allowed his subconscious mind to run free, as he turned his head under water, looking for the disturbance. He forced himself to remain calm and serene, in control of his meditation, but his heartbeat had jumped slightly as he remembered the many times a case had been solved in meditation, while he, without the constraints and distractions of reality, became one with the facts and evidence, his mind speeding through data more swiftly than any computer could, and suddenly there it would be, a face swimming next to him, and he would have it all, would ascend back into the now with the answer he had been searching for, and had known all along, somewhere, somehow, on some level in his mind.

Proving it, of course, was another matter altogether. Judges didn't smile upon police officers asking for arrest warrants based on metaphysical conclusions. But he would know, with certainty, who the bad guy was, and that made his job and his life a hundred percent easier. All he had to do then was concentrate fully on the suspect, and eventually, as they all did sooner or later, he would fuck up.

So now Mick studied the disturbance in his meditation, wondering which of the seven open files he might solve today, mystifying Vic and the rest with what they called his "hunches," until he realized it was not in his meditation, this disturbance. This was someone, some *asshole* knocking at his door before the sun came up. He always disconnected his phone before meditating, but had yet not found a way to keep people the fuck away from his front door. He dragged himself back to the floor, away from the loveliness of the refreshing blessed blue waters, and padded barefoot to his basement apartment's front door to allow entry to his buddy and partner, Lou Michaels.

He would not ever mention that his meditation had been interrupted, that was not allowed by the Way, anger was not a part of his life, and it would not be honorable to invite a guest into your home and insult him, at least before serving tea. But throughout the day Mick would know he hadn't had his full half hour. He would feel dragged down, worked out by lunchtime. By the end of the day he would need all of his mental strength even to keep his eyes open. Maybe, at lunchtime, he could grab a half-hour, sneak back to his apartment, and do it right, allowing him then to go forth without sleep all night and into the next day if need be. He tried not to think of cuss words as he warmed the tea, tried to remain positive and accept the intrusion for what it was. Tried to put it in perspective.

Karma. Fuck it.

Ray Tomczak heard the car pull up in the driveway and thanked God he hadn't yet put on the storms up here, on the second floor. This weekend, if the kids and his outside business would allow it, and, of course, if Tina didn't have the kid. . . . He had been in the academy with Franky Meadows, an old-timer back then, at twenty-five, and he was thirty-eight now, the oldest man in the unit, and he cursed himself and his lousy luck every time he thought of a man Victor Perry's age being a lieutenant, even though he himself had more money squirreled away than Perry would ever see even if Vic made Chief of Police some damn day, which wasn't out of the realm of the possible, seeing who Vic's fucking rabbi was.

Now he opened the window and waved down at Lou

and the Mick—smiling inwardly, thinking, fuckin' Irish bastard playing Chinaman—and signaled that he would be right down. He put on his bathrobe, smiled kindly down at the very pregnant belly of his wife, thinking, please, let it be a boy, God, please, then let himself out of the bedroom and walked softly down the steps, wondering why, knowing damn well that the other three kids would already be awake and watching cartoons, fighting among themselves quietly, terrified of waking up Daddy. And he was right, there they were, looking at him with wide eyes, frightened, wondering what a car was doing in their driveway this early in the morning. Ray opened the back door for his fellow officers, listened to the news, and waved them to the kitchen table. He put on the coffee and laid out the cream and sugar, happy that he would, at least for today, be taken off the dead-end fucking murder case Perry had assigned him to work—alone, mind you—happy to be back in the saddle, going after a hot one, by God, one where the body would still be warm when he got there. He brought in the paper and told the men he'd be right down, help themselves to the fridge, and went into the living room, got assurances that the dog had been let out and fed, and the beds were all made, teeth all brushed and faces all washed, breakfasts all eaten. Good kids. Self-sufficient, like their old man had taught them, like *his* old man had taught *him*.

He walked back upstairs to dress and say good-bye to his wife, and leave her a scrap of paper with the Fourth Precinct's phone number written on it, in case she thought the kid was coming.

Ray Tomczak had his worries, and he was involved in some things, but he knew in his heart that everything he did he did for his family, and so that made it all right.

* * *

Franky Meadows was a wild redheaded lady-killer, and one of his conquests was beneath him now, in his small garden apartment on the North Side, a place for which he paid eight hundred a month because it was on the seventeenth floor and he could see the lake through the sliding glass door that led to his garden—fifteen square feet of balcony, a garden apartment in a high-rise, for Chrissakes. Only in Chicago, he figured, could a builder have enough clout at city hall to be able to advertise garden apartments on the seventeenth floor. The phone rang as he was grunting with orgasm, pounding wildly into the little bit of fluff beneath him, curing his slight hangover, starting his day off the right way. He rolled off her cursing, went to the wall phone in the tiny kitchen panting like a racehorse, and told Vic Perry he had just come in from jogging when the lieutenant asked him what the fuck was the matter. He listened for a minute, muttering "Christ" every few seconds, pissing Vic off, he knew, but genuinely outraged at what had been committed that morning. He hung up and went to the fridge, took out a pre-mixed vitamin breakfast supplement, and drank the whole thing. He took out a couple of eggs, cracked them into a coffee cup, and drank them raw. Ahh. Breakfast. He turned to the woman on the bed.

More girl than woman, now that he got a good look at her. The night had made off with some of her beauty, but she still looked pretty good to him, even after. That was the mark, to him—how they looked after. All women, to Franky, were lovely and mysterious before. He smiled and said, "So, you want a roll or anything before you take off?"

THE EIGHTH VICTIM

* * *

The team was all together now, sitting and standing and lounging in the room the Fourth Precinct had given up for them, set up with a Mr. Coffee machine, all the comforts of home except for their own telephone line, which would be put in that morning. An old blond wooden desk was against the far wall, with a matching chair in which Vic sat. The walls were the institutional green common in police stations around the country, except maybe in some progressive places like Beverly Hills. There was an urgent mood to the group. They had been out already, gathering bits and pieces, assigned by their boss, who had stayed behind, administrating, getting the okay to go ahead with this one at full speed, getting his other seven files reassigned until they cracked it. Lou was speaking now, and the other detectives listened carefully.

"Father Campeau's right, then Skelker missed the guy by a couple of minutes, tops. He said he heard somebody crashing through the bottom-right swinging window as he came in through the Sacristy for Mass." He stopped for a swig of coffee and to take a bite out of a doughnut Vic had brought in from the Dunkin' Donuts on Commercial Avenue, a block away, then continued.

"Priest comes in, same as always, him and his pastor switch 5 A.M. Mass every week, and obviously they made enough noise to scare off the asshole, who ran for the window he had busted coming in. No glass missing but the lock was busted off; maybe we should be looking for a twisted pro, who could get in without breakage?"

Victor looked up from his cup, which he had spent the last half hour staring into. "Forget it," he said. "That lock's been broken off since I went to school there, for Chrissake." He looked at Ray. "Make a note, Ray. After we split up, go over to the school, get the records of every kid ever went there, as long back as they keep them. There'll be pictures inside, and handwritten notes from the nuns, explaining every infraction of the school rules the kids ever committed, and the punishment they got. I'm betting the guy went to school there, and if he grew up to be able to do something this sick, by the eighth grade *some* sort of sick behavior would have been noticed. Those nuns might have scared the shit out of us, but they were sharp."

Ray looked aghast. "You know how many fucking kids went through that school since they opened, Vic?" he asked. "Shit, gotta be thousands."

"Ray, by noon we'll have a hair color and blood type. That'll cut the records at least into thirds. Cross-index, I'll get you a bluesuit to cull out the ones don't have the right hair or blood, you get that from the school nurse's card in the kids' jackets, then you go through the others. Get your list and get ahold of me. Got it?"

Ray nodded, still mad, but not wanting to push it in front of the others. Fucking hot dog, he thought. Then had an idea. "Vic? What if the killer's just a random transient, or, keeping in mind that he knew about the window being busted, how about he maybe didn't go to school there, just church on Sunday? For that matter he mighta just been walking around the church, trying windows. Could be a waste of time." He looked hopefully at Vic, who just stared back at him. Long seconds passed. Ray looked away. "Right, Vic. I'll have the list soon's I can."

Vic turned to Bobby Franchese. "That's a good idea about the transient, though. Hit all the boardinghouses, all the rooming houses, all the places with rooms-for-rent signs in private houses. Talk to the owners, managers, whatever, find out if any boarders been acting strange, talking funny. This doesn't play like some stable All-American Boy who just freaked out. Odds are we got a loner, this kind of behavior. Shit, who'd want to be friends with a psycho like this?"

Bobby smiled without humor. "Other psychos, Vic," he said. "You got it."

"Franky?" Vic said.

Meadows turned away from the window, itching for action, hoping his wouldn't be some shit detail like Ray had caught.

"God's still in heaven, Franky, calm down," Vic said, getting a laugh. "And remember, I'm Catholic, too, huh? When we break up, you go down the hall, talk to the dicks, find out the names and addresses of anybody arrested the last couple of years for any kind of the crazy stuff—killing animals, bizarre rituals, anyone suspected to be members of any satanic cults, anyone caught writing anything about Satan or the like on public buildings.

"Mickey, go over to the high school, talk to the principal, counselors, disciplinarians, if they still got those around, find out who if anyone writes '666' on the lockers, on their notebooks, the same thing as Franky's doing, only on a smaller level.

"I figure it for a local, either a kid caught in a prank that got way outta hand, or some weirdo honoring Satan on Halloween; either way, he's local. Priest heard nothing after the guy escaped, or else, if the guy *was* in a vehicle and parked it further away, where the priest wouldn't have heard it, he'd probably head right for home, clean up, get the shit off his legs. If it was someone out of the precinct, he woulda gone ahead and done his thing in his own neighborhood. Let's get to it and clear this one up, we can get it over with and have this animal off the street before Ray's Tina has the kid. Hey, Ray, you gonna name the kid after me?"

Ray looked at him, his mad over, itching for action now, wanting to get the shitwork over with and into the action part, and he tried to hide the smile fighting to break through the deadpan exterior that was his trademark. "Yeah, Vic, I wanted to, honest to Christ, but Tina said no kid of hers would ever be named Asshole Tomczak." He abandoned the battle then and grinned, and Vic smiled back while the others laughed. It was okay now between them.

They spent another half hour rehashing the statements they had been given by others at the scene, and came up with nothing else. Outside of the assistant pastor, no one had seen or heard anything. Or claimed to, at least. They split up, Vic making sure the Mr. Coffee was turned off, no use repaying fellow cops' kindness with a fire, and as he walked to the door, buttoning his coat against the early chill outside, Ray asked him where he could reach him if he needed him.

"Well," Vic said, "what's left to do?"

Lou shrugged his shoulders. "Interview the nuns at the convent?"

"There's hope for you yet, Lou," Vic said, adding loudly, to the milling detectives, "One more thing I want to make clear—" when he was interrupted by a knock at the door. Lou opened it, puzzled; any bluesuits would simply have stuck their heads in the door, and any other detectives would have barged in as if they owned the place.

The young man outside was dressed in blue work clothes, with an ILLINOIS BELL patch over the left-hand pocket of his shirt. He was sweating, in spite of the cold, and when he entered the room the web belt of tools around his waist made a loud clanking in the dead silence he had caused.

"Installation?" he said.

"Card?" Lou said.

"What?"

"Where's your card?"

"Which card do you mean?"

"Hey, chico, lemme tell you something," Lou said. "We're fuckin' *cops* here, our own people put in the lines, for Chrissake." He chuckled, and the other cops walked out past the young man, shaking their heads at his stupidity, clocking him already for what he was, ignoring him, too much to do to waste time getting mad at his childish trick.

"You need to have a card, pal," Lou told him, playing with him, having some fun. "Since all the old ladies were opening their doors to any asshole went down to the Goodwill and got a used pair of work clothes from Ma Bell, then went around, banging on doors, raping and robbing. A card with your name and picture, proves you work for the phone company."

"I left it at home," the young man said, acting a little pissed now, wondering why the hell this guy was giving a working stiff a hard time. "I didn't think you guys would be worried about it, you know?" Sarcastic now, putting the cop in his place. "Tell you what, though, I'll go get it, okay? Then you all gotta wait maybe another three hours to get your phone installed."

"I already told you, we do our own stuff around here," Lou said, tired of arguing with this dipshit when he had better things to do. "Now, what paper are you with?"

"Okay, all right, look, let's just forget about the whole thing, okay? Fuck it." He was sweating terribly now, and his tongue darted out constantly, wetting his lips. He turned to leave, and Lou shook his head, turning to look at Vic.

"Hold it," Vic said.

The young man stopped dead in his tracks, one hand on the doorknob, and turned slowly to eyeball Vic. "Lieutenant Perry? Look, I don't want a problem, all right? Just let me take off, this never happened." He was scared now, thinking of what his editor would say if Vic Perry, MCU squad leader, called him and beefed about this thing.

"What paper you with, kid?"

The reporter sighed. "I'm Dooley, *Times.*"

"You're under arrest, Dooley, *Times,*" Vic said, trying not to smile, enjoying getting a little bit back for a change. "It's illegal to come on as a telephone repairman, didn't you know that? Impersonating a public worker, could get you a year and a day in the County." He turned to Lou. "Go get a bluesuit in here, will you? Have him process this guy for us. We got enough to do." He turned to Dooley as Lou went out. "Up against the wall, Dooley, spread 'em."

"Aw, come on, goddammit," Dooley hissed, "I'm a reporter, man, not some rapist!"

"You're a lawbreaker," Perry said calmly. "Now you and me, maybe we could have straightened this thing out, Dooley, like a couple of men. But you have to come in here, insult my intelligence in front of the entire unit. I gotta bust you, even if you don't *like* it and even if I don't want to do it."

"Look, can't we talk this over, Perry?" Dooley said, alone with Vic now, trying to understand the cryptic message Vic was sending him. "I mean, you don't want to bust me, and I don't want to get busted. That's established. Now, what can I do to get off the hook, make up for insulting your intelligence?" There was no glimmer of sarcasm or guile now.

This was even better than Vic had hoped for. He had no idea what he would do with the kid, now or in the future, but it never hurt to have a reporter owe you one. He walked over and perched on the edge of the desk, eyeing Dooley closely, evidently wondering if he should let him go.

"I cut you loose, Dooley, give you a break, I save you a lot of face around the newsroom, save you a lot of bullshit, editorial ethics review, court appearances, like that, right?"

Dooley nodded his head, not trusting himself to speak.

"I let you go, you owe me. A big one. And I don't want you running back to the paper, writing some bullshit column about me or my unit, you got that?"

Dooley swallowed as Vic spoke, knowing that his face had given him away. It was as if the cop had read his mind.

"On account of if you do that, Dooley, I swear, I'll haul you back in, instate the charges. I got a year to make up my mind on you, kid. Don't forget that."

Lou came back into the room with a uniformed officer, raising his eyebrows at his lieutenant, who winked back. He turned to the bluesuit and dismissed him, thanking him for his time, then turned his full attention to Dooley, enjoying himself, giving him the full weight of a stare that had broken more than one hardened convict.

"We got a deal?" Vic said. "Or do I call the officer back in?"

"We got a deal, Lieutenant."

"Good." Perry ignored him now, turning to Lou, and Dooley stood there, frozen, afraid to leave without dismissal.

"Vic?" Lou said. "What were you going to say, before, when Dooley here made his grand entrance?"

"Oh, yeah," Vic said. "No talking to the press on this one, not even to friendly reporters." He turned to Dooley now, looking surprised to see him.

"You still here?" And he smiled at Dooley's back as the reporter swaggered to the door, getting some of his cockiness back already. Vic was wondering how he could put this newly "friendly" reporter to his best and greatest use.

Chapter Three

Rebeccah Lesco was exercising early Halloween morning, as usual. Up at dawn, a quick brisk run down Ewing Avenue to the park, down to the sand, then south along the beach as the gray was just creeping into the sky. She was moving at a slow, easy pace now, through the Forest Preserve property behind the city itself and before Lake Michigan that was like a buffer between the eternity of the water and the fresh upstart that was Chicago. Then back onto sand again, somewhere along the line having crossed into Indiana after running less than three miles. On the beach, staring off, a little angry as she watched the foam break with the waves onto the golden sand, the bastard child of the chemical companies and the refineries just across the way. Catching her breath now, her long red hair damp with sweat—no, women didn't sweat; she laughed at the memory of her mother's words, laughed aloud, alone there on the beach; women *glowed*. Animals sweated, men perspired, and women glowed. Then remembering her father, the Reverend Francis P. Lesco, smiling down from his towering height upon the two women he loved the most in the world, being tolerant, saying something to his wife you wouldn't imagine in your wildest dreams a reverend saying, such as, "I well remember a time when I made you work up quite a sweat, my dear." And that would be it, he and Rebeccah would be rolling and rocking with laughter as her mother blushed and muttered to herself, trying not to smile.

She remembered her mother just about every morning when she ran there along the polluted beach in Indiana, in the summer smelling the dead fish that had washed ashore, but the air clean and fresh now in the early fall, and she would smile. Mother, in another realm of existence, watching over them, maybe, guiding them gently, where pain was but a soft memory and the White Light was all.

This morning, as she often did, she sat down in the sand, her knees up and her arms wrapped around them, and watched the sun rise majestically, imperially, straight out there over the water, getting smaller and smaller as the light from its heat grew brighter. She could look a little bit to the north, move her head maybe three inches, and she could see, clearly on most mornings, the Hancock Building with its twin antennas reaching into the sky, looking like a monster in a Japanese movie. Another quarter inch, there was Sears Tower, making the Hancock Towers look puny. Big black ugly thing, but scary. From here, it looked to Rebeccah almost like a model.

She got up and brushed the sand from her pants, thankful she had worn the full warm-up suit this morning. It was getting cold. Snow, maybe, next month, and she'd *really* have to bundle up.

She began to run toward the north, going for home, blowing white plumes of breath before her as she went, feeling everything loose and feeling all oiled up and ready, everything working the way it should.

She reached her front door less than hour after she had locked it behind her, and stopped and warmed down for a while, walking around back, getting the house key out of the hiding place under the fifty-five-gallon drum in the alley, which had been painted black and had their house number on it in orange. The old garbage can. If the number weren't painted on it, even it would have been stolen by now. She decided that she was exposing herself to maybe a little bit too much of the city's negativity, and decided she would say a prayer and burn some sage when she got inside, ask for a little help. It couldn't hurt.

But she never got the key into the lock.

As she was reaching out, the door flew open and her father was there, in his bathrobe, bundled up against the cold, his eyes wide with apprehension and relief, his face a mask of . . . of what? Fear? Rebeccah was astonished. She had seen her father grieve when her mother had died. She had seen his heart broken, she had even, at times, seen him shaken by things that had happened in their city, in their neighborhood, but she had never, ever, seen him afraid. He reached out now and held her protectively in a bear hug, his powerful arms encircling her. She could feel them trembling slightly.

43

"Papa?" she said tentatively, a little scared herself now. "What is it?"

He pulled her into the house and shut the door, bolting it behind them. He looked at her, his piercing eyes nailing her to the spot, but losing some of their power, their hypnotic, tremendous power, to the fright windowed there.

"I had a vision," he said.

Rebeccah understood then.

He had had three visions in his life, to her knowledge. Three only. She had seen one of them. She had no desire to be in his presence, ever, when he had another one.

It had been when her mother had been dying. He had come home from the hospital to try and eat and maybe get a little bit of sleep before returning for the death watch. He had been at it for weeks, and had finally come to the conclusion that his wife, his friend, was dying. Before that he had tried healing her, hours at a time, his hands over her belly where the dark malignant child was growing in her, praying, asking God to extend to her the same miracle He had once given himself. But it was no use. Some could not be healed. Some were not meant to be healed. His eyes had suddenly rolled up into his head that night long ago as Rebeccah had stood bravely at the counter, trying to be a source of strength for *him* for once, and she had been frozen there, watching, as his throat expanded, veins standing out in almost impossible widths. She had imagined a large snake crawling into his throat and choking him, a boa constrictor, something like that. He had fallen to the floor calling out in a language she had never heard before, rolling around, his hands clutching at his head. For long minutes she had stood there, afraid to move, and at last he had stopped writhing and had sat up, but the fear was not there, only a deep, deep sadness, grief etched into his face, reflected in his eyes.

"I am sorry," he had whispered softly, "but I have just seen your mother pass over."

Rebeccah was a cheerful woman, sunny, warm, almost always smiling softly, but now, in the early morning sunlight streaming in through the kitchen window, worry lines were etched in her forehead and she went to the counter to put on her father's coffee, there in the kitchen alone with a mystic psychic healer who had just had another vision.

Her father lighted a Camel, asked softly for an ashtray, smiling now, almost back to normal, the strain of the vision leaving him; he was getting back into control. "And stop hiding them, will you?" he said. Rebeccah smiled at him.

When the coffee was poured he told her she was in danger.

"From what?" she asked.

"From within," her father said.

"Papa? Come on, I'm not one of the congregation." She saw him look up sharply, a reprimand on his lips, but he softened when he saw the smile on her lips. "I mean," she said, "you've never been cryptic with me, so don't frighten me. You say from within—do you mean, inside me? Am I going to get . . ." She could not bring herself to say the word. Cancer was a reality to her; she had seen her father cured of it and her mother die from it.

"No," he told her.

She waited patiently. He'd figure it out in his own good time. At last he rubbed his face roughly, lighted another Camel, and gave it another try.

"I wasn't being 'cryptic' on purpose," he told her,

throwing her a good-natured shot, smiling at her now with his mouth *and* with his eyes. "This time, honey, I went out, *some*where, and saw, no, *saw*'s too strong, more, I *felt* grave danger, yes, but not for me, for you."

Now that he was smiling again, Rebeccah let herself relax a little. She sipped her coffee, gave a pointed glance to his cigarettes, began to notice things again. The blue wallpaper. The little figurines on the kitchen shelves. The damn smoke in the air. He had never been wrong before, her father, not once.

"So you thought maybe I'd been run over by a dune buggy on the beach, or what?"

Lesco smiled back. "Nothing like that. It's personal danger, Rebeccah, from a human being. From a man, a man we know, a member of the congregation, from our own church! But I couldn't see who."

"Papa? Do you think maybe . . . well, you *were* asleep when I left, after all. I mean, you know, maybe—"

"You think I was dreaming."

"Well, after all, Papa, you counsel most of the congregation, don't you? I mean, if any really weird ones were out there, don't you think you'd be aware of it by now?"

Lesco knew she was right. In his church, especially, there was more than enough gossip to go around. They were an elite group, his, and subject to ridicule from outsiders, so they socialized together more than another congregation might, and sometimes they went to extremes in their beliefs, giving them all a bad name, perhaps, with their strange professions to the outside world, but if any member were deeply disturbed, on the fringes, he would have known. Or should have.

"The danger I saw. It appears to be neutralized by

another man, a different man, a stranger to us. But I see him as very, very sick. He has a disease, a physical disease, and his spirit is in great disharmony."

"Oh, great, terrific. Finally I find a knight in shining armor, and he's got a disease." Then, teasing, knowing her father, Rebeccah said, "I hope it isn't herpes."

And then, less than fifteen minutes from his fearful visitation, the Reverend Francis P. Lesco of the Church of the Spiritual Redeemer went from the grip of terror to having to hold himself up on the table, that's how hard he and his daughter were laughing.

Chapter Four

Vic and Lou rolled to a stop in front of the simple stone building on the corner with nothing to distinguish it from the other bungalows on the block except the statue of the Virgin Mother, surrounded by lights, keeping a vigil in the front yard. The lawn was neat, mowed recently despite the cold spell, the grass radiantly green, without a weed. The windows sparkled, although the draperies were drawn this morning, in mourning, out of respect for the fallen sister, the Bride of Christ who had died in His service.

"First rule of a stakeout," Lou said, staring down the street, "leave your engine off so the exhaust fumes don't give you away." Down the street, a Cadillac sat idling, two forms recognizable in the front seat. "Want me to check 'em out?" Lou asked.

"That's okay, Lou, go on inside, start without me.

Call for a squad car, though, from their phone, all right? I don't want these two to take off, they see me using the mike."

"You gonna bust 'em?" Lous asked, surprised. "What for?"

"They're Tommy Campo's boys, Lou," Vic said, "and I'll bust them for jaywalking, loitering, whatever comes to mind. Maybe, if I'm lucky, I'll get them for resisting." He stared hard at Lou, who raised his hands defensively, saying, "Okay, okay, I'll call in."

Lou went in to the front of the convent while Vic walked down the middle of the street, right in the Cadillac's path, so they couldn't take off without backing all the way down the block, in which case, at this point, with the way Vic felt about their boss, he planned on jumping on the hood and maybe shooting them through the windshield. He had to use no such measures, however, because the driver's window powered down as he approached, showing a smiling face, toothpick and all. "What's the problem, officer?"

Vic smiled. "Get out of the car, scumbag."

"Way I see it, Joe," the driver said, "we got us a little police brutality here, whaddaya think?"

"Cool it, Nose, just cool off, now, the lieutenant just wants to have a little talk, right, Lieutenant?" Smiling now, sweet-talking, talking down to the flatfoot who might make, on a non-credit union payday, maybe a fifth of what he pulled down, getting out of the Cadillac smiling, hands on the top of the car, still smiling, saying, "Tommy sent us over here, Lieutenant, keep an eye on the ladies, in case the asshole killed the first one's still around. Make sense?" He winked. "We're here, sort of, to help you guys out; you ain't got the manpower keep officers sittin' around all day, guardin' the front door of every church in town, you know what I mean?"

Vic was looking at the one still in the car, Nose. "Get out of the car, now."

Nose gave him an insolent stare, slowly, casually got out of the car, and leaned against it, his ass against the fender, crossing his arms, the toothpick bobbing up and down, giving him away, showing how nervous he was.

Vic said, seeing how to play him, "Don't put on a show trying to impress Joe. You get tough, you'll get hurt. You don't think so, just ask Joe." Vic looked over the roof at the one standing on the other side of the car. "Tell him, Joe."

"I already *tole* him, Lieutenant."

"Tell him again."

Joe raised his hands off the car in a gesture of appeasement. "I *tole* you already, Lieutenant, Tommy just sent us down here to keep an eye on the nuns."

"Tommy Campo suddenly got religion, Joe? All I know, you guys did the nun. All the world knows you so-called tough guys are sex perverts, jumping each other, raping your women, I think you gotta go in for questioning, maybe get charged with something, maybe not, but I'd like to see Nose here with the El Rhukins in the County lockup, see how he handles himself, see if he's half as tough as he acts."

Nose looked at Vic, scared now and showing it. "Lieutenant," he said, "come on, for Chrissake, don't tell me you don't know," then looking at Joe so much as to say, see, he knows already, I ain't giving him nothing, just keeping us out of jail. "Tommy Campo, Father Joseph Campeau, they're brothers, for Chrissake. Joe changed his name to sound French when he went into

51

the monastery or whatever it's called. Lieutenant, give us a break."

"Nose—" Joe started to warn his partner.

Vic looked at him and said, "Shut up, Joe," then turned to Nose again.

"Why would Tommy send you out here to guard the nuns, Nose? He got a little problem, maybe one of his business partners comes out, gives him a warning, kills a nun, telling Tommy he could be next, or his brother?"

Nose was staring at Joe now. A prowl car turned the corner, saw the lieutenant in conversation and slowed down as it cruised a little bit over to where they stood. Two young guys got out, well built, shoulders filling the leather jackets. They put their hats on as they got out of the car, putting their batons in their holders, moving with authority over to the boss.

"What's the problem here, Lieutenant?" the driver said.

Vic looked at him, searching his memory for a name, got it. "Johnny, these guys were staking out a convent. Seems a little coincidental to me, two punks like this got religion and just decide to guard a bunch of nuns, do them a favor, it ain't like punks, ya know? So run them in, John, and I'll question them when I get around to it." He winked at the officer.

"Got no room at the precinct, boss," John said, catching on and knowing his own ass was covered, he was just following orders. "Want I should run them down to County, hold them for you there?"

"Shit," Vic said, winking again. "Well, if that's all that's open, what are you gonna do?" He turned to the two men by the car. "Sorry, fellas, but I'll try and get back to you before your forty-eight hours are up, okay?

We can't hold you over for questioning on suspicion any longer than that." He turned to the uniformed officers.

"Just make sure they're kept apart, fellas. I don't want them to have time to put an alibi together."

The two officers walked toward the suspects, hands on their pistol butts, telling them to assume the position, reaching for their cuffs.

"Hey, Lieutenant!" Nose yelled after Vic, "stick around, okay? Maybe we can talk this over!"

Vic answered without bothering to look back over his shoulder. "I don't bargain with the help. I'll talk with your boss in a while, straighten him out."

And he walked toward the convent, watching Lou in the doorway smiling, and he smiled back now that his two detainees couldn't see it, and he ignored their curses, smiling wider at the scuffling sounds. They were resisting. Out-fucking-standing.

Lou opened the door. "They need any help?"

Vic shook his head, looking in at the nuns seated around the living room. They regarded him solemnly, arms resting on embroidered doilies, handwork for the off-hours. An idle mind is the devil's workshop, Vic thought, wondering if he had first heard that from Sister Mary Bonaventure. "Let's get this over with," he whispered to Lou, and, face a mask of compassion and understanding, walked with his partner into the home of the sisters.

They learned about as much as Vic thought they would; not much. Nuns aren't in the habit of making enemies. No one had seen anyone hanging around the church, no one remembered Sister Mary Bonaventure getting mugged recently or arguing with anyone on the street. In short, there really was no reason for her death.

Back in the car now, thinking about it, what amazed

Vic was their acceptance of the brutality just visited upon their lives. They took it in stride, as if there were no adequate occasions for anger, for outrage, for tears. He wanted to shake them, to get *some* kind of reaction, get anything out of them other than the humble acceptance of God's will in their lives. God's will? Vic wondered. Did a God of *any* religion expect His flock to accept something like this without emotion? For that matter, could rape and murder ever be thought of, truly, as God's will? Not the God Vic prayed to. He turned to Lou.

"We're making a quick stop, Lou."

"Sure, Vic, what's up now?"

Vic said softly, "I want to make sure Tommy Campo stays the hell out of this thing."

Lou raised his eyebrows. "I want in on this little trip, Vic, to cover your ass. Ill-advised as it may seem, if you must go in and brace the fat little motherfucker, I'm coming with you. He's got a lot of pull."

"That's why I *don't* want you with me. This way, if anything does come down, he got the pull to hurt anyone, it'll just be me and no one else. And just because he got the juice doesn't make it right."

"He's not *supposed* to have zip, Vic. He's supposed to be in a cell somewhere, or a cage. But he's federal now, and you know it. We can't touch him, he's got too much clout. There's nothing you can say that's gonna scare him."

Vic looked over at him, taking his eyes off the road, something he rarely did when driving. "It's not what you say, it's how you say it. I'm going to say it in a way I don't need you to hear, so you'd better just stay in the car, okay?"

"Stay in the car?"

"I'll call you if I need you."

Chapter Five

Chicago's history is rich with crime. Tradition has it that the most vicious gangsters in the country reside there, men so wild and vicious that other criminals leave them alone. That does not mean it is an open city. Far from it. Chicago is, perhaps, one of the tightest and most well-run combines of crooks in the world, with their own laws and regulations, their own crimes, and their own very permanent punishments. But this does not change the fact that in the thirties, when Lucky Luciano was conscientiously organizing the whole country's criminal elements into one national mob, the Chicago Outfit was almost unanimously rejected from the ranks by the other mobsters. Al Capone was just too much of an animal for them.

Little has changed over the years. The friends are more sophisticated now, of course. They have control of many, many legal enterprises and businesses, and have a lock on the concessions that service said businesses. Gino's restaurant, for instance, might have Vito's vending machines, jukeboxes, and pool table in it, while Carmine's laundry had the towels in the washrooms and Tony supplied the fresh meat and vegetables. Gilly the Fish might control the waiters and liquor licenses through his connections at City Hall. Business as usual.

But the lion's share of the Outfit's cash flow still comes from traditional sources: old-fashioned loan-sharking; prostitution; drugs, the biggest money-maker of them all; jewel thefts; fencing operations. And, of course, what they back this all up with, what keeps the working stiff from the docks on Ninety-fifth Street from running to the law and bitching about paying back six for five, is murder.

Murder is very, very big business in Chicago.

And the littlest coward with the most deranged mind can make it as soon as he convinces himself and his superiors that it takes real balls to pull a trigger rather than a mental handicap, such as lack of conscience. Such as lack of morals. Such as the ability to blow a man's brain right out of his head and then go home to a good Italian spaghetti-and-meatballs dinner and not give the day's work a second thought.

Vic Perry hated them all, the greaseball gangster punks, from Tony "Big Time" Acavino on down to the two-bit hustlers running the junk from dope house to dope house, taking numbers, breaking legs. These characters gave his people, the Italians, 99 percent of whom are decent, hardworking people, a bad name. A reputation to overcome. Which is why, when Vic had been born, his father had changed the family name to Perry, to give the kid a chance in the legitimate world, without a strike against him up front.

He hated them passionately. Had seen too much of their violence up close to romanticize them into the kindly dons and the wise *padrones* so fashionably, and profitably, portrayed in movies and novels. And at the bottom of this pile there was Tommy Camponaro, aka Tommy Campo.

Tommy was one of the St. Charles graduates that Vic had stayed away from in his youth, although they had gone to grade school together for eight long years. Even then, as a child, Tommy had been a bully and a loser, a sicko, a cootie they had called the oddballs back then. Always in trouble, always suspended for smoking behind the school in the alley, always being given "just one more chance" after his widowed mother came sobbing to the nuns, begging them to forgive him, poor child, he had no father or uncle to show him.

Tommy had begun as a car thief, had graduated to headbusting for the sharks, and then branched out, getting permission to take the horse action on the Southeast Side, over in Hegewisch, part of the *Bolita* numbers action over the state line in Indiana Harbor, and before long he was made.

Vic knew the circumstances, knew the hit as well or maybe even better than Tommy Campo himself did, but he had been powerless to stop it from happening, just as he was now powerless from arresting him for it and locking him up for the rest of his life. But when the smoke cleared and the bodies were counted, Tommy Campo had three notches on his belt and was given permission to take all that he could plunder from the far South Side of the city. The gambling, the narcotics, the whores, they were all his all the way into Burnham on the south to Seventy-ninth Street on the north, west all the way *down* the way to the village of Blue Island. The lake was east, and one of Tommy Campo's favorite lines to a would-be pretender to his throne was that the newcomer could have "all of the action east of Lake Shore Drive," which was, of course, no action at all, unless the fish were gambling. These words were always said with a smile, but there was an apposite threat behind them. Back off, Jack, or sleep with the fishes.

And he had gotten to the top of that heap. He was the Godfather of the South Side, and he lived and acted the part.

He stayed there, in his home territory on the East Side, near his roots, in his brother's parish, less than two miles away from where he had been raised. He welcomed Vic like a long-lost brother, waved the bodyguards away from the door, stood awkwardly with his hand out, waiting for Vic to shake it, then rubbed it against his shirt, then turned and said, "C'mon," over his shoulder, saving face in front of his crew, being the badass. Vic followed him into his den.

Tommy made himself a drink and sat down behind a big dark wood desk, put his feet up on it, swiveled back and forth a little and said, "That ain't right, Vic, coming into my house and giving me the cold shoulder in front of the help."

Vic shook his head. "They're not help, Tommy, they're hired flab, and I don't shake hands with bums like you."

Tommy let out a long-suffering, impatient sigh. "Been a long time," he said, "since I had to lose sleep over what some two-bit small-time cop thought of me." He sat up, slamming his feet to the polished hardwood floor, gazing off at his shelf of books.

Vic looked around, checked out the room. No class, no style. It was about what he expected. The shelf of books was exactly that, a shelf. No bookcases, no leather-bound volumes, no classics. Just a long shelf running the length of the wall filled with dog-eared paperbacks. Iron pistol bookholders held them up on either side. Two leather chairs faced a deep fireplace, where Vic guessed the master of the household sat on cold winter nights, his feet up on the leather hassock, lips moving as he tried to make his way through one of the novels.

And baiting him now, this big-time Outfit punk. Calling him small time. No respect. Vic was not about to get into a name-calling contest with Campo. They'd done that years ago, many times. He sighed, wondering how to play it, wanting to pick Campo up and throw him through the wall, get his attention.

Campo was drinking now, looking at Vic over the rim of a heavy rock glass filled with a dark brown something. Light from the window bounced off the crystal facets, sending ovals of multicolored lights across the ceiling. Vic concentrated on that for a moment, enjoying its beauty even here, in the den of the viper.

"Look at you," Campo said. "Curly hair all in place, properly dressed." He lighted a Camel with a gold Dunhill lighter and blew smoke at the ceiling.

Vic's anger at having to be there gave way to a wave of fatigue. How many men like Campo had he seen in his career? How many of them had gone down, one way or the other? Almost all of them. If the law didn't get them, someone closer to home did, and they ended up in a car trunk, rotting in the sun, waiting for a garage attendant or a concerned citizen to notice their damn smell. And Campo would go down, too, one way or the other. He wasn't worth getting angry at, wasn't worth the trouble it would take to throw him through the wall. Campo would understand that kind of reaction, it would make Vic easily understood, but then he would be just like Campo, and he would quit the force the day before he ever allowed that to happen.

"So?" Campo said.

"I just busted a couple of your people; they were down by the convent, hanging around. It got me to thinking, maybe one of your competitors is trying to move up in the world, take your place, and warning you by acing a nun, get you excited, let you know that your brother's next. Or maybe you." Vic made it up as he went.

Campo said, "I handle my own problems, if I have any, Perry. And you can get that thought out of your head. Nobody'd fuck with me in the crazy way you're saying, not in my own neighborhood, and you ought to know, family's out, for God's sake. What'd we have, everyone had a beef went around killing their enemy's family, huh? Anarchy, I think. And nobody would tolerate that. Not in his own backyard." He lighted another cigarette with a flourish.

"This is a murder investigation," Vic said, "not some 'problem' of yours. Every muscleman you send out is going to get busted and locked up. Suspicion, whatever it takes. I'll handle this case, not you. We'll protect the nuns. That's the job we're paid to do. But you can do me a favor and keep sending them over. Hell, until Nose told me, I didn't know that the parish priest was your brother. You never can tell what little tidbits I'll pick up, questioning your goofs. Maybe enough to put you away, Tommy."

Campo was staring at Vic now, not hiding much.

"You harass my employees, Perry, my lawyers will have a field day with you. Now get out of my house."

Vic allowed himself a small smile, enough of one to let Campo know that he'd done what he'd come to do, just get under his skin. He was pretty sure that Campo would pull his men off the stakeout. Vic's news about prying information out of them had hit home.

Vic knew also that Campo's two guys were in a world of hurt for even opening their mouths to a cop, let alone telling a cop intimate details of Campo's family life. As if Vic hadn't suspected. As if he'd grown up with Campo and his brother Joe and never figured that Joe had gone off to the seminary. Jesus, but these mob guys were dumb. And thank God for that.

He turned on his heel and walked from the room and out of the house, ignoring the hired muscle in the living room, clocking a couple of new faces in the crowd, staring coldly at them, filing their features away for future reference. It hadn't been a wasted trip after all.

He got into the car and made sure Lou drove away slowly.

"Hey, Vic, I was getting worried," Lou said. "Another few minutes, I was going to have to come in after you."

Vic smiled at Lou, the cavalry. "Sorry it took so long," he said. "We were shooting the shit. You didn't know that Tommy and me went to school together, did you?"

Lou shook his head. "Did you get his ass straightened out?"

"Think I did. But you never know, with Campo being way out of my league. I mean, I could never touch him. He's *fed*eral."

Lou looked over at him and saw he wasn't smiling.

Vic was sorry he'd said it before the words were out. But he'd been pissed off and a little hurt by Lou's earlier statement. He'd smooth the ruffled feathers later.

Hey, the hell with Campo, Vic thought. As long as he pulled the stakeout off the convent, what did it matter if Campo thought he'd stepped on Vic, made him look bad?

"Hey, Lou, I didn't mean to sound wiseass."

"No problem, Lieutenant."

"Lieutenant?"

"Vic."

"Okay."

"Hey, Vic?"

"Yeah."

"Look, you figure, I mean, you don't feel that maybe we got us a mob war here, do you?"

"Not at all. Lou, those guys may be nuts, but what we got here is psychotic, way beyond just some goof doing a number for his boss. What scares me, Lou, is that it could be *worse* than a mob war."

"You mean a psycho, gonna try and get all the nuns in the city or something?"

"It's a thought."

Lou made the turn onto Eighty-Seventh Street, which would bring them back to the Fourth Precinct house. "Oh man," he said.

Vic was thinking about it, some maniac out there, figuring on doing all the nuns for some reason he alone could discern. " 'Oh man' is right," he said.

Chapter Six

Ray Tomczak sat in a burrito parlor on a lunch break with the bluesuit assigned to help him sift through the hundreds of records going back to the fifties, looking—for what? For a kid with a disciplinary problem? What kid who ever went to a Catholic school in the history of the world didn't have a discipline problem at one time or another? Jesus, but once Vic got something into his head, you had to beat it out with a shovel. But Ray wouldn't have his job, no sirree. It was hard enough being a follower on the force these days, let alone a leader, with everyone looking to drop the blame on everyone else, ever since the new mayor got elected. And now the guy the voters all thought would be their savior turned around and fucked them. Sure, he got them raises, put the force back up to strength, got units together like this one, but man, did he crack down on the old ways and means, came down *hard* on the guys got caught making a few extra bucks.

But what the hell, Ray had a pretty good life. With the extra four or five grand a month he could pull down from the gamblers and pimps, he'd managed to provide for his family fine. He wasn't like some guys, on the take for the dirty money, the dope money. Ray had never taken a penny of dirty money. Drugs, or kiddy porn, stuff like that. Hell, when those bastards were running their porn shops and massage parlors on Escanaba Avenue, he had been one of the first to get a name for himself by getting into disguises and fake mustaches and long-haired wigs, doing everything he could to close them down.

His father had been a cop on the North Side, a long ways from the grim dirty streets he worked in today, on this fucking nun's murder, and here he was doing shitwork, looking through files, while the scumball was roaming the streets, maybe looking for another nun to do. A good cop, Raymond Tomczak, Sr., had been. Courageous, fearless, ready to run into a burning building or walk up and grab a killer with a loaded gun pointed at him, anything to serve the public, anything. His father would go to any lengths to help the poor folks he had sworn to protect. So, having taken all the risks and all the chances, having put it all on the line for a paycheck and a quarter a week, hell, could anyone in their right minds blame his father for getting what he could from the gamblers and the pimps? This stuff, gambling, being paid to get it on, this wasn't illegal, this was victimless to the elder Ray Tomczak, and he had taught his son young and well. No matter that mouths were not being fed because Daddy had lost it all compulsively rolling dice—if he hadn't dumped it there, he would have been out at Balmoral Park or Sportsman's or Arlington, one of the perfectly legal horse tracks, and lost it all there, right? And then, so far from home, he wouldn't even have car fare. At least in the neighborhood, he knew how to walk to his own house. If he had one. And the whores, hey, don't hand him any of that bleeding-heart stuff about johns' cutting them up or pimps' brutalizing them. Who made them become hookers in the first place? Not Ray Tomczak.

But Ray, Jr., knew he had to watch himself. If Vic Perry ever suspected that he had land in Wisconsin or long green in safe-deposit boxes in his wife's name in banks all over the city, the shit would start to fly. Hell, Vic wouldn't even let a restaurant owner comp him to a fucking lunch, the straight-arrow asshole. Busting his ass chasing perps, making what, six bills a week, maybe? For what, for going nuts trying to put all the niggers and beaners in cages where they belonged?

And speaking of beaners. . . . What the fuck had happened to South Chicago? There they were, two cops, out for lunch, and all they had to choose from was the taco stand down the street or the sit-down bean joint across the way. He didn't even recognize his partner there, for Chrissakes, the blueshirt, didn't know if he could be trusted to brace the owner and get lunch for free. Fuck it, he'd pay. And be seen doing it.

Still, any way you looked at it, he had it by the balls. Good home, healthy kids, so why did he even want to be on the street running down this creep for, when for sure and certain he was the luckiest guy in the unit. He had it dicked today, really.

A quick call and he had a hair color, black, and a blood type, O positive. And the first thing he had said, he had asked the medical examiner, that old Jewball, "What do I need the blood type for? I got the hair color; the school wouldn't know the blood type, would they? I got enough to do." And the M.E. had told him, "What happens, a kid gets hurt at school, needs blood, of *course* they'd have the blood type." Jesus, what a self-absorbed asshole.

But he had thirteen kids with black hair and blood type O positive, and maybe half again as many records to go through as they already had done. Piece of cake. And the office had a phone, naturally, and they were closed today, so there were no nuns or kids or office people running in and out, a day of mourning for the dead nun, and so with the phone he could call and check on Tina, make sure she was all right, Jesus, his kid due any day now and he had to get involved in a nun's murder.

Ray Tomczak signaled for the check, waved the patrolman's money away, and popped for lunch for both of them. Another hour, two tops, they'd be done. He could take it easy the rest of the day, maybe get Perry to let him go home early, take care of Tina, stuck there by herself with three kids already.

And he had a good lead, he thought. With tons of records to go through, the cop was kept pretty busy, but Ray had the time to read all the records the uniform pulled for him, and of the thirteen, twelve were pretty much normal kids, with the usual pranks on their records. God, there ought to be laws against teachers, especially nuns, writing down their beliefs and opinions about children's behavior, and the reason for it. How many kids, Ray asked the uniform, were really *bad* in Catholic grade school? And how many nuns, teaching grade school until they get old and retire to the nun's academy or wherever the fuck they retired to, have psychology degrees?

He had told the uniform of the story he had heard in the Academy, about the applicant, first in the class, now a captain in Division, who had applied for a position with the FBI, and Hoover's agents had found some petty infraction in the man's school records, some nonsense, but the teacher had written him up about it, saying that in her *opinion* his behavior was the manifestation of other, deeply rooted emotional problems, and this alone had been enough to keep an otherwise all-American kid out of the FBI Academy. He had fought it in federal court, and had won a settlement against the school and the teacher, but still could not get into the FBI, which had to give no reasons for washing you out, the bastards. And so the guy had joined the force.

But still, this young kid here, the dates of schooling would make him in his early thirties now, he seemed like a candidate for trouble. Had been caught playing around with a second-grade little girl when he was a sixth grader, and had been suspended again in the seventh grade when he was caught tying a cat's tail to a washline during lunch hour. Sexual hang-ups and cruelty to animals, classic signs of psychosis. He put this folder on the top of the pile, for Vic to look at first, and every subsequent folder that the officer gave him, three more fitting their profile, went to the bottom. Vic wanted folders, he'd give him folders, sixteen of them, with the well-read contents in order, showing what Ray thought to be the most bizzare behavior from top to bottom.

* * *

Bobby Franchese threw his cigarette into the gutter and kept walking, slowly, staring intently at each house he passed, looking for separate entrances, dormer additions, other clues that would tell him the house was a possible for boarders.

He had begun his search at the church itself, walking around the block, writing down possibles in his notebook, not stopping yet, not checking with the owners until he had scoped every house in a two-mile radius. Then he would begin with his first house, asking questions, being polite, just checking, he would tell the owners, looking for any signs of unnatural behavior in boarders or renters. All two-story houses automatically went into the notebook, to be checked in his slow, methodical way, the only way a detective should be, Bobby figured.

He didn't have Frank Meadows' anger or Ray Tomczak's impatience. He did his job the right way, carefully, knowing that almost all police work was slow compilation of evidence, the steady, relentless pursuit of causes and connections, of putting together the proper case, in the right way. None of this kicking in of doors, he'd leave that for the eager-beaver patrol officers who wanted his job someday. He'd plod along, taking his time, doing it by the book, and continue his perfect record of never having a case thrown out of court for improper procedure. He was not in a hurry. But that did not mean he was lazy.

He did often act on instinct, but he always knew the facts up front. He had called in and learned the hair color of the killer, taken from the pubic hairs found at the scene, and had disregarded the blood type for the moment. He wouldn't be needing it in his investigation.

But he did learn the finger span of the killer, learned from the choke marks on the nun's neck, and knew from the ME's report, given over the phone, on the spot, off the record, that the killer would not be a big man nor especially powerful. He hadn't been able to choke the nun to death; she hadn't died from strangulation. Her death had been caused by having her head beaten repeatedly on the marble floor while the killer tried to choke her. Jesus.

And so he would be looking for a weak white male, with a seven-inch finger span between thumb and forefinger. Small-handed white boy. Bobby knew well enough that it didn't take a great big hand or bulging muscles to pull a trigger or to put a sharp knife in somebody.

Bobby Franchese once had spent two hours on a lonely fall afternoon listening to an old, shriveled black lady tell him and his first homicide partner about her life with her dear sweet darling husband, listening to her sitting there in her rocking chair, telling them how she couldn't imagine anyone ever wanting to do such a wonderful man harm, why did he get shot? They'd ask her the same questions again, phrased differently, and after a while some of her answers did not ring true. And as Bobby was deciding that she was covering up something relevant to the murder, his partner was thinking maybe she had something to do with it. And as they walked away, Bobby, listening to his partner saying something like a little old woman couldn't maybe *lift* a good-sized pistol, why, that sweet little old crippled thing had begun potting at their backs, and she killed Bobby's partner and ran into the house and it took three hours to talk her out. And she *had* killed her husband, knew with a shrewd intelligence born on the streets fifty years back that Bobby's partner was getting too close, that it was about over; knowing he had to be shut up before he could convince others she was guilty, she had snapped, and killed him cold on the street. So Bobby Franchese never, ever was careless with people suspected of murder, no matter how small, frail, or innocent-looking.

His instinct came into the game as he passed an obvious boardinghouse, second story with two separate private entrances, first floor with an enclosed front porch, steps to the right on the inside leading to the top, door to the first floor on the left. There were five mailboxes on the shingled wall beside the door. Bobby began to write down the address in his notebook, for later investigation, when the front window in the first floor had its draperies parted and a fleshy old white arm appeared and taped a "Room for Rent" sign right in the middle of the picture window. "Inquire within" was written in a spidery scrawl along the bottom border. Bobby was not a superstitious man, but this was too good to be true, and he walked to the door casually, like someone who had seen the sign going up, which he had, and rang the bell.

Mrs. Calloway was on the phone with the Widow Jasek, talking about the terrible murder at the church that morning, when her doorbell rang, making her jump. She hung up the phone abruptly, as was her way. Mrs. Jasek was someone to talk to when there was nothing much else going on, and Mrs. Calloway never thought twice about hurting her feelings when something more interesting came along. She walked heavily to the door, *knowing* that she had a new boarder already, that her reputation for running a clean house was legend, that they were probably waiting in line for a vacancy.

The smile left her ancient face when she saw him, a big, tall, lean, mean-looking black fella, standing there on her stoop, dressed to the nines, she had to give him that, but didn't they have a reputation for being sharp dressers and good dancers? Probably had a big Cadillac around the corner, too. She debated whether to open the door or to ignore him, but he had seen her now, no telling what one of them might do if they were angered, so she slipped the night chain on as unobtrusively as she could and called through the crack, "Yes?" as if she didn't know already what he wanted from her. She was shocked as all get out when he held a badge up to her face. As soon as she checked the ID picture she forgot her trepidation and threw the door open with a flourish. Mrs. Calloway respected the law. And the law transcended race, although she could remember when the only dealings a black man around here had with a badge was when he was getting arrested by somebody wearing one.

"Yes, officer?"

"Ask you a few questions, ma'am," the man said, and Mrs. Calloway saw him looking past her, at her apartment door standing open behind her to the left, and the stairs leading to the rented rooms on the right. She was standing in an alcove, with the outside door open, knowing how important it was to hide her feelings, having lived with a drunken Irisher for forty years who would act up over the tiniest thing. So she kept a smile on while he asked his question, but her mind was asking, *What does this jigaboo want with me?*

"About the room?" she asked, cursing herself because her composure had slipped; her voice had cracked. Her husband had been dead too long. She couldn't keep up a front like she used to.

"No, not at all, ma'am. I got a place to stay. What I wanted to ask you about was the last boarder you had here."

"Well, he just left today; I just put the sign up in the window. Before the doorbell rang. Maybe five minutes ago."

"I know that, ma'am," the black fella was saying, all smiles. "I saw you, as a matter of fact. If you let me in, we could talk about the fella; while we're at it, I'd like to ask a few questions about all of your boarders. And maybe you could help us out, with this investigation we're working on. You see, ma'am, I need to know what's going on in the neighborhood, I'm not from around here, and I'd like some information about boarders in this area, and maybe you could do the department a big favor, save me a *whole* bunch of steps."

And that was what had hooked her, his saying that she could help the department, and hadn't they been right there when her hubby had had the final attack, hadn't they been there in five minutes, and hadn't the officers, God bless them, raced him in a squad car down to South Chicago Community Hospital? They wouldn't even consider taking any money for it; she'd asked them, later, after her hubby'd died. So if she could do anything to help now, she would. She wouldn't be gossiping, she'd be helping. There was a big difference there. And so she threw the door wider still and stepped back, allowing the first black man ever into her humble home, and said, "Would you like some coffee, officer?"

And Bobby knew he was in.

THE EIGHTH VICTIM

* * *

He drank the coffee, looking around him, letting her get to it in her own good time, listening to her rattling on about how she had nothing against Negroes, checking the place out as she felt him out. Bright, airy colors, with the aroma of a good piece of meat roasting in the oven. Droplets of water forming on the kitchen windows. A good kitchen in a good home. Hell, he didn't even blame her for her apprehensiveness when she'd come to the door. She remembered how it was in this neighborhood forty years ago, so how could he blame her for being afraid of a black face showing up on her doorstep?

As the woman spoke she waved her arms in expansive gestures, wattles of fat jiggling, but her eyes crinkled and she smiled often, and he liked that.

And so when at last he got around to asking her about the empty room and why it was newly vacant, he was shocked by the change that came over her; the coldness in her voice when she spoke of the previous tenant; the anger under the surface that he could tell she was fighting down.

"That Thomas Geere, I'll *tell* you," she said, getting into the gossip now that he was more of a nuisance remembered than a threat close and real. "He never flaunted the rules in my face, not really, or I'd have had him out of here in fifteen minutes, I'll tell you! But he tried to give you the impression that he was pulling the wool over your eyes all the time, that he knew a secret you didn't know, that he was sharper and smarter than anybody else.

"I've been renting out the upstairs rooms since my mister died, eleven years back, it was; the cancer got him, he caught a cancer from years of smoking them darned Camels, God rest his soul, and I don't mind telling you that of the men that stayed there, I've matched up six of them with good women, who made good wives. I've always tried to stay with older gentlemen, no smokers at all, no drinking allowed in the room, no women at all in the house; I don't run that kind of establishment. I'll tell you, that Thomas, if it wasn't for his momma being such a good woman with the church all them years, I wouldn't have allowed him within ten feet of the upstairs of *this* house, I'll tell you for a fact. But he swore he didn't smoke, and when I go to change the sheets the first Friday after he's here, there's ashtrays filled to the top up there, and some of them cigarettes weren't regular, I could tell by the skinny little butts in the ashtray, the end twisted, and *stink?* So it was good riddance when that one left, I'll tell you, he won't be missed around here."

Bobby sat there, nodding, taking it all in, waiting for something useful, knowing she was building up to something, patiently letting her take her own sweet time to get there. But even then, it shocked and surprised him.

"And you want to know the worst of it?" She leaned forward, a conspirator, telling the law about her ideas and deductions. "He's one a them devil-worshipers, I really think he is."

Bobby sat forward too; she had his attention with that one, and he wanted to keep her rolling. "How do you know that?" he asked.

She had been waiting for it, and now took her time, filling his coffee cup, offering doughnuts, homemade. He took one, dying for a smoke, but not seeing ashtrays and knowing about her poor husband, ah well. At last she settled down in her chair and smiled at him, making him wonder when was the last time anyone had sat down with her and really listened to what she had to say.

"I'll tell you," she finally said, "I'd of had him outta here months ago, except I was a-scared. He'd sleep all day, then take his empty bottles out with him at night, thinking he got up early enough to fool *me,* and he'd skulk the street with his teenage friends all night, sneak back into his room with the sun, and lay there, listening to one of them little recorders lets you turn the sound way up but no one around you hears nothing? And I'd go in there sometimes, the smell would be *terrible,* and he'd be laying there, a bottle of wine or cheap booze right there on the floor, a cigarette burning in the ashtray, smelling of booze and passed gas and marijuana, and one of them funny lights on, when it hits one of them posters it makes it shine kinda scary-like? And he had a poster on the wall, of a devil outta hell, it was, I'll tell ya, and it liked to scare hell outta me when I'd go in there, but I had to, you understand? He mighta burned the place to the ground the way he acted.

"But that's not really the reason I was scared of him. What really got me was the upside-down cross hung over the doorway. *That* scared me. And I couldn't dream of a way to tell him I knew it was there, you understand, or he'd know I'd been in his room when I shouldn't a' been. When I change the sheets the cross is never up. Only when he's home, like he carries it with him or something when he goes out, maybe to a black mass, you think?" Bobby nodded, not wanting to break her spell. She was getting into it now, words spilling over one another in their rush to get out of her mouth. She had been bottling this up for a long, long time. And who safer to talk about it with than a cop? He looked as interested as he could, which was not hard to do. He blessed his luck, he had *never* had such a break, in all his years on the force. But he tempered his enthusiasm with caution. This world was full of nuts, and this one didn't necessarily have to be his boy.

"But there's one more thing, scared me so bad, I was gonna call the police today myself anyways, if he hadn't moved out." She stopped then, staring at him expectantly, wanting to see how closely he had been paying attention, and he leaned even farther forward, inches from her face, and gave her what she wanted.

"What's that, ma'am?"

"Last night, he didn't go out. First time in all the time he's been here he didn't go out at night. I was so scared, I didn't know if he was alive or dead, so around four-thirty—I could hardly sleep, I was wondering what was going on—and I woke up, came out and put the coffee on, and got so worried I couldn't take it, so I went upstairs, quiet-like so as not to wake the other men, and I went into Thomas' room. He wasn't there."

"So," Bobby said, "he *did* go out after all sometime last night, and you didn't hear him leave, right?"

"No, I heard him banging around up there until eleven, dancing or something, God only knows, and then it quieted down. It was only after I was up there that I wondered if it was the door closing that woke me up, when he left. And I found some modeling clay, like little kids use? It was all over the floor and on the desk, and then I hear the church, down the street, Our Lady of Sorrows, was desecrated this morning. Mrs. Postalik across the street came home from Mass early and told me a nun was killed there, that someone had gone to the bathroom on the altar, for goodness' sake. And I started wondering."

"But you didn't think to tell the police."

"I'm telling them now, ain't I," Mrs. Calloway said. "Mrs. Postalik—God rest her husband, he used to drink and raise hell with himself before he died—she goes to early Mass every day, rain or shine. She told me that before the cops got there the nun was laying there dead, naked, and she and a few other ladies milled around the church lookin' at it all before Father Campeau got the presence of mind to ask them all to leave. And she said there was something stuck on the crucifix, and while she was tellin' me, shaking and crying, she was, poor thing, Thomas came home like a bat out of hell, pardon the expression, racing up the steps, into his room, and it wasn't a half hour later he came roaring down, bag packed, left the key on the desk without even telling me he was going. And after Mrs. Postalik left I went upstairs and he was long gone, everything, poster, funny light, cross, and all."

This is it, Bobby thought. I'll be goddamned. He looked at Mrs. Calloway.

"You didn't happen to notice if there was any of that modeling clay left lying around, did you?"

"It was all gone by then," she said, and smiled when his face fell. Then she gave him the good news, feeling sorry for him, and they were getting along so *well.*

"But I did pick up a handful of it before I came downstairs the first time. Don't know why, really. I suppose I was going to ask him about it. It's in the pocket of my housecoat; would you care to see it?"

"Yeah, Mrs. Calloway, that would be nice." But then, "Wait a second, Mrs. Calloway," Bobby said, as she began to heave herself out of her chair. "First, do me a favor, will you? Take that sign out of the window, real quiet-like, okay? Don't tell Mrs. Postlick or whatever her name is, don't tell your other renters, no one. I want to rent the room for a week, seal it off right now, no one in or out, okay? Now there's gonna be some men down here, take fingerprints, stuff like that, some pictures, maybe, and that can't get around either, we don't want to let anyone know what's happening. How much you charge for a week's rent, ma'am?"

"Well, that's the biggest room, got its own entrance, its own bathroom . . . I'd say fifty dollars ought to do it," Mrs. Calloway said, wistfully, hopefully.

"Now this fifty dollars," Bobby said, smiling to take the bite out of his words, "it goes a long way to keeping this to yourself, right?" She nodded and started to say something, but he spoke first.

"How," he asked, "would you like to take a ride downtown and make a statement, tell some fellas the same story you just told me?" He took out his money and dropped five crisp bills on the kitchen table.

Mrs. Calloway reached down into her bra and came out with an old, worn leather change purse, snapped it open and stuffed the bills into it. She replaced it in her bra and smiled at Bobby.

"Best place to keep it," she said.

" 'Specially with boarders like this Geere fella."

"Mr. Calloway left me well protected from hoodlums like him, officer."

This got Bobby's attention. "And just how did he do that, Mrs. Calloway?"

She smiled. It was a child's smile, a secret smile, an innocent yet somehow guilty smile. She said, "In my bedroom, the mister and I always stayed in separate beds, you see. Well, next to my bed, I have his old service pistol. Just as good as the day he brung it home from the war. He was an officer, and when the neighborhood started to change, he took me down to the dumps at night and made good and sure I could use it. I'll tell you, how he used to scream when I'd turn and the pistol was pointing right at him, he didn't know I did it on purpose, had the safety on the whole time." She saw his skeptical glance and hurriedly added, "And, yes, it is licensed, so don't be thinking about running in a poor old woman on some trumped-up gun charge."

Bobby broke out laughing. "About that ride?" he said.

"I'd be delighted."

Bobby looked at her, understanding her now, and she understanding him, allies now, no longer adversaries. "I thought you might be," he said. "Now how about you and me take a little walk upstairs? You can show me the room I just rented."

Chapter Seven

Vic had given Lou the hunk of clay and sent him on a canvas of the area, a two-mile square around the church, checking at five-and-dimes, drugstores, kid's stores, anyplace that might sell clay, anywhere their killer might have bought it in the area. It was a long shot at best, and Vic felt that maybe they were putting all their eggs in one basket and if the basket had a hole in it he'd be in deep trouble.

He got into his personal car and drove quickly from the scene, cursing himself just a little, knowing he had a full house, eight victims, a dead nun among them, and here he was, taking time off to check on a goddamn drunk. For maybe the fourth time that day he tasted Scotch at the back of his throat, had a craving, a sudden wanting, and it gave him renewed certainty that he was heading in the right direction, doing the right thing. He couldn't just turn his feelings off. He wasn't built that way. If Claire were anybody but his ex-wife . . .

But she was his ex-wife, and had stayed with him through years of suffering. He'd tormented her, abused her emotionally. And maybe he just might have had something to do with her drinking. Maybe he could help her out, get her dried out, maybe; maybe there might even be a chance—Vic cut himself off from that train of thought right *now*, before he got into something he couldn't handle. Hey, he was an alcoholic, helping another one if he could. Nothing wrong with that. He had to put this first, always. Above work. Above the eight victims. Especially when he was going around, thinking about drinking, tasting alcohol in his *mouth*, for Chrissakes. He'd been doing something wrong or he wouldn't be feeling that way.

Okay, Claire had been his wife, still was, as a matter of fact, in spite of the fact that he thought of her as his ex. She wasn't a big part of his life anymore. Her night-time calls had turned into a pain in the ass. But she was still a flesh-and-blood human being who had once been extremely important to him. And maybe he was putting himself a little bit up on a high pedestal. Maybe he was looking too far down at her, calmly telling her off in superior tones the way Campo had told him off that morning, thinking he was better than she was instead of just luckier. Thinking not, There but for the grace of God go I, but, Look at this wretch I'm saddled with.

And she had been the one who'd given birth to Elizabeth.

He pulled to the curb on East Ninety-fifth Street in front of 7363, got out of the car, and made sure all the doors were locked before he walked to the stoop of the three-story house. The outside door was broken again, allowing entry to anyone who felt like dropping in, and Vic made a mental note to get on the ass of the landlord, whom he'd had words with earlier, when Claire had taken up residence in this flea trap.

Up the steps to 2B, which was a joke, calling it anything other than maybe Room 2. "Apartment" was way too nice a word for this place.

What if she was with a man?

Vic almost backed off at the thought, down the steps and into his car; he had eight victims, what in the hell was he doing here? But he kept going, right up to the door. If she wasn't alone, he'd handle it when he got inside. Insurance companies got fat from people worrying about things that never happen. He couldn't afford the luxury. He had enough problems in the real world without making things up.

Knocking lightly now, calling her name softly, fighting back a sour taste and wiping an arm roughly over his eyes. How had it ever come to this? He knocked harder.

Then feet padding across a tile floor, smacking wetly as she plodded dizzily toward the door. Vic composed himself. This wasn't his weight to carry.

Softly, almost a whisper, in a raspy, cigarettes-and-vodka voice: "Hello?" He heard fear there, creeping through on the last letter, as if she expected death to be on the other side of the wood, waiting.

"It's me, Claire. Vic." He was surprised at the strength in his voice. Maybe she'd go with him this time, check into detox. Hell, she couldn't get any worse. Could she?

The door swung open.

When she'd left she had been a bottle blonde, tall. Still a looker, even with her head too far into the neck of a vodka bottle for the past couple of years. She'd been proud of her appearance, good and vain, always staying home until every hair was in place, every strand combed, every stage of makeup artfully and expertly applied, covering all sins. Making them late to the social functions to which they were less and less frequently invited. Since she had left, he had watched her quickening decline with a distasteful anger, watching her lose her self-respect, her dignity, her pride. But this was too much even for him to handle.

Her bathrobe hung from bony shoulders, the tops of her breasts exposed in a display that saddened him rather than exciting him erotically as it once had. Her hair was dark at the roots, the split ends curling around her shoulders. No makeup. There were dark circles under eyes that once had shone with life, vitality, mischief. He recoiled from her. Death *was* visiting; Claire looked like someone with two or three weeks left to live. He had a sudden vision of himself pulling out his piece and ending it for her right then, and just as suddenly hated himself for the thought. She was fighting a disease for which there was no known cure. He knew she needed sympathy like she needed another day without a bath.

He walked into the apartment as she stepped back to let him through. Her hands shook with an almost imperceptible rhythmic twitch. With her heartbeat. The shake, he knew, would not get better from this point on.

"Claire."

She did not answer, just closed the door behind her and went unsteadily over to the table in the middle of the filthy kitchen, dropping heavily into an old fold-up metal chair. "Blaine's Mortuary" was stenciled on the back. Vic sat in another chair like it and looked at her, wondering how to start.

Claire searched through the mess of newspapers and half-eaten food on the table until she found a crumpled pack of cigarettes. She shook one out, raised it slowly and carefully to her lips. She wrecked three matches trying to strike one, and finally threw the wet book down in disgust and groaned as she got to her feet and staggered to the stove. She lit the front burner and leaned down until the cigarette tip was aflame, then quickly pulled her head back, shutting off the gas and staring at Vic.

All right, Vic told himself. Don't lose it. He took a deep breath through his mouth and let it out slowly, then again, until he felt his heart slow down a little. He watched Claire tromp back to the table, holding the robe closed over her breasts, the cigarette dangling from her mouth.

"Claire," he said again, and she looked at him with loathing, as if he were interrupting her life unfairly, as if he reminded her of another time, a better place, a different Claire.

"You said last night you'd like to come home," he said softly.

"I didn't call you last night. Why would I want to call you?"

He made up his mind then. She was dying, of that there was no doubt. He could sacrifice a little himself, to help her out. Others had given more. Before he could think about it, he jumped in with both feet.

"I want you home, Claire," he said. "With me. A family again. You and me. Like we used to be. You get yourself cleaned up, dried out, like I did, come home then, pick up the pieces. I could help you whip this thing, Claire."

"Come *home?* And where would I sleep? In the

baby's room, maybe? Or with you? Is that why you came by?" She stood now and almost fell and she reached out quickly and grabbed the edge of the table. The thing shook with her effort, and Vic stood hurriedly, afraid it would tip its load of garbage onto him. Claire grabbed the robe with both hands and flung it open.

"You want this, Vic?"

He was afraid he couldn't maintain control. And then he didn't care. He leaned across the table, looking her full in the face and she didn't back off, he had to give her that, she stood her ground, all five feet eight inches of her, standing in slop in her kitchen with her ravaged body bared, she didn't give an inch. The tears were in his eyes now and in his voice when he spoke.

"Claire, you're fucking *dying*. Let me help you!" He looked at her and she stared back as if she were winning a battle, playing her sick game again, and he felt her weight, which he had sworn to leave alone, settle slowly on his shoulders.

"Get out," she said, closing the robe now, sitting back down with an odd grace he hadn't known she had left in her. "Just get out." Her teeth were bared and he thought she might lunge and take a bite at him. Or would if she had the strength.

Vic got to his feet and walked slowly to the door, wiping his eyes dry, vowing not to shed another tear over her. She didn't want help, his or anyone else's. She wanted to die. So be it. With his hand on the doorknob, though, he gave it one more shot.

"If you won't listen to me, I could ask Earl—"

"Get the fuck out, you baby-killer!" Claire shouted, strength in her voice now, powerful and cutting. "Now!" And Vic opened the door and stepped through quickly, wanting to cut himself off from that ghastly sight as quickly as he could.

He waited in the hall for a full minute. If he heard one sob, one cry, one sign that she still had some human feeling in her along with the hatred, he would go back in and drag her off to a detox. She would give him the sign.

But she didn't.

Chapter Eight

Mickey Muldoon was already feeling the effects. He hadn't had his full meditation time, and now he felt distracted, a bit resentful—for which he admonished himself—and tired. And this asshole guidance counselor at Washington High wasn't making it any easier on him.

He was sitting in the man's office now, a wood-paneled study was more like it, designed, Mick guessed, to give errant students the sense that they were inside a psychiatrist's office instead of a teacher's. He had *explained* that he was investigating a homicide. He had *told* this character that he wanted only to spend a little time talking to some of the more troublesome students. And what had this guy said?

"Do you have a warrant?" That's what this guy had said. Too much television, that was the problem. Mick

himself didn't even own a television set, and if he did,
he wouldn't waste a second of his time watching any
damn cop shows. He smiled now, wondering how to
play it. If this were a bartender or some other kind of
businessman, he'd just threaten him. Lightly, of course,
but still a *threat.* Surprise inspections. Tell him he'd
have electrical contractors and building-code inspectors
down around his head so fast it would make his head
spin. But how do you threaten a teacher? Tell him, Hey,
Jack, do what I want, or I'll close down the school? He
decided to try another tack.

"Mr. Adams," Mick got that right because the stiff
had a big desk nameplate right on the edge of the desk
there, maybe twice the size of normal ones. "Mr. Adams, I don't think you comprehend the gravity of the
situation. I am investigating a homicide, a murder. We
have reason to believe that the perpetrator might be
involved in some kind of cult, some kind of occult worship. Now, if you don't want me to spend time here,
talking to any students you suspect of having ties to
such an organization, I can understand that. No problem. How about you give me their names? I can look
into it after school hours."

"Do you have any proof that your, er, perpetrator is a
student here at this school?" Mr. Adams wanted to
know.

Mick was quick to reassure him. "Oh, no, Mr. Adams, that's not the point here. We suspect that there is a
vague connection at most. But you know as well as I do,
I mean, this isn't LA, this is Chicago, we don't exactly
have a large amount of devil worship around here. So if
our man is a member of such a cult, it's logical to assume that he might have told his plans to other members of the cult, and it's common knowledge, within the

police department, that this school has a small but active group of students who gather with the purpose of worshiping occult gods."

"I think what you're telling me is that you're on a fishing expedition."

Mick sighed heavily. "No, what I'm telling you is that I am investigating a murder. And when we get this guy, which we will, if I can prove a connection between him and a student at this school, then you, Mr. Adams, having tried to prevent me from doing my job, will be facing a charge of obstructing justice. Who is your superior?"

Adams flushed and put his hand out as if physically to hold Mick to his chair. After a couple of seconds, he composed himself enough to speak.

"Firstly, I am the chief guidance counselor here at Washington. The principal, naturally, is considered to be my boss. And there are several others, outside of the school itself, to whom I must answer.

"I think, detective, that you misunderstood me. The point I'm trying to get across to you, sir, is that the students who seek help from our offices are, for the most part, in some sort of trouble, and not necessarily only here at school. Now we spend a considerable number of hours trying mightily to win their confidence. If I were to give you names, even just one name, it would undermine my credibility with all of them. That, I believe, I cannot do."

It sounded to Mick as if the guy was already planning his defense, talking just to see how it sounded, like to a jury. Mick had to admit it sounded pretty good. He rose from his chair and didn't bother to extend his hand.

"In that case," he said, "I think I'll just wander

around the school awhile, see what I can find out on my own."

"We can't have—"

"Sure you can," Mick said, and left without a backward glance.

Franky Meadows was having considerably better luck with his part of the investigation, at least the initial phases thereof.

He was trading ass-stories with a young detective from the Fourth Precinct Detective Division, a skinny, blond-headed kid who looked fresh out of uniform and eager to impress the MCU guys.

"For dark meat, now, if that's the way you swing, there's no place better on the South Side than the Burning Spear, over on Eighty-seventh Street. Young, good-looking stuff, man? The best around, if you swing that way."

They were sitting in the cramped squad room that had to serve a complement of twenty-four detectives, eight to a shift, with third-rate rank who caught the squeals, two-man teams to a shift, with eight roving sergeants supervising, making the big decisions, catching any heat from upstairs, or from the lieutenant who worked an eight-hour day while the sergeants and the other dicks often put in twelve- and sixteen-hour days trying to get the bad guys while the trails were still hot. There wasn't time, with a work force like that, to sit around shooting the breeze about pussy. But Bill Windauer was two weeks in the division and had yet to see that a promotion to detective rank was not a license to take it easy. He sat on the edge of an old, cigarette-scarred desk, calmly talking to the redheaded fireplug of a man before him with the easy air of the foolish, while

Windauer's partner ran through the files stuffed in the corner in disarray, cursing as he searched the cabinet, knowing that the detectives filing anything in them could well put something pertaining to drugs under "Dope," "Narcotics," or even under *J* for "Junkies." The partner's name was Elroy Kidwell, and he thought that his young partner Billy Windauer was a lazy, incompetent, jack-off son of a bitch, a fact that he would share with Bill before the week ended. Bill Windauer winked, man to man, at the MCU man, and began to go into a recital of the previous night's conquest, a tale of a little chicky he'd met while investigating the report of a B and E at her premises.

"Hey," Elroy Kidwell said quietly from his squatting position in the corner, and Franky Meadows looked up gratefully, got out of his chair, and put his coffee cup down on the desk. He walked quickly over to Kidwell, dismissing Windauer without realizing that he and the young detective had a whole lot in common.

"Got a goof here," Kidwell said, "shows up under 'Drugs,' and under 'Demons.' Believe it or fucking not. You'd think we'd have a file for 'Occult,' but whoever popped this guy, he decides to put 'Demons' down, start a new file. Cute." He looked down at the scrawled signature on the bottom of the report. "Figures," he said.

"Files here start from the first of the year, for our own information, go into boxes in the basement at the end of the year, stay down *there* for a couple more years. Everything's over at ID Section, anyway, and in the computer. This is kind of just for us, you know?

"Now what we got, under the 'Demon' file, is a guy got caught in a drug bust, a loser in a dope house. Reason the jack-off put the cute little demon flag on him was this guy had an upside-down cross hanging under his shirt, and spouted off some smart shit about his 'dark Master,' the report says." He looked up at Meadows, a little ashamed of his workmate's stupidity, and said, "The lieutenant, he sees this 'demon' shit in our files, he's gonna have a baby, believe me."

Franky allowed that he knew how lieutenants were, wishing the guy would hurry it up, get to the meat and potatoes. He needed a name, not a lot of background shit. Hell, he could read it himself from the reports.

As if he were reading his mind, the detective handed him four reports, or, rather, mimeographed copies of four reports. Meadows scanned them quickly, liking what he saw, not hoping for anything yet, it was too soon to get his hopes up. This was probably a dead end, but worth looking into just the same.

"Geere," he said, reading the name from the top report. "Listen, thanks a lot. I'm gonna run, get ID to send a picture, and prints." He lifted the reports. "Thanks for these, and while I'm running him down, do me a favor. Check with the other guys, see if they can fill us in on anybody a little *weird,* let's say, maybe some cult involvement, a devil-worship group, a satanic church—whatever—within the precinct."

"I'll check," Kidwell said, "but I can't promise anything today. Halloween; we're gonna have our hands full of jerks wearing masks with the city's blessing, busting into houses after people open the doors for 'em, not to mention the razor blades in the apples, the poison candy—shit, we'll be lucky to be able to talk to each *other* before the day's over."

Franky remembered, from his own days in the First Precinct, the special troubles policemen had on Halloween, and he made a mental note to type up a request of what he needed and have copies made. He could put the note on all the desks in the detective squad, and give one to their lieutenant. The lieutenant would make sure the detectives cooperated with the MCU. Or it would be his ass. He thanked the detective again, walked past Windauer without even a nod, and headed back to the MCU temporary squad room, hoping like hell that the phone had been installed. He had to call ID and get a picture and prints sent over, get the guy's rap sheet, too. Hell, maybe they'd get lucky.

Vic's beeper went off as he was driving back to the Fourth Precinct, and he tore his mind away from Claire. It took a great effort to do so. He'd been wrong, he knew. Going over there had been a mistake. Just mail the check, that's all he was obligated to do, but no, he had to go over there, Mr. Intervention, going to save her ass. Well, it hadn't worked, and the slight taste of Scotch he'd been tasting all morning was now like a fresh and real thing in his mouth. He was *thirsty,* dammit. He pulled to the curb and went into Alfred's Cut-Rate Liquors, looking for a phone, his eyes searching the rows of bottles hungrily.

The old man behind the counter eyed him cautiously; it wouldn't be the first time he'd been robbed by a well-dressed man with a haunted look in his eyes. The old man reached down to get a grip on the .38 under the counter.

"Police," Vic said. "You got a phone in here?"

"Got some ID?"

Jesus H. Christ, Vic thought, then noticed the hand under the counter. "I am reaching my hand into my back pocket. All that'll come out is my wallet with my badge in it." The man's hand did not move. Vic showed him the shield and photo-ID, and the man loosened up.

His hand came back above the counter with a touch-tone telephone which he placed on the glass top.

"Can't be too careful, you know," the man said. "I mean, it ain't only the jigs you got to worry about nowadays."

Vic punched the numbers showing on his beeper readout and identified himself when the other side picked up. It was Skelker.

"Thought you'd like to know, Lieutenant, one of the other uniforms searching the area found a bunch of clay in a garbage can less than two blocks from the church. I called on the phone thinking you didn't want this over the airwaves."

"Good thinking, Jim," Vic said, the excitement in his voice. "Get it down to the lab, *now.* I need prints. Jesus, do I need some prints." The taste was in his mouth now, not of liquor, of Scotch, not anymore, but the coppery taste of the chase, the real manhunt beginning. It was a taste he knew well. "What was the stuff shaped into?"

"Well, it's hard to tell, Lieutenant, the first hunk I seen, it was like two hunks shoved together, coulda been anything. But the second hunk, no doubt about it, it was shaped like a big cock, balls and all."

"Detectives on the scene already?"

"Michaels is, sir. He took the stuff with him, to the lab already. Told me to beep you, let you know." Skelker was doing more than his share, Vic thought, obviously trying to make up for choking that morning.

"Best news I've had all day, Jim, thanks," he said, and hung up the phone. Without thanking the man behind the counter, he left the store and jogged to his car.

Things were starting to shape up, and he had to be on

top of things and stay there, for more reasons than he cared to think about.

There were five phones in the office when he got back. Thank God. He sat at the desk in the crowded little room, sipping hot coffee, looking at the folders Ray had lined up for him, listening to Franky Meadows talking into a telephone, excited about something. Excitable kid. Especially about women, Vic thought.

He himself had already taken two calls in his first few minutes back. One was from his friend and superior, Earl Flynn, the commander of all the MCU teams throughout the city. Earl had calmly told him that the mayor was hoping for a quick arrest on this one; it had been in his ward, where he'd started his political career, for one thing, and the elections *were* less than a month away and he did not need a psycho running around, giving the opposition Republican candidate ammunition. Not that a Republican had a chance of winning a mayoral election in Chicago, but anything less than a blowout would be considered a loss in a lot of circles by a lot of powerful people. Vic dismissed this. He didn't care one way or another about political pressure. He'd get this guy, and as soon as he could, but not for the wrong reasons.

The second call was from the lab.

They'd lifted a clear set of prints from the clay penis. They were running a search on them now, and if the man had ever been arrested or in the service, they'd have him. In the meantime, the sperm sample they had would be enough, along with the pubic hair taken from the nun's groin, for a conviction. All they had to do was get a suspect. Chromosonal analysis could prove if he was the one. So Vic's job was to get the guy, and the conviction would be ensured. Great.

Vic was under no illusions about the department. He picked up the top folder, looked at the note attached. "Vic," it said, "baby on way, at SCCH if urgently needed," and it was signed "Ray." A postscript was scribbled hurriedly on the bottom, a forgotten but important piece of information. "All the records here that match the perp, check top one."

Vic was thankful. Ray's laziness and attitude had been a problem recently, and he did not cherish the thought of having to go to the school and look through all the records himself. He scanned the top folder, concerning one Thomas Geere, as he picked up the phone and dialed the number next to Bobby Franchese's name. It was marked "Urgent" and underlined with a red pencil.

A half hour later Vic and Bobby stood outside the boardinghouse, in back. They were trying to keep a rein on their excitement, being cautious, paranoid, even. They couldn't lose this one on a procedure error.

"What about a warrant?" Vic asked.

"Rent paid by the week, due Saturdays," Bobby said, then, noticing the pained expression cross Vic's face, he hurriedly added, "No sweat. It's *four-weekly*, not monthly, rent. He was late, last Saturday, didn't pay on time, as usual, you could say he was three days late, really, with the rent. Receipts all in order, nothing'll pop up at us in court, like early payments. No warrant needed; Mrs. Calloway invited me up, suspecting Geere already, searching her soul to see if she should call in the law anyway, figuring she had a bad guy on her hands after talking to her neighbor and hearing about the murder. All it took was me at the door, she spilled her guts."

"You certain she'll play it that way in court?"

"Already talked to her, Vic, over and over. It was her civic duty to call us, she just didn't want to bother herself till I came strolling along." He told Vic then about walking past the house, seeing the window being hung with a "Room for Rent" sign, stopping in on instinct. The incredible luck he had enjoyed for the first time in his career. Probable cause for a search, after talking to the landlady, no problem. And how the room was thoroughly cleaned, no evidence to be found.

"Make sure your report reads this was the fourth or fifth house you stopped at, understand?" Vic said.

"Oh, yeah, Vic, way ahead of you. Already sent one of my bro's down the block to check out a couple other of the houses I had written down. Some lawyer asks them, 'Did a black detective come to your house Monday morning, asking about roomers, before, say, three in the afternoon?' they gotta say yeah, no problem; hell, all us niggers look alike to the people in the neighborhood here. The badge throws them off, they never look past that. It's covered. F. Lee Bailey couldn't get this search thrown out, believe it."

Vic sighed his relief. "Thank Christ." Then he told Bobby, "The Mick struck out at the schools, counselors, principal; they wouldn't even tell him any problem kid's names, protecting the little angels from the fascists, I guess. But he *did* get one of the kids to open up some in the weight room. A wrestler. Said that maybe half the kids in the school write weird shit like '666' on their books, listen to the goofy music backward, trying to get messages to Satan, said the kid and his buddies ignore 'em, there's an established pecking order, the burnouts and dopeheads wouldn't dream of even being seen in the same room with one of the jocks.

"Frank got the same asshole here on record from the precinct, popped three times the past year, possession of controlled substance, got to court, had *doctors* with him, for Christ's sake, said he's being treated for depression, had to have the drugs to function. So there's money there, someplace. Frank's at the shrink's office now, wasting his time trying to get something. Guy'll claim physician-patient rights to privacy, we won't even be able to get him into court without a lawsuit against us." He looked around him, shrugged his shoulders in his coat, wrapped it around himself tighter. "C'mon, Bobby, let's get out of here."

Back in the borrowed command post they sat huddled around the desk, thinking, talking, putting together all of their information, everything they had gathered in the past two hours on Thomas Geere.

"Local boys think he's some kind of, well, 'leader' is too strong a word," Mick was saying, "so is 'idol,' but he's sort of an authority figure to the local dropouts and toughs; he decides where they go on any given night, when he says leave, they all follow; he gets the dope, buys the booze for them, a funny uncle. We break up here, I'm going over to the schoolyard, where they meet most nights, try and get a line on him through the local punks, see if they might give him up in return for future favors. Ray called in, Tina's in labor now, Ray's with her, in the room, grabbed a doctor, wouldn't give her anything for the pain." He shook his head, smiling at the veteran copper's antics.

Frank Meadows looked up, concerned. "They throw him out of the room?"

Mick shook his head. "Nah, they calmed him down. Hell, you think he'd be used to it by now."

Vic nodded his head, remembering his own concern for Claire when she was in labor with Elizabeth. "Want to all kick in then, buy the kid something?"

Franky Meadows beamed. "That'd be nice, Vic, but let's wait till it's born, see if it's a boy or a girl."

Vic nodded, then turned to Lou. "What have we got on the clay?"

Lou smiled broadly. "This is a lucky day all around, Vic. First, this puke, he was in Sanfretto's dry goods day before yesterday, Saturday, bought the old man out of red and white clay. Sanfretto remembered him on account of the punk was pissed off he didn't have more. Remembered wondering what the hell the guy wanted with a ton of clay. Prints match from the clay, ID and FBI file show it's Geere, all right. Also, they match the prints Bobby's team lifted from the boardinghouse. I'll bring the old man in soon as we get this kid in, for a lineup; he'll be a great witness in court, the kid's dumb enough to try and fight it." He looked at Bobby Franchese. "Great work at the rooming house, Bobby. How'd you get on to it so quick?"

Bobby could not remember the number of times he had chastised his teammates for going on gut hunches. For operating outside of established investigatory techniques. He wasn't about to tell them that he'd had a hunch. "Got lucky quick," was all he'd say. Thank God Lou let it pass at that.

"Vic?" Lou said. "I want to tell you, we got this guy, dead. Sperm sample, pubic hairs, chromosomal analysis, now fingerprints from the clay. He's convicted, for shit's sake. Airtight, right? It's almost as if God was sending this guy to us as a present.

"What I'm getting to, Vic, is, we get this character next door, in interrogation, can I get first shot at him?"

Vic understood completely. They had it all, as Lou had said before, airtight. Wrapped up in a little gift-wrapped package, maybe from God, maybe not. But they had him. No doubt about it. Yet sometimes things went wrong. Sometimes, over the tiniest little mistakes, scumbags like Geere beat cases that were airtight. Vic knew that Ray Tomczak's folders from the school could never be used as evidence in court. Not unless the comments written were done so by a nun with a degree in psychology. Fortunately, they had enough other substantive evidence that the matter would never come up.

What Lou was getting at, though, was a confession. And if anyone could get a confession out of Geere, it would be Lou Michaels. Vic had seen him wheedle statements out of some of the fanciest and smartest tough guys on the block, as easy as rolling off a log. Incriminating statements that wrecked the defense's case. And the crooks had copped. Pleaded guilty. If they could get Geere into interrogation, squeeze him a little bit, get him to open up and get a confession that would stand up, their lives would be easier by far. This was no ordinary case. All of the team members were a little shocked by this one. And would take extra precautions to protect the integrity of the case.

"You got first crack, Lou," he said, then addressed the rest of the crew.

"First thing we do is, we have to get him in here to crack. Now, this punk, he's probably running around, doing his normal, average everyday thing. Acting like he knows nothing. He has no reason to suspect that we've got him cold. We need to get him in here." He spoke directly to Franky Meadows.

"Frank, get a batch of copies of this guy's picture. Have the duty sergeant distribute them to *all* uniformed officers. We don't want this guy spooked, so no talking to the press. I'll get Flynn to release a statement, 'An arrest is imminent,' the usual bullshit they put out. The last thing we want is for this guy to book out to New York or LA. We want him feeling safe, secure.

"Mick, get back to the schools, find out who this guy is tight with, then get a backup and make some visits. Get *inside*. Geere's doing one of three things right now: staying with a friend, if he has any; renting another room somewhere; or hiding at his family's home.

"Bobby, you've got a good list of boardinghouses in the area. Get a bluesuit, check them all out, find out from the landlord or landlady if he's checked in anywhere.

"Lou and I'll take the family. If he's there, it'll be best for the two of us to be there. I'm betting he ran home, but he could be anywhere. The address current from the files Frank got?"

Lou checked, and nodded. "Last arrest three months ago, case still pending. Address given over on the East Side, *not* a boardinghouse. Same as the one given on his Army discharge papers. Family home, no doubt about it."

"Okay, let's hit it." As the men filtered from the room, converging on Frank Meadows for the latest on his buddy Ray's problem at the hospital, Vic motioned for Lou to stay in his chair as he picked up the phone and called Flynn again. He wanted Flynn to use up a big favor with a judge, get a John Doe warrant out for Geere. If they used his real name, the press would have it in an hour and spread it all over the front pages. All over the television screens. Geere would fly away, and he might never be caught. They'd had too much luck on this one, it had come too easy, even taking into account the low intelligence of your average thrill killer. Never planned ahead, any of them. Mostly always got caught. But if this guy ran, went underground, he could hide out in a city the size of Chicago forever unless they got even luckier, which Vic did not count on. He got the okay from Flynn, checked his watch. He hadn't even thought about lunch, and he'd missed breakfast, wouldn't have been able to eat even if someone had popped for a big time at the Palmer House. They'd grab something on the way.

He turned to Lou. "Ready to roll?"

Lou was looking at him quizzically. "Vic? You sent the other guys out, running down good stuff, sure, but you figured all along this guy'd go home, right?" Vic used his best defense and remained silent, looking at Lou. "I mean . . . hey, Vic, we *are* planning on bringing this guy in, aren't we? You're not planning anything, are you?"

"If I were, would I bring you along?"

"Hey, sorry, Vic, it's just . . . I'm getting paranoid here. This nun, she was your teacher, years ago; this guy, he shits in your church . . . I was just wondering, was all."

"You can quit wondering, Lou."

Lou felt a little ashamed and annoyed at himself. He knew Vic better than that, should never have brought it up, should have kept his doubts to himself. Hell, Vic would never murder a suspect in a murder case just because the guy might beat it, would he?

Would he?

Chapter Nine

Thom Geere had raced from the church terrified, not believing what he had done, feeling like a desperado, man, like Jesse Fucking James after holding up the California Express. Butch Cassidy and the Sundance Kid, that's what it was like, after they held up the *Flyer* and the next train came along and a thousand cops came flying out on their horses, chased them till they got them, shot them dead in Bolivia. He'd have to get Petey the Pear in on it, quick, to play Butch to his Sundance, let him in on it; Petey already knew about the church scene, would be able to figure it out as soon as the news hit the television . . . shit, Petey'd *never* read a paper, unless he heard a buddy got busted, and then only to make sure the kid didn't turn *him* in and he'd better pack up.

He had run down alleys, through gangways, in the

dark, leaving the church only after hearing someone's key in the lock in one of the doors. Shit, he was having fun until he heard that. Squatting down, looking at the marble-white cold dead flesh maybe a foot away; dressed already, just looking at his handiwork, grooving on it, feeling a strange kind of detachment; thinking, hell, that wasn't so bad after all. No lightning struck the church, no blood seeped from his pores, no giant ghostly hand came down from Heaven and slapped the hell out of him. He began to giggle a little bit, hunched down there, waiting, maybe it'll come up again . . . who knows? Maybe try for seconds, no fear at all now, hell, she had asked for it, coming at her schoolwalk badass pace, robes swishing, hand up, ready to hit him; shit, he hadn't let anyone hit him in—how long? Years, man, years—and the last time someone hit him and got away with it it was right next door, right in that school, and it had been a nun. Well not this time.

If she'd'a just split, screaming, running, he might have run too, scared, waiting for the cops to come get him; but not this one, she had to get all righteous.

She had asked for it.

And then he heard the steady, heavy tread of steps on the wooden porch leading to the sacristy, where the priest and his altar boys would enter the church from for Mass, and the fear hit him hard, sent him scurrying out of the window, away from the church and out, taking the long, long way home, forgetting about the shit on his pants, thinking, slyly, that if anyone heard his footsteps pounding down their driveway this early in the morning, they'd call the cops, give them a hot lead a mile away from where he was really heading. He wasn't worried about the cops. They had been chasing him for years, down alleys, through gangways, and the only three times he'd been caught was stone-cold stupidity on someone else's part, when he was carrying and they came down looking for some jerk and he'd been caught in the roundup. Twice in dope houses, once at Petey the Pear's crib, the dumb fuck.

He had run until he felt the first real signs of fatigue, a sure sign the speeders were wearing down. He turned and headed for home, down the dark alleys, the big lights Mayor Daley had said would make the alleys so safe all broken now, shot out, with pistols, BB guns, making the late-night alleys sinister, fearful places. A place where Thom Geere felt safe, secure, in charge. And he made it to the rooming house, safe, in the dark, looking at the light on in her kitchen window, seeing that Holy Roller bitch from down the street holding her head in her hands, crying.

So Mrs. Calloway knew. And her friend, the church-goer. Okay, fuck them. They knew *nothing,* and even if they *did* call the cops, he'd be long gone before any of those duds out of the Fourth Precinct would respond to a 911 call, suspicious character. Hell, they had a dead nun to contend with.

He waited, patiently, cautiously, until the woman left, then raced for his side entrance, up the steps, into his room, into the bathroom without even thinking, taking the dirty pants off and into the shower with him, scrubbing them like mad as he stood under the steaming spray. When he was sure all traces were gone from them he tossed them into the corner, scrubbed himself from head to toe, vigorously, carefully, making sure that each and every square inch of him was clean, soaped down, doing double duty on his cock, soaping it and rubbing it until it was red.

He was shaking now, scared. He dried himself carefully with a towel that smelled of mildew, humming to himself, trying to get up some courage. He dressed in a pair of jeans and a Black Sabbath T-shirt, threw on his leather jacket and a black watch cap to cover his still-wet hair, and began jamming his few worldly possessions into a dirty white laundry bag.

He searched the room after he was done, muttering, cursing, hand-swept the few remaining pieces of clay off the floor and the desk, shoved them into the palms of his hands, compressing them into a tight ball, then flushed them down the toilet. He hung his cross against his chest, upside down, hanging there from a rawhide string, making him feel a little more on top of things. He tore down his poster, crumpled it into a ball, shoved it and the black light into the bag, and hung his Walkman from his belt, the earphones hanging around his neck, the machine off still, his ears straining for any sounds downstairs or out on the street.

Finally, when the room had nothing left in it to show he'd even been there, he opened the door and peered out into the hall. Seeing no one, he went for the stairs as quietly as he could, out into the street, running now, laughing to himself, feeling his pockets for his speeders, dropping two of them on the run and then two more, waiting for the rush, planning his alibi already, and where he would ditch his stuff.

When he had been asked to leave his mother's home he had given up the key to the front door. He had kept the key to the back door. Left it on his ring with his key to the front door of the rooming house, just in case. She had a couple of portable color TVs, a stereo, and usually had a few bucks stashed around the house in obvious places, like in the cookie jar. If he ever really needed money fast, he had planned on going there one day while she played her games at the church, and taking whatever he could. The key came in handy now as he came up on her house from the alley, looking around. The neighbors knew that there was bad blood between him and his mother. They'd probably call the police if they saw him around her house in the early morning, while she was at work. After about a minute, satisfied that no one was looking, he ran to the door, unlocked it and hurried inside, shut it quietly and stood listening. Ginny, the German shepherd his mother kept for protection, came barking in from the basement with teeth bared.

"Here, Ginny," Thom said softly, not moving. "Here, girl." The dog stopped barking and stood a foot away, the hair on her back standing, still cautious, sniffing. She put her nose in Thom's crotch, and he scratched her behind her ears with his right hand, cooing gently, letting her remember who he was. "Good girl," he said, then squatted down, rubbing her vigorously, and when she backed off, tail wagging, he felt safe enough to ignore her and began a careful search of the house, room by room. He had seen it done on TV.

Satisfied that he was alone, he dropped heavily onto a chair, his right hand instinctively going out to pat Ginny's massive head, his left hand rubbing his face. He yawned heavily, the hinges in his jaw popping, filled his lungs with air. He began to laugh.

It was going to be so easy. No matter what happened now, he had it made. He had fooled them in the Marines years ago, and he'd be able to pull it off again. A shrink is a shrink. As long as they didn't send him back to one of those Marine psycho houses, he'd be all right, everything would be all-fucking-right. Even if they *did*.

He began searching through his laundry bag as he

reached for the phone. The poster, black light, and all the clothing he'd worn earlier had been dropped into different trash barrels on his way over to his mother's. There was no physical evidence linking him to the crime now. He thought fleetingly of the sperm he had left inside the nun and the crap on the altar. Could they learn anything from that stuff?

He had a moment's panic as he thought of the clay he had taken with him on his mad rush from the church. He had thrown the pieces into a trash can not a block from the church. Damn. Probably had prints all over them. Christ, the cops would surely check the alleys close to the church for clues. But he hadn't wanted to be caught with them in his possession. And so he'd fucked up, because he had panicked. Well, all right, but it did not have to go any further. Three times now he had been busted since he had started dealing, and all three times he had walked. He would walk again, because he planned ahead.

He held the phone and dialed Petey the Pear's number.

"Hello, yeah. Who's this?"

"Wake you up?" Thom asked.

"Geere!" Petey shouted, fully awake now, and fear in his voice. "Hey, hey, man, fuck this, don't be calling *me* no more."

Thom felt a shiver in his intestines. "Fuck you sayin' to me, Pear?"

Petey the Pear was apologetic. "Look, Geere, we was up, man, listening to the radio, night rock, featured the Mammy Jammers all night, man, and when the news come on before daylight, oh, god*damn,* Geere, when they said a nun'd been *killed,* man, I knew it was you; I remembered you telling me about putting some dildo on the cross or something. Christ Almighty, but killing a *nun,* man, uh-uh, too heavy for me, you stay away, man."

"Who's 'we,' Pear?"

"Hey, hey, Geere, I didn't say nothing, not to *no*body. You think I want one o' them punks to call the cops after dealing with a guilty conscience all day, giving them my name? No, uh-uh, man, fuck that. I got a new load of Colombian in last night, sold it away to the kids, you know, some of them stayed around, didn't wanna go home stoned. Loaded up with some white crosses, jammed and told lies all night, couple o' burnouts was all, but I didn't say *shit* to none of them, honest to God."

"Pear, you cross me, I'm gonna tell the cops you was in on it with me."

"No, man, relax, willya? I ain't told nobody, no-fucking-body. And I ain't gonna, okay? Just do me a favor, man, stay away till we find out if they know it was you, okay? I don't need the hassle, man."

"You sure you didn't tell nobody nothing, Pear?" Thom was shouting, because the Pear was lying and now there was no alibi.

"I swear to Christ, man. Honest to God, I ain't tole nobody nothin'." The Pear sounded like he had no idea he was sealing his fate.

"You're using the name of the Christian God a little too much, Pear," Thom said, throwing him a curve to keep him from thinking about what he had just said. Then Thom gently hung up.

He searched through his small tattered black telephone book, cursing the drugs in his system that made his heart beat too fast and his fingers shake, trying to form a plan on the fly, going to his second line of defense.

There were three psychiatrists Thom saw intermittently, depending on which prescription drug he was having a hard time finding on the street. Two were paid from the state welfare funds; Thom only having to hand over his green card in payment. The third was the shrink at the Veterans Administration. Petey the Pear loved that scam, getting the drugs free and legal, but Thom hated going to the VA. It reminded him of the months he had spent in the psycho ward waiting for his Section Eight. And besides, the fucking shrink was a jig. Always looking at him like he was jiving, like he knew what was *really* going on. Well, fuck him. He was getting a disability pension because the war had made him nuts, had made him terrified of the dark, of close spaces, of gooks. Four-fifty a month, tax-free, the first of every month. And all the sleeping pills he could con out of them.

He called the first doctor in his book, and got a service. He hung up and tried the second. It rang a long time, but a flesh-and-blood receptionist answered.

"I gotta talk to the *doct*or," he moaned, putting terror and tears into his voice, looking for a heartfelt reaction. The voice that came back at him was crisp, cool, unaffected.

"Doctor is in with a patient right now. Who is calling, please?"

"This is Thom Geere. Please, get the doc, will you? I'm losing it, lady, *I'm losing it!*"

"Can you leave a number where I can have the doctor call?"

"I need the doctor!"

"Would you care to leave a number, Mr. Geere?" He

had her now, she was getting excited. Mad, though, instead of concerned.

He shrieked into the phone and hung up, cursing, then hurriedly dialed again.

"Lakeside Veterans."

"Dr. Russell's office, please," he said, trying for the Oscar, looking at himself in the mirror on the opposite wall, making faces at himself while his voice cried out for help.

This was good. The woman on the other end knew who Russell was, for *sure,* and his voice had gotten to her. The normality went out of her voice and she said solemnly, "One moment, sir," and put him on hold.

He stared into the mirror, hoping he could pull it off, annoyed that he had to call Russell, the black fuck. But he was better than nothing.

"This is Dr. Russell." Sounded like a white man, almost, but the ghetto came through loud and clear, he wasn't kidding anyone.

"Dr. Russell! Thank God I got ahold of you. This is Thom Geere. I need . . . I need *help,* Doctor." He paused. There was a silence, and he could picture Russell sitting back and lighting his pipe, drawing on it while he thought things over, while, for all Russell knew, he was sitting here bleeding from both wrists. He let a little bit of panic into his voice.

"Dr. Russell, are you there?" The right mix, a little overcontrolled, a little hysterical.

Almost a soft sigh, he thought he heard, before "Yes, I'm here, Thom. What seems to be the trouble?"

Got him. "Remember what we were talking about the last time I was over there?" Let him come up with it, show he's got a good memory.

"Yes, I believe we discussed demonic possession, and drug abuse, didn't we, Thom?"

"Yeah, yeah well, Doc, listen to this: I'm losing *time* out of my *life,* Doc! Hours at a time, and I think—I think I'm being possessed, Doc. I woke up this mornin' with blood all over me, Doc, and I—I—holy shit, Doc, *I don't know how it got there.*"

"Where are you, Thom?" Dead-serious now, concerned. Thom saw him slap his big nigger feet down on the floor now, leaning forward, taking him seriously for a change.

"I'm at a pay phone, Doc, I don't even know where the hell I'm at. I cleared out of my rooming house this morning. I was, I don't know, trying to run away from the devil, I guess."

"Now listen to me carefully, Thom. Do you want to commit yourself this time? I've tried to get you help before, you know, and you've never wanted to come in for a month or so. Do you want to try inpatient for twenty-eight days or so, Thom?"

"Yeah, yeah, I think that's what I need, Doc." Let relief in, now, as if the good doctor has offered a way out; come on, look into the mirror, let it show, man, you are relieved and saved. "Yeah, that's what I need, Doc, thank God. At least I won't be able to hurt anyone if I'm locked up."

"Now, Thom, give me the numbers from the nearest streetlight wherever you are. I'll have someone right down to pick you up. In an official Army car; you won't be able to miss it."

Thom hadn't expected this kind of service. Hell, Dr. Russell hadn't even come to court with him one time. Had always acted as if he was wise to him. He stopped, mouth half open, looking at his reflection turning slowly pasty-white. Setup. Could it be? Naw, the man had acted bored when he first came on the line. But he hadn't known who it was, had he? Or had he told the receptionist?

"Thom, are you there?"

"Doc, the blood, it's all *over me.* Doc, I can't wash it *off!*" Cry a little, buy some time.

"Thom, if you committed a crime, the court will bind you over for psychiatric evaluation. I can convince them to release you into my custody, into our facility here, since you've been under Army care for over seven years. The state people can come see you here, I'm sure of it. Now tell me where you are."

"Doc, the cops will try and pin anything they want on me if they think I can't remember!" That was a way out now, one even Russell wouldn't be able to argue with. "How do I know they won't try and pin every fucking crime they got open on me?"

"Thom, I won't let anyone hurt you, you know that, I—"

"Like hell you won't! Remember when I got in trouble those times, you wouldn't even come to court and tell them you were seeing me! You hate me, like all the rest!" He slammed the phone down hard. So far, so good.

He went to his mother's bedroom, mind racing, but physically spent, exhausted. The drugs were keeping him alert and awake, but his body was having a hard time responding. He had to crash. And soon. But first, he had something to take care of.

If they were looking for him, they would have an easy time of it with that thick, wavy black hair that stuck out even from under a hat. He would take care of that before he slept.

He found scissors, and his mother's electric razor. Taking a copy of the paper out of the rack, he began to cut his hair off, letting it fall onto the paper. When it was as short as he could make it, he took the electric razor and trimmed it to the skull, shorter than it had been in basic training, right to the skull. Then he cleaned out the razor and threw the paper, wadded up, down deep into the garbage pail. He oiled his hair and felt the tiny bristles under his fingers, cursed, and went through his mother's bathroom, looking for dye. No good. All right. Into the kitchen, under the sink; there it was, the brown shoe polish. He dabbed it, applicator over his eyebrows gently, not wanting to paint it on, getting a natural look.

He pulled down the steps leading into the attic, checked the house to make sure that he had left no signs of his visit, patted Ginny, and climbed the steps, pulling them up behind him.

The attic was small, cramped, with plywood sheets over the beams. His father had never gotten around to finishing it before the divorce. He had never gotten around to a lot of things. Thom bent down and duck-walked to the far corner, the only light a sliver of sunlight coming in through a crack in the roof between the gutter and the wall.

He found an old trunk and opened it, shivering in the morning cold, and wondered why the heat from the house didn't rise up into the attic like it was supposed to. He took two winter blankets out of the trunk and duck-walked to a far corner, away from the sunlight. He used one of the blankets as a pillow and one to cover himself. His mind was racing from the speed, and although he was physically exhausted he could not sleep.

He was trying to figure out a plan. Okay, if he got

busted, if those dumb-ass cops somehow caught him, which he doubted would happen, he had set up an insanity defense with Dr. Russell. But what if he kept going and got away clean? What if he picked up the money over at the spiritualists' church tonight, as he'd planned all along, their whole weekly take? Then what?

He was remembering himself and Petey the Pear, taking a ride south in a hot 1983 Toyota, Petey driving, going to score some coke down in Miami and get set up as drug kingpins, like Al Pacino in *Scarface*. All the way to Miami, last summer, in a hot car with three grand in their pockets, for a start, to get into the main dope trade. Finding a Cuban guy named Emilio Juarez, a street-level supplier for one of the big movers, one of the real badass Colombians who brooked no shit from anybody, who cut the heads off babies to make a point. Thom's kind of man. Emilio had listened to their plan with patience at first, but inside of a minute he was sneering at them. What did he, Emilio Juarez, need with a couple of *falicos* from Chicago, never did anything worse than steal from their mamas to buy some grass? He'd leveled them with his stare. Sitting there at the outdoor ice-cream parlor in his eight-hundred-dollar suit, with his mustache dripping, smelling of sweat, and had said to Geere, "Come back when you're something, man," and it was all Thom could do not to jump him right then.

Well, he was something now, by God. He'd killed a nun, fucked her, too. The Colombian killers, the guys who were whacking out wives and children in New York every day to get through to their daddies, they'd respect that. Especially if Geere came down with some real money to invest. Money and balls, that'd send him up the ladder.

So he was set. If he *did* get busted, he'd beat the case. Do a year, maybe two, in the nuthouse, but he'd been there before. There were worse places to do time. And if he got away, like he planned, then he'd go to Florida and wind up living in a house the size of St. Patrick's Cathedral.

Thom fell asleep.

And dreamed.

Of his mother, having other men in while his father was working his ass off, trying to be a provider. Of the real reason they'd gotten divorced, when he'd come home from work and found his wife in there with a man he'd thought was a friend.

Dreamed of watching, through the big old-fashioned keyhole of his mother's bedroom door as she gave away what belonged only to his father.

And knowing that she knew he was watching. She was getting off on it, enjoying the idea that her young son was getting an eyeful, and that he didn't know what to do about it.

He had raced to his bedroom to masturbate guiltily, while his mind gave itself over to visions of himself with his mother, doing what he watched the other men doing. She was falling in love with him, marrying him, not doing anything with anyone else but him ever again. Lying there spent, later, filled with remorse, hating himself. But sneaking back for one more look.

Getting caught in school for rubbing himself as he sat at his desk in the back of the room. The humiliation. The pain. The *bitch.*

And after the divorce, when it was too late, she'd changed.

Got religion. Became fanatic about it.

118

THE EIGHTH VICTIM

Put toilet paper into the keyhole, so he couldn't even watch her sleep alone. . . .

Geere groaned in his sleep, troubled, terrified, fully alone. He turned quickly, hitting his head on the stud coming up from the wall, moaned and went in deep again, his plans for the future devoured now by dreams out of the past.

Chapter Ten

Rebeccah Lesco was cleaning a pew, thinking, from tiny acorns. There were two sets of thirty pews, each twenty feet long. Before the night was over, she knew, there would be standing room only in the church, which had started as a small unofficial gathering in the basement of their home. Hundreds came now, Fridays and Mondays, to her father's church, to hear her father's words. And one would be healed.

She called across the church to the other aisle of pews, where the church's single employee, Leona Geere, was working. "Do a nice job, Leona, we wouldn't want any dirty backsides tonight!" Rebeccah giggled at the small blasphemy, enjoying the sound of her voice ringing in the empty building. Leona shot her a look of cautious fun, as if they were children misbehaving in a classroom, and Rebeccah laughed aloud. What a find Leona Geere was.

Rebeccah was a tall woman, she got that from her father, who was almost six and a half feet, and his military bearing made him look even taller. He could be intimidating, until he opened his mouth. Then any uncertainty you felt looking up at his height or his silver hair or his intent blue eyes was forgotten, as he transformed you into a listener, a seeker of his truths, willing you to believe.

She had gotten her five-feet-nine-inches from him, as she had gotten the startling good looks; the flaming red hair and bright green eyes came from her mother. The hair was soft, straight, not kinky and frizzy as her mother's had been, thank heavens, just curving slightly at the shoulders and down past them almost to her waist. She had a classic beauty and wore it, as she wore the world, like a loose garment; it was a gift from God, nothing to get all worked up over; nothing to act prideful about. And yet how many times had she caught men in the congregation staring at her, and how many times had she smiled inwardly, but then spoken to her father about them, letting him know that their minds were not on church business, that they could not be trusted with positions of authority. There were damn-sure enough people trying to run them out of town as it was, so the church and the men who governed it had to be above reproach.

Which was one of the reasons why, at the age of twenty-nine, Rebeccah Lesco was still a virgin.

She had a feeling of flesh-crawling distaste suddenly as she thought of Leona Geere's son, Thom, who insisted that he be addressed with the *th* sound instead of plain old "Tom," like anyone else blessed with the name of Thomas. Remembering the night—was it over a year ago already?—when Leona had made him come with her, God knows how she'd forced that miracle, and the little, well, little *shit* had spent the entire service staring at her, in her favored position beside her father, handing him his water and hanky as he spoke. And Thom had licked his lips with terrible intent when she looked at him. That night her father had told her that she had truly seen evil, and had risked Leona's wrath by asking that the young man not be allowed into the church again.

It was not right, hatred, Rebeccah knew. It had no place here, within the walls of the church. Oh, there had been times, in college, especially, when anger had gotten the better of her, anger brought on for the most part by the sight of chapels empty on Sunday while students partook of the pleasures of the young and foolish—an extra two hours in bed, the hangover brought on by the excesses of the night before, all the excuses and reasons given her by the agnostic, the atheistic, the new breed of students who worshiped the dollar instead of God, and to whom education was a ticket to the corner office rather than a way out of their ignorance.

But she had fought that anger as she fought this anger now, by remembering her father, his gentleness, his love that had never failed her. She had returned to service in his church, service to a God unknown by most, but that, too, was changing as her father's ministry caught on, as he swore people to the service of God, letting them know at the outset that he was no guru, just a teacher blessed with some special gifts. And then he taught them a belief that dated from before the time of Christ.

She supposed if she had been a man she would have

married by now and started a family. The sexual revolution had passed her by, and she had not felt a moment's insecurity because of it. She watched as her girlfriends gave up their gift to unworthy men who treated them like whores afterward, like slaves. Watched some of them drop out of school to have babies, watched the heartbreak as these children faced life by acting like the parents whose wisdom they so doubted. And so she had waited, always popular, always well liked, always with a date for any given dance, and my God, at the prom she had had to turn down a half dozen offers.

She had waited for someone worthy.

Daddy dear, where does one find such a noble creature?

Her dates these days found her old-fashioned and prudish. Usually, even the most ardent admirers would throw in the towel after a half dozen attempts at her gift. And sometimes she would cry afterward, as she matured, became older and less sure of herself in this world, feeling out of place because she was not with it.

And he had always been there, her father, and then it would all be all right, because he would say the right man was coming, the worthy man, and he always seemed to know things before they happened.

As he had known that time when she was ten and there was no snow at Christmastime, and none expected. He had asked her what was wrong, and she had said, "Oh, nothing," and he had let it go. But, by golly, when she got up Christmas morning, the streets and the walks and the houses had been covered with snow, a foot at least, big, white wet flakes, and he had looked at her, and asked, "Now, why were you worried?"

As he had known when the doctors had shown him the X-rays and told him to put his affairs in order. He had waved them off, had only been talked into another set of X-rays when the professor at IIT had talked to him for over an hour, there in the living room, after he'd stayed alive, and now he had the before and after pictures in his desk drawer. He had cured himself, or, rather, God had cured him, had given him the healing power, but even the professor from IIT could not get the results published. The others, the ones who wanted nothing to do with men like her father, had spoken of *spontaneous remission,* and forgery and fraud, but not one of them had the intellectual courage to speak of miracles and of divine intercession.

But the word had spread, and quickly. *Time* and *Life* had done articles, then *Newsweek* and even *People* had sent a man out. Letters and cards from around the world had poured in, begging her father to come quickly, they were dying and alone. Some of the letters were stuffed with checks made out to staggering amounts, which were all returned. He answered every card himself, telling the people that the power was within them, also.

Then the death threats had started. Some of them were the work of cranks, but others were eerily frightening, seeming to know everything about her father—his habits, his hours, where he was at what time. He had refused to take any of them to the police. If it was his time to die, then it was his time. Even now, all this time later, there would be protesters outside the church tonight, carrying picket signs, denouncing her father as the anti-Christ. That was the only good thing about winter, to Rebeccah's thinking. It kept the crazies from their door. Maybe his ideas were all different from what most people had heard before, not recognized by their leaders and spiritual counselors; but did that mean that he did not have the right to teach? This Jew turned spiritualist who dared to preach his beliefs? Isn't that the same thing Jesus Christ did?

Yes, Rebeccah thought, and look how *He* wound up.

And this great man, this healer, had known her fears and touched her face and held her gently as she cried, had rubbed those tears away and had told her that he knew, that he *knew* that the right man was coming for her.

She believed him.

But, boy, did she wish that fella would come along.

And thinking about him, about the special man, she was smiling. And when the door opened and Vic Perry walked in, with Lou Michaels trailing behind, the smile froze there, and she stood staring, wondering in the back of her mind, who these strange well-dressed men were but really thinking that the taller one, the older one, had the most beautiful aura she had ever seen.

The brightest, most colorful aura she had ever seen surrounding any man, or, for that matter, woman, in her entire life. God, it was yellow and gold and red (mmm, passion there!) and blue, like a rainbow! And it shone around him like a body-sized halo, bright and pure and true and good and she was dumbstruck, because he was so tall and powerful-looking, yet there was a gentleness in his eyes that spoke of compassion. And the best part, the very, very best part was that he was staring at her the same way she was staring at him.

Vic and Lou had gone to the home and rung the bell, knocked for a while, and had even toyed with the idea of a little B and E when they had spotted the neighbor across the street standing suddenly in her front yard, appearing out of nowhere with a rake in her hand, slapping at the perfectly mown and raked lawn and trying not to look at them too obviously. So they crossed the street and had a chat, and yes, she did know where Mrs. Geere was, and no, that good-for-nothing son of hers had not appeared at the house for months, and yes, she'd surely know, being as how her sitting room window happened to look directly onto the front of the street. She knew most of the comings and goings around the block, that was for sure. And so they had headed four blocks over, to the Church of the Spiritual Redeemer.

And had entered the sun-washed church through the big double wood doors.

And Vic had encountered Rebeccah Lesco.

It took him a moment to take it all in, this full-figured redhead in front of him, smiling at him benignly as if she had been waiting for him all of her life, her green eyes shining in her light-skinned face, her hair falling gracefully damn near to her waist. Her face was a little flushed; Vic hoped it wasn't from working with the rag she held forgotten now in her hand.

"Hello," he managed.

"Well, hello," she said.

"Vic?" Lou said, and Vic had to make a physical effort to look at him, see what the hell *he* wanted.

"Police," Lou Michaels said, flashing his gold, flipping it shut, and Vic reminded himself that this was not supposed to turn into a social visit, goddammit to hell. He turned back to the Vision and introduced himself.

"I'm Lieutenant Vic Perry, and this is my associate, Lou Michaels. We're sorry to bust in like this—"

"Don't be," the Vision said. Then: "But how can we help the po*lice?*" Vic thought he saw some anger there, maybe a little bit of disapproval.

"You are—?" he inquired.

"Rebeccah Lesco. This is my father's church."

"A pleasure, Miss Lesco," Vic said, to see if she'd correct him, tell him it was *Mrs.* She didn't. "Is your father here?"

"No, my father doesn't come here until almost time for services. He's storing up his strength, he has a healing tonight."

Vic knew about the Reverend Lesco, and took it no further. "Well, may we talk to you, then, Miss Lesco?" he said, letting it roll off his tongue. What a name, sounded a hell of a lot better than Mrs. Whatever. "We're conducting a murder investigation, Miss Lesco, and we'd like to speak to one of the, er . . . church's employees. A Mrs. Leona Geere?" And sometimes it happened like this, sometimes it all falls right into your lap. A silver-haired woman appeared from the other side of the church, her hair wrapped in a bandanna, beads of sweat on her forehead.

"Is it about Thomas?" she said, and Vic and Lou looked at her.

"Mrs. Geere?"

"Yes."

"I'm—"

"I heard you introduce yourself to Rebeccah," she said. "Did Thomas do something?"

"We'd like to speak with you about that, if we may," Vic said.

"Then ask away," Leona Geere said, steady now, like a rock. Vic admired that. No fear of policemen in this woman. She'd probably been waiting for this day for a long time. Maybe even wondered why it had taken so long.

"Would you like to step outside?" Vic said.

"No, no, we can speak right here." Vic recalled the Catholic church of his childhood, with nuns running up and down the aisle taking the names of anyone even suspected of making a sound. Here he immediately felt comfortable and welcome.

Within ten minutes it was obvious that they'd need a statement in writing. Geere had been calling his mother for weeks, threatening her, saying he had something special for her. It had been loyalty that had stopped her from reporting the threats to someone.

Vic saw his chance and asked Lou to take her down and get her statement while he questioned Miss Lesco about Geere. Lou looked at him funny, but went along, and so now he was talking to her, writing down her remarks about the time Geere had been to the church, asking her if perhaps Mrs. Geere could spend a couple of days with her and her father while they staked out the house. There was no telling what Geere might try to do now that he'd killed once. She said that Mrs. Geere certainly could.

Vic could sense that the two of them were like high school kids, feeling each other out, knowing something special was happening but not quite what. Pretty soon he ran out of official business to discuss.

"Why didn't you say anything before?" she asked him, filling in the moment's silence.

"Before what?"

"Before." And she turned full face to him. She was some looker, it was a little much to handle. "Before, when I said my father needed to build strength for his healing."

"You said 'storing,' you said your father was storing his strength because he had a healing tonight."

"You paid that close attention?"

"I paid that close attention."

"That doesn't answer my question."

"I know who your father is and what he does. I know he cured himself of cancer. I know he heals people, and teaches them that they have the same power within themselves." Vic had been careful to say, "cured himself of cancer," not, "he is supposed to have cured himself of cancer."

"You don't think we're crazy?" she asked with a smile that invited him to say, well, yes, actually.

"Crazy?" Vic repeated, being careful again. "No, I don't think that. As a matter of fact, I believe the single dumbest thing I can do is to have contempt for something prior to investigation. And I don't know enough about your church to make any statements one way or another."

"But you do believe that my father cured himself of cancer and heals others?"

"That's been documented, and written up in reputable journals. I believe in God. I don't know Him, don't want to meet Him, just yet, but I believe in Him, and don't see much percentage in second-guessing things that appear to be His work." He wondered if he should tell her about the things he *had* seen, like the time his father had died and he'd seen him at the end of his bed, looking down with a sad, yet somehow serene smile, as if he'd come to say good-bye. And at the time he'd been sober for the past three years. Save it for later. If there is a later.

Rebeccah was still smiling, and he had come to relate the smile to the person. She seemed to send out a sense of peace, of calmness.

"Lieutenant—"

"Please, it's Vic."

"And I'm Rebeccah." She shook her head and the mane of hair shimmered in the sunlight filtering in through the high windows.

"Vic, by tonight, this place"—she waved a hand around her— "will be full. Standing room only. Outside there'll be a handful of picketers and protesters, which we've learned to live with. In here, a quarter of the people will be the faithful, the folks who come twice a week. One quarter will be the curious, people out on a cheap date, or looking for some fellowship, or to have something to talk about in the office tomorrow.

"The full other half, Vic, at least a hundred people and growing every week, will be those needing to be healed. The lame, the cancer patients, the insane and infirm, the old people staving off death, hoping my father will be giving them the secret of youth. They'll line up, Vic, and my father will come to one who's ready, and he'll touch him or her, and that one'll be healed. No logical explanation, Vic, at all. None. But it happens twice a week, and no one ever gives much thought to the amount of energy he must expend to do a healing, to do a complete cure such as he does.

"Now he could put together a fortune, Vic, could be on TV and everything, like the phony healers, could get rich off his power. But he won't, and that's not my point." She touched her hand to his arm. "The point I'm trying to make," she said softly, "is that thousands of people pass through this place every month, and you're the first one to come here and send a friend off to do your job for you so you could spend some time with me."

She moved her hand away then, and it was as if she had removed a vital and lifelong part of his body. He heard the door open behind them, Lou and Mrs. Geere coming back.

"It may be necessary for us to talk to you again later," Vic finally managed.

"As often as you'd like," she said. Damned if Lou and the old woman weren't walking up behind them.

Vic made his mind up as he and Lou took their leave, that it sure as hell would be necessary to see her again, and soon.

"She was hitting on you," Lou said, driving again, in the precinct car, the heater rattling softly and throwing a warmth into the late afternoon chill.

Vic ignored him.

"Good-looking head, too," Lou said, "Jesus, did you see those—"

"Watch it!" Vic said, with feeling, and Lou looked over at him, obviously wondering what the fuck was wrong with him *now*.

"Hey," Lou said, "I've got some bad news from Franky Meadows."

"He's back already?" Vic asked.

"It's after five, Vic."

Vic was startled. He'd spent over an hour and a half with Rebeccah and hadn't noticed.

"Ray and Tina lost the kid. Stillborn."

"Oh, no," Vic said, truly sad.

"Yeah, and it was a boy, too." Lou made a disgusted sound through his teeth. "Ray really wanted a son."

Chapter Eleven

Victor Perry was sitting at the desk in the command post, going over statements, reading his officers' reports, waiting for Flynn to call, fighting the feeling that he was losing it, losing this punk. And not knowing why. They'd ID'd him, they'd done what they had been formed to do. Of course, they still had to grab him, but that should be easy, a dumb-ass punk like him. They had the evidence; they'd get a conviction. Especially now that Operation Graylord had kicked so much judicial ass in Chicago. No judge would dare play around with this suspect, not when they could prove that he'd gone in with stealth and premeditation. No judge would even think about sending him to a state mental health home for a couple of years. Would they?

The punk had some heavyweights behind him, that was for sure.

At all three of his court appearances he had been represented by Craig Bertram, who wasn't your usual downtown ambulance chaser. Flamboyant, highly visible, a gambler and a playboy, Bertram had been the link that had led them to the name of another figure at all three trials, Dr. Matthew Loudine. Geere's shrink. Or, rather, one of them. The records showed that he was seeing three at any given time, two private, one from the Veterans Administration. Vic smiled. Franky had the pictures out to every cop in the district. Mick had been out talking to everyone who had been involved in previous court appearances—Bertram, Loudine, and the other private psychiatrist, Caesar Porter—and had wasted his time with all three. Mick had learned that Bertram represented Loudine, billed Loudine for all legal work done for Thomas Geere, and Loudine had probably, Vic would bet, billed the state.

Loudine and Bertram had made headlines when they had successfully sued the state to pay for a sex-change operation for a young ex-con on welfare. They had argued that his mental health and his life were in danger by his being forced to remain trapped in a man's body. And they had won. That was the type of case that Bertram lived for. It got him the attention of a news-starved public. It would be like him to go to court with Geere for free, just as a favor for Loudine, judging by the amount of newsprint the relationship had gotten him.

Mick had gotten no further than that with either shrink. They had represented the defense in court, period. Anything else was privileged and confidential, and Mick's anger showed in his report.

Vic sat back, grinning a little. That's all right, Mick, he thought. We'll get a little bit back at them when I go over to the VA Hospital. Vic had an in there. A very strong in.

If they could pick Geere up right now, they could make a case. Get him before he got a chance to get to Loudine or Porter or the other guy at the VA Hospital —what was his name? Russell. Bring him in, throw him in a cell, let him see it up close, sweat him for a while, until the drugs and alcohol were out of his system and he was craving them with all his heart and soul, withdrawing in the County, with the really *bad* dudes, guys who would like nothing more than a sweet thing like Thomas Geere to keep them happy while they waited for trial. Let him detox in a County cell, holding his guts and rocking back and forth, puking himself, sitting on a cot going back thirty years, moaning, sniffling and sweating while the drugs left his body and his body said, uh-uh, don't go, old friends.

Vic knew detoxification, the pain involved. He had detoxed for five days in the basement of his house in Avalon Trails, sitting on a cot, rocking back and forth, sweating it out, calling friends he had met two nights earlier who warned him about it, calling them at two and three and four in the morning, puking, crying while his entire body called out for alcohol, wanting to know just what in the fuck he thought he was doing to it after all these years. And it sure showed him. It kicked his ass for five full days and six nights while the liquor slowly dried up and out of him. He tried to figure it happening to somebody alone in a cell, with no one giving a shit. He shivered. That was it, all right. The trick was to bring him in now, let the little prick suffer and hope for the best. But they had to find him first.

There was a knock on the door. He straightened up and called, "Come in," but it wasn't his boss, Flynn; it was a plainclothes from the precinct with a sorry look. A Not Again look. Vic smelled trouble but kept the anxiety out of his voice.

"What's up?"

One of the benefits of being with the MCU was the cooperation you got from the precincts across the city where you worked when you were called in. Vic had expected problems at first, resentment at the outsiders showing up for the headlines. Instead, the detectives accepted them with open arms, for they were there now to take all of the heat, all of the pressure, all of the public outrage from the community members who demanded to know just *when* did they plan to clean up the city? Vic also suspected that many of them harbored ambitions one day to join the team themselves.

And so they seemed happy to take the statements, to drive witnesses back and forth, to do the shitwork of any big city murder investigation, without getting a lot of the credit. And the detective standing there now had been assigned some of the shitwork. Taking statements. Vic raised his eyebrows expectantly at the man.

"Got a problem, Loo. I caught it taking the Postalik broad's statement, thought you'd want to know." He didn't wait for a reply, but hurried right into it, as if he were embarrassed to continue.

"Maybe I had no business going through all the statements, Lieutenant, but I remember reading the Calloway broad's statement, about the perp racing up the steps while she was yakking with Postalik about the murder. That ain't the way Postalik remembers it, Lieutenant."

Vic was out of his chair now, reaching for the papers, pulling them out of the detective's hand. "What's wrong?" he shouted.

"She claims never to have heard the perp come in, Lieutenant. Says she had a little coffee with Mrs. Calloway, they talked about the murder for a while, and she left. I asked her half a dozen times, and the story still's the same. She swears he never came in and Mrs. Calloway must be confused."

Vic listened with half an ear and read the statement in his hands, signed there in a tiny scrawl by Mrs. Postalik, who still signed her name officially with her husband's first name. He looked at the detective, relieved that it had been caught.

"Great work, detective, great work. Christ, if we'd gone to court with two conflicting statements, they'd have tried to prove that we coached the witnesses, and maybe even gotten the search thrown out.

"Now look, you get down to Mrs. Calloway's *now*, and tell her what you've learned. Sweet-talk her, threaten her, whatever, but you get in here with her and get her to write another statement, jibing with Mrs. Postalik's. We don't need to lose this bastard because of some old woman's memory gone bad. Got it?"

"Got it, boss. I'm on my way."

"Detective? Good work," Vic said. "What's your name again?"

"Detective Ralph Jordan, sir."

Vic nodded. "I'll remember."

Jordan nodded and left, leaving Vic certain now that he had to get this guy within the next forty-eight hours, before somebody made a real whopper of a mistake.

He wondered what Craig Bertram would do with this kind of thing in court. Conflicting testimony from the landlady and her friend, testimony that had been at the base of their search of Geere's room. Jesus, he might even get the clay ruled as inadmissable evidence. And that might help to blow the case; everything that followed, all the investigatory procedures they had gone through pertaining to the clay and all facts gathered since might go right out the window with the clay.

"Come on, Earl, goddammit," Vic muttered, and as if in answer to his prayers the door opened. But it still wasn't Earl Flynn who entered, as if he'd come in person rather than call, as if Vic's case were that important to anyone but himself. No, it was Ray Tomczak.

Ray had been floored twice in one day, which had never happened to him before. It was a rare day when he had even one thing go wrong. His life was regimented and structured. Had to be, with the stuff he was into. But today he'd been body-punched twice, the old one-two, right to the heart, and he did not know where to turn.

First the baby, the worst blow. Jesus. Stillborn. No reason for it, really, just the one time out of a hundred and fifty thousand normal births when the child was born dead. Tina in shock, out of it, under heavy sedation. He had gone to relieve his mother and to break the news to the other three kids, but he never got past the hospital steps.

The OPS boys had got to him there, right there, dishonoring him in his time of greatest sorrow. Office of Professional Standards.

For three hours that had seemed like three days they had grilled him, throwing times and days and dates and names at him, tripping him up and nailing him until there was no doubt in his mind they had enough not only to bounce him from the force but to put him away for a long, long time.

Then, when it had looked as if he would indeed not

be leaving custody, would go right from here to the County to await trial, the bastards had offered him a deal.

Work undercover. Help bust up the MCU teams, prove them to be dirty. As all of the elite and so-called "special" police units had to be dirty. The lure of easy money was too much for a cop to handle. That's how they had it figured. So, Ray's life and honor and career could be salvaged if he'd go undercover, to help prove Flynn's MCU to be an idea whose time was past.

He'd leapt at it.

And had terrible, crippling doubts as soon as they'd let him out on the street.

He'd called and told his mother about Tina over the phone, a terrible way to do it, but what could he do? He couldn't face her tonight, or the kids. They wouldn't understand that their father was going to be a rat, a stool pigeon, for their sakes. They'd never understand. He hoped to God they'd never know.

He'd stopped for a couple of drinks at a jive-ass South Side gin mill, hoping one of the suspicious black faces would mouth off and give him a reason to vent his frustration.

Then he'd gone back to the unit. Home, really. The only place he ever felt really and truly comfortable. With other cops.

And he'd found Vic alone.

And here Vic came, around the desk now, his hand out, his face a mask of concern, forgetting about shaking hands and throwing his arms around him, muttering his sorrows, and Ray couldn't help it, he'd choked, sobbed, but not for the dead son he'd never even seen.

Sitting now, facing Vic, a cup of coffee in his hand,

wishing it were bourbon, Ray found himself talking about anything but what was on his mind.

"I need to work, Vic," Ray said, expecting an argument, knowing Vic'd give him some shit about resting and taking it easy and amazed when he didn't.

"All right, Ray, got something for you. Flynn's supposed to call. Tell him I had to go out to the VA Hospital, check on one of the shrinks out there. The guys should come around soon, and I need you to coordinate them. Lou's on the street, trying to get a line on Geere with the junkies and the street hustlers. A favor for a favor."

"Geere?" Ray asked.

"Shit, you've been gone. The first folder you left me? He's our man. Got prints, everything else we need to convict. It's all in the reports here on my desk. Read them while I'm gone. Bobby's checking boardinghouses and transient hotels. Mick's on the street, talking to the kids. When he gets back—Bobby, I mean—send him home. He's been on his feet walking since dawn. Frank and Lou, they can go over to this doper's house here"— he consulted one of his reports— "Peter Petrovich. Geere was popped in his crib on a drug thing, maybe he'll know something.

"Then, Ray, I need you on stakeout. Mrs. Geere, the mother, has been getting hate calls from her son, and maybe, if he's gotten high or if he still thinks we're not on to him, maybe he'll go over there and try something. She's gonna be staying for a few days with her local preacher"—the thought of Rebeccah passed through his mind and he missed a beat— "so we got a key and her blessing. Pull all the shades and stuff, you just use your best judgment, you know what I'm saying. Call in when you're settled in, let somebody know you're in position.

There's some chance he'll show up there, Ray. The kid
hates the mother."

Ray Tomczak figured that for bullshit, icing to get
him to eat a shitcake, that's all. But it was work, and he
was in no position to argue. Vic was in a position to
send him home, even suspend him if he gave him an
argument. So he'd go. Fuck it.

"Anything else I should know?"

"Popped a guy this morning, from the *Times*. Name
of Dooley. Called in the favor already. Got him writing
up a scare report for us, from an unnamed source in the
coroner's office, saying the perpetrator's shit had traces
of blood in it, make him think he's got cancer. Late
paper should be hitting the street about now.

"Maybe it'll scare him, maybe not. Maybe he'll see
through it, Ray, but it'll be hard for him to shake off.
My bet is he'll try a call to one of his shrinks by morning, crying about a terrible pain in his gut he never had
until he read the paper."

"What if he don't read the paper?"

Vic looked at Ray as if he were crazy. "Are you serious? Hey, Ray, *all* these guys love to read about themselves. He'll see it, I guarantee you that."

Ray was wondering if maybe Vic's trick with the reporter was a piece of information that could buy him
some time with the OPS. Maybe, maybe not. It was
worth a shot. He'd see.

Vic came around the desk, his hand out, and he
shook Ray's hand, holding on to it while he spoke.
"You all right?"

"No," Ray said, "but I'm gonna be."

"I lost one too, you know. My baby died."

"Yeah, but I ain't got no bottle to hide in, Vic," Ray

said, before he could think about it, before he could stop himself.

Vic's silence made him feel worse than any comeback could have, and, embarrassed at what he'd said, Ray left the room before Vic could change his mind and pull him off the street.

He nearly laughed out loud, though, thinking of being "on the street." He was baby-sitting a house, that's all he was doing. A nothing job, a small-time, do-something job from the great Vic Perry, who was feeling sorry for him because Vic had lost a kid, too. Well, anything was better than going home, seeing the kids right now. Maybe crawling into a bottle wasn't such a bad idea. No, now that he thought about it, crawling into the jug and pulling the cork in after him sounded pretty good at the moment. It would keep his mind off the lost baby, off Tina. When he got drunk, which he rarely did, he went blissfully numb. And what could be more therapeutic than that tonight?

Chapter Twelve

Vic walked through the double glass doors of the VA Hospital, thinking of Dr. Richland Masterfield as he checked in with the receptionist, assuring her that he knew his way, amazed at the thought that it had been eighteen years since they'd first met. Almost two decades. Where the hell had the time gone?

He remembered a soldier, specialist, combat medic—himself—and on R and R in Hong Kong, leaving 'Nam behind for a few days, a desperate young man looking for a few days' pleasure to wipe out the memory of months of blood and terror and destruction and always death, right *there,* not some specter to be faced years in the future, when you got old. Death had been real then, and violent, looking you in the face every day and visiting Vic in his dreams, telling him, "You're next."

It was in a bar in Hong Kong, away from it for a

week and the whole time feeling guilty because his buddies were fighting and dying while he drank and sang and punched it out with the grunts in these dingy clubs.

Masterfield's bars had been a barrier at first, but the unit knew. But he had an out, a good excuse outside of the booze. He might never see this man again. If Vic bought it out there, if they got him, if the bad guy caught a hold of his young wild ass one moonless night, this man would never know, would never tell his secrets now that he was gone for good, would never gossip about him after he died, at least not to anyone who mattered, and so he told him about his immigrant shoemaker father who worked from the dark of morning to the dark of night so that his son could go to school and be a doctor, and that was why Vic was a medic now, seeing if he liked it, the blood and the guts, and the helping, of course, seeing if he had what it took to be a doctor.

"But you really don't want to be a doctor, do you?" Richland Masterfield asked him, and Vic nearly dropped his drink; it was as if the man had climbed into his thoughts.

"If you really wanted to be a doctor, Vic, you'd be in college now, not humping out in the field, playing medic. You'd let the government pay you to become a doctor, and owe them two years' time at the end of your schooling. Like me. They offered me three years in a noncombat situation, or two years if I did a year in 'Nam. You know something, Vic? I'm gonna re-up."

"Why, Doc?" Vic had asked, confused, not quite knowing how they had gotten off him and on to the doctor.

Masterfield looked at him with a drunken gaze that was unexpected in its intensity. "Because, Vic," he began slowly, from the heart, "I could never, ever in my life waste my talents again for some rich bastard who thinks he's doing me a favor by coming to me. Not after that over there, not after putting back together the pieces of guys like you. After this, I don't want to be listening to some asshole complain about a pain in his chest when he weighs a hundred pounds more than he ought to and smokes three packs a day and hasn't had any exercise since he jumped the old lady last month after the board of directors' meeting. I just couldn't do it."

"So you're gonna be career, Captain?"

"Don't call me Captain, goddammit. I'm a doctor. A fucking medical doctor."

"I'm sorry, Doctor, Jesus, I didn't mean—"

Masterfield's face sagged. "I didn't mean to jump on you, Vic. Just none of this rank shit on R and R, okay? Doc will be fine, or Rich, but please don't call me Captain. Any asshole can be a captain. It takes long, hard years to be a doctor."

And, Vic wondered, how many years did it take to become as idealistic as this man in front of him? Especially when his friends who made it to the world in one piece were writing back about how some hippy chick spit on them at the airport or threw chicken guts on their uniform before they could even get home and get out of it.

They drank into the early morning, a bond forming, and the friendship had, at least on Vic's part, been forgotten and written down in his life as exactly what it had been: a drunken night of philosophical bullshit between two scared and homesick soldiers.

Two months later, while on a normal patrol in the South, in deep-shit country, Tigerland, where you had to keep a *tight* asshole, Vic's company was engaged in battle in a place called the A-Shaw Valley. The Marines came by the score, and then by the hundred, and for the first time in Vic's memory the gooks fought into the day, well into the day, and that day turned into night and the blood poured like the rain in monsoon season and Marines just died while their reliefs, the men who had come to save them, charged the hill again and again, screaming KILL-KILL-KILL and they dropped like flies as the gooks from the high ground cut them off; but still they came, pissed off now, maddened that a ragtag bunch of riceburners could hold off the country's finest, and at last the hill was taken but at what a cost? What a terrible, terrible price had been paid.

And Vic had ended up there, right at the front, pulling the wounded Marines back to safety, patching them up, dragging them back, then going back for another, passing up the ones obviously dying, looking for the ones he judged savable, and doing all he could to keep them alive, charging the hill right next to them, picking up weapons from his fallen comrades there at the end, discarding them when the barrel became too hot, or when they ran out of ammunition, grabbing another, screaming, charging, knowing somehow that he was not to be caught hold of this day, that he was gonna *get some* off those yellow bastards today, and when it was all over the second lieutenant had, against all regulations, summoned everyone who could still stand to attention while the flag of the United States of America was planted atop that hill and they all saluted, Vic with tears running down his cheeks, remembering Shotgun and Monkey and Wildman and Stony and Killer and China and Mungo, who were gone now, who put their lives in his hands before and had always made it back.

146

THE EIGHTH VICTIM

When the brass came, the assholes, and made them take down the flag and leave the hill, walk away from it right there for the fucking gooks to come and take *again*, Vic had noticed with amazement that he had been wounded. Not bad, but a round had torn into the flesh of his thigh and he had lost some blood, so he'd taken down his pants and seen that it had gone clean through. Well, he'd pour some alcohol on it or piss on it and it'd be all right. But the lieutenant, the same lieutenant who had broken the rules and allowed them to plant their flag, he had taken a look and ordered Vic back onto the next helicopter out.

And it was then, back in Cam Rahn Bay, just about the safest place a man could be in the whole damn country, that he ran across his old drinking buddy Richland Masterfield.

The tall, haggard doctor had been walking down the tents, stopping at each bed, making the rounds, looking dead on his feet. He had probably been up the three days the battle had been fought, tending to the wounded, sending the serious casualties back to the chest men and the neurosurgeons in the operating tents, with their big red crosses on the top, while he supervised the stitches sewn by the medics, gave shots to those waiting for operations, patched and tended, put casts on and set the broken bones, shot the morphine into the ones too far gone to be helped, at least allowing them freedom from terror in their last moments on earth, as far from home as it was possible to be.

He saw Vic sitting on the bed, jittering, shaking, his fatigue pants soaked through with his blood, his eyes gone, way past the limit. He sterilized the wound carefully, gave Vic a shot of morphine, and when the jittering abated a little, when the eyes became less terror-filled, when the brow smoothed out some, he looked at him closely, and even through the morphine high Vic could see the compassion and caring in those eyes, those eyes that seemed to be doing as much for him as his doctor's hands, and when Masterfield spoke it was so softly that Vic was never sure if he had actually heard him or had read his lips.

"Your war is over, Vic," he said, and he put Vic's legs up, covered him with a blanket, gave him two fresh canteens of deliciously cool water, and told him he was in shock and needed to rest. Then he was gone, to the next bed, and Vic closed his eyes, feeling safe for the first time since he had left his mother and father's home to come here, and he knew it would be all right.

For the first time in almost a year, Vic slept soundly.

He became Masterfield's assistant, and not once did Masterfield ever mention that battle, which Vic appreciated. He had enough back-line assholes with stripes and bars and leaves and twigs on their sleeves asking him about A-Shaw, so that they could write home from their electrically lighted tents and tell their loved ones about the terrible battle they had been in, sending pictures and bootlegged Cong ribbons, the lying bunch of dinks.

There was a cook and a barber, and there was Masterfield. They were his only three friends, they and the bottles of whiskey he would pour down his throat at the end of the day to help put him to sleep, to keep the nightmares away, to get him through these last three months, the tough ones, the short-timers' last ninety days, when so many of them seemed to get it.

And Masterfield would come, never judging him, never discussing the increasing amounts of alcohol that Vic needed to help get him through the night, never

THE EIGHTH VICTIM

saying a word when the tent Vic had to himself smelled of strong sweet Asian grass.

And they would talk, joke around sometimes, but Masterfield was not a man for serious laughter, and, for that matter, neither was Vic. Not anymore. Not since A-Shaw.

When Vic was getting on the plane out, Masterfield took a day's personal leave to drive him there, to shake his hand, to smile sadly at him and wish him well, extracting his solemn promise to stay in touch, as had the others, the barber and the cook.

But it was only to Masterfield and to the bottle that the promise was kept. And when, years later, and after a battle with his drinking that made A-Shaw seem like a cakewalk, Masterfield got the commanding officer's post at Lakeside Veterans' Hospital, the occasional letter and the Christmas phone call became occasional dinners and long nights in conversation. They discussed all sorts of things, things Vic could never discuss with his fellow officers.

He was Colonel Richland Masterfield now, and his stringy body had filled out, his hairline retreated to the middle of his head, but he still had the values; he was still the idealist, the man of compassion. And he still insisted that Vic call him Doctor, or Doc, or Rich.

Vic was sitting in the waiting room of the outer office leading to the CO's private one, and the orderly kept staring at him, giving him the eye, so Vic said, "Do I know you, soldier?" and when the young private turned away, embarrassed, Vic felt guilty enough to ask, "What's wrong?"

The private laughed, red-faced, shook his head. "Sorry, sir, I've just never been able to understand the colonel, sir. He seems so calm, usually, but since you

149

called, he's been running around like a little kid—" The private's face fell, and he looked ashen. "You won't tell him I said anything, sir? It's not what I meant, sir."

Vic smiled, shaking his head. "Your secret's safe, private." Then, by way of explanation, he said, "We go back a long ways, me and your colonel."

But the private was back in control now. "Yes, sir," he said, briskly.

As if on cue two men in white jackets with major's oak leaves came out of the office, talking, and right behind them was Masterfield, smiling widely, hand out already in greeting as he walked quickly toward Vic, stopping the two majors to tell them that this was the best damn assistant he had had in all his years with the Army. Vic smiled back, shaking their hands, amused at their confused looks. At last Masterfield ushered him into the inner office and closed the door, telling the man outside that he was not to be disturbed.

The office was large, as befitting the head man in a hospital this size. A bar stood against one wall, bottles gleaming in the dying daylight, made brighter by their reflection in the mirror on the wall behind them. Vic looked at their amber shining with an almost aching feeling in his stomach, ghost pains, like an itch in an arm that had been amputated.

A rich leather sofa dominated the center of the room, surrounded by leather chairs. Conferences were held here, management discussions, the occasional ass-chewing. There was a sign Vic loved, painted in gilt on the glass doors leading into the hospital, done in script to take the bite out of the words for all the high-ranking officers who passed through. "Abandon your rank here, all ye who enter," it read, and it had been Masterfield's idea. And to this day the clinic and hospital emergency rooms were assigned on a strict first-come first-served basis, regardless of rank, and emergencies came first. Vic liked that.

"Vic, Vic, Vic. Three weeks, I can't get you during normal working hours, nor at home. Where have you been? Then you pop up here. The last place I'd expect to see you!" He was smiling, the old eyes still wise, still calm, still filled with compassion. Vic wondered at him, even after all these years. The typical doctor, the doctor you'd want to take your family to all your life. Just about unknown now, in this day of HMOs and Blue Cross. And the only place you could find this kind of doctor was in a veteran's hospital, not in your neighborhood clinic, nor in the big-time office buildings.

"How are you, Rich," Vic said, his eyes narrowing in concern. "You look tired."

Richland laughed, waving a hand in the air. "You'd think now, after all this time, I'd get to stay home at night with the wife, wouldn't you? I was here until dawn, for God's sake. Well, I wasn't here all that time, got a call around midnight; this you won't *believe,* Victor.

"Busy night, last night. The outpatient clinic was full up, people waiting in line outside, everyone mad, all the dependents of the retired sergeants, the wives of dead soldiers, all wanting to go first. Had to press the ambulance drivers into service, not that they do anything anyway, but you know rules and regulations, Vic. Those guys, they kill me. Not one of them over twenty-five and they get what, three calls a month, maybe? This isn't an Army town, for Chrissake, it's Chicago! But still, gotta have them. Rules. Then when they have to work for a change instead of standing around looking at dependent girls, they get mad.

"Well, they had one of their infrequent runs last night, Vic. A private on leave went to Cabrini-Green to see his mother, and fool that he was, went in his fatigues, you know they all are issued camouflage fatigues now? Shot him dead, the bastards."

Masterfield was talking slowly, savoring the discussion, glad to be talking to someone who wouldn't blab everything he said around the entire hospital, someone who wasn't out to get his job, someone who wasn't interested in office politics or getting a promotion over the dead body of a person who had been a close friend.

"The ambulance drivers are scared to death to go out there to pick him up, so the paramedics take him to the morgue, and my guys pick him up there. Bring him back here. He can't be packed, we're using every single medic and doctor on duty to keep our heads above water, so we put him alone—mind you, against the rules—in a storage room, on a wheeled stretcher, room eight. The drivers go on duty at the desk, pulling records, what have you, and this one, this Rogers fella, cocky six-year man, waiting to get out next month, he's taking the new patients' history, being an ass, acting the role, *he's in charge!*

"Black woman comes in, her head hurts. A headache, for goodness' sake! Her husband's retired six years, she's been here maybe every other week, some minor complaint, so Rogers tells her, 'Lady, come back in the morning, don't you see how busy we are,' and she goes off on him, gives him hell about how she and her husband were protecting the country since before he was born, blah blah blah, and Rogers tries a couple of more times, she won't budge." There was a glint in his eye now. Vic smiled to encourage him, not that he needed it.

"So Rogers, this dummy, he tells her, 'Okay, okay, lady. Take it easy!' He pulls her file, does it all by the book, really official, old Rogers is, and he tells her, 'Here, take this down to room eight, the doctor will be in in a minute.'

"She looks at her file as if she's never seen it before. 'Room eight?' she asks Rogers, 'I ain't never been in no room eight before!' Rogers reaches for her file, like he's going to take it back. 'You wanna see the doctor or not, lady?' he asks her, and she waddles away, Rogers and his just-as-dumb partner following discreetly.

"She turns on the light, takes one look, and screams her lungs out, then goes into a dead faint.

"That's when she calls me, after Rogers and his partner revive her, trying to hush her up, never thinking they might have given her a heart attack, and I have to come down in the middle of the night, to . . . to . . ." And that was it, he was laughing now, off and running, and Vic was rolling in his chair, trying to keep from falling to the floor. These kids, the closest they had come to the war in Southeast Asia was maybe getting into a fight in a Chinese restaurant, Vic said to Masterfield, and they laughed harder still.

"So what happened?" Vic managed at last.

Masterfield was wiping his eyes. "Rogers, God bless him, pleaded ignorance, said he 'forgot' the soldier was in room eight. I had to let him go on his own word. Ignorant that boy certainly is.

"The problem was the duty officer. It's a heavy rap, Vic, leaving a dead soldier unattended. He's supposed to be guarded from the moment we get him until he's turned over to his family's mortician. Had to write the man up, it'll go into his record. Maybe hurt his chance for promotion. Doubt if he cares much, he's just doing his time until he can get out and go to work chasing the big buck and the heart attack that goes with it. But you didn't come down here to discuss the goings-on in M.A.S.H. Midwest, did you, Vic?"

"No, no Richland, I didn't. I have a favor to ask."

"You say it, you've got it."

"Not so fast. It might be against your personal and medical ethics." He tilted his head toward the door, meaning the outside world.

"Well, tell me and I'll let you know."

Vic told him, starting with the nun's murder and giving him everything, without worrying about any leaks to the press. He told him about the deal he had cut with the reporter, Dooley.

"You mean you trusted this reporter, this guy who made a run on you in your office, and gave him the killer's name and all the information you had on him? I don't get it."

"One hand washes the other, Richland," Vic said, "I give him the real goods, he gives me his word not to use it until I say so; this way he can do all the background work, get a major story ready while the other papers and the TV news crews are still in the starting gate. In return, he prints a rumor, anonymous, of course, not attributable to anyone, that the medical examiner has learned that the killer has colon cancer."

"You clear it with the ME?"

"Yup."

"But what do you possibly hope to come of that?"

"That is one of the things I was hoping you could tell me. Not you, precisely, but a certain doctor . . ." Vic checked his notebook. "Avery Russell. A shrink."

"Know him well, Vic. Just a moment." Masterfield walked to his desk and made a call. He came back and

154

sat back on the couch. "Avery will be here in a minute, Vic, with the records."

"You've got no problem with this, Richland?"

Masterfield smiled. "This is martial law here, we're Army, Vic, not civilians. That patient-doctor crap doesn't play very well here, it wouldn't be practical. The MPs come in here, Vic, they ask, 'You got a guy named so-and-so confessed to his shrink about a murder?' I might play dumb, say none of your damn business, but you bet your ass if their commanding officer gets on the line I'll have to give him up. It's a lot different from the outside world, Vic, or have you forgotten?"

Vic looked at him. "I won't forget this, Richland."

"You won't? That's too bad, Vic, I've forgotten it already."

And then Russell was knocking once and entering quickly, a stocky black man with short hair. A worried look was on his face. Under his arm was a folded copy of the *Times*, in his hand a cream-colored folder, and he was saying, "Jeez, Rich, did you see the paper?"

Chapter Thirteen

Monday, Wednesday, and Friday. On these days, at precisely 8 P.M., no matter who had been killed, Vic Perry and Earl Flynn, called the Swashbuckler behind his back, turned off their beepers and attended closed meetings of Alcoholics Anonymous. It was through steady attendance at these meetings that Vic Perry had been able to last almost ten years without having to pick up a drink. Though God knew, he'd come close.

Ten years back. A *long* time. Unlike most alcoholics, Vic could not give you the exact date he had stopped. But he remembered with chilling clarity, as if it were yesterday, the circumstances that led him to make the decision.

Captain Flynn had been his boss then, Vic remembered, sitting with Flynn after a meeting, having coffee in Dunkin' Donuts, quiet, enjoying the solitude, the peace. To this day Flynn still wore a red tie every day with a white shirt and a sports coat.

Flynn had tried, really tried, back then, to like Vic, but Vic's quiet, bitter nature ran contrary to Flynn's outgoing and happy personality.

"You're *young,* Vic," Earl Flynn would say, "young, and a detective already; what more could you want to be happy?" And Vic would give him the eye, telling without words that he'd never be able to understand.

Until one day it came to a head.

"You don't know what it's like anymore, Captain," Vic said in Flynn's office, "you keep calling me in for these little pep talks, giving me the line about sunshine and happiness, life being too short, all that crap, but you're not *out* there anymore, Captain, all due respect. When was the last time you saw a little girl raped and murdered by her *daddy?*"

Flynn's Irish temper had swelled. "Who in the fuck are you, Perry? God, the conscience of the world, *what?* You're going to carry all the sins you see home with you, to Claire, you're going to spend your life bitter and full of hate because of what people do to themselves and each other? Then maybe you're in the wrong line of work.

"And let me tell you another thing, Perry. At first, when you were assigned to me, I thought maybe it was inexperience, shyness made you quiet, then word got back you were suffering for the fuck-up in Vietnam, *where I lost my only son,* I might add, and I look at you, and it's just too fucking late to be carrying the war inside you, so now I see you transfer it onto this job, *when all the time it has nothing to do with the war or the job, does it now?*

"Face it, Vic," Flynn said softly, sitting down on the

158

edge of his desk now, ignoring Vic's deadly stare, "the department or the Fire Department are the only two jobs you could have taken, aren't they? The only two jobs that would allow you to see enough pain, to suffer enough so you could have a tailor-made excuse to go out and get drunk every night." He held up his hand to tell Vic that no argument would be tolerated.

"You're an alcoholic, kid, admit it. You got a major problem here, and I'm telling you, you have to do something about it, and now."

Vic stared his hate and contempt across the room, afraid at first to speak. His face had turned red, and his hands gripping the arms of the chair had knuckles turned white. His body seemed coiled to strike, and Flynn actually balled his fists, expecting him to try. When he spoke, he bit off the ends of each word viciously, as if he were speaking to a child molester instead of his superior.

"You got a problem with my life-style, Flynn, if you think it's affecting my performance, write me up, take it up with my union rep. You got no business sticking your nose into my fucking personal life, you understand me?"

"I was expecting some bullshit, Perry," Flynn said, pissing Vic off endlessly. "And I have written you up. Your jacket will reflect my belief that you have been drinking on duty. I'll back that suspicion up with a breathalyzer test every time I think you've been drinking, and if you refuse to take it I'll fire you on the spot, and you can go six, eight months without a paycheck, lose your house, get divorced, probably, waiting for your hearing, and I promise you, I *guarantee* you, you'll lose the case. I haven't spent twenty-six years with the force without having at least a couple coming to me, and believe me, the department won't lose a night's sleep over you, not when I tell them you're a fucking lush. You got any idea how many millions of dollars are lost every year on this department due to cops' alcoholism? They'd be *grateful* I bounced you off before you got a pension guaranteed."

"What the fuck you talking about—divorced, Flynn?"

"*Captain* Flynn, Perry, goddammit; I'm your superior officer, and you show me respect or I'll bounce your drunken ass off my walls."

Vic stood now, angry, embarrassed, ashamed that his secret was out. Maybe he did stop off now and again for a couple, maybe he did close the bars most nights he stopped, but that was his business, it had nothing to do with alcoholism, he wasn't *sick,* for Christ's sake, he just had some things he liked to forget once in a while. To forget the A-Shaw Valley, to forget the look forever frozen on the face of a ten-year-old child who had been sexually molested, then murdered.

Hell, why didn't fuckhead here jump all over the kids in the locker room, smoking joints at the end of the shift? Why was he fucking with *him?*

And he understood clearly and totally now. Captain Flynn would never understand, because he hadn't been *through* it.

He unclenched his fists and sat back down. Losing his head and his job would not help matters any, and it was well known that Flynn had clout over just about any inspector in the department, let alone other captains. His tentacles reached all the way into City Hall, and if he gave a cop the kiss of death it was only a matter of time until that cop was tending bridges somewhere.

"I'm sorry, Captain," he said, thinking he would

bullshit his way around this, as he did at home, with his wife; in bars, when he was short; to creditors; his family; everyone who knew him. "Listen, boss," he said, "I've been having problems at home, with Claire. *She's* drinking heavy, and I'm spending half my nights chasing her down. I know she called you, Captain, she's been threatening to for months, to get even with me if I didn't leave her alone, stop harassing her about her drinking. It's not like you think, Captain, I just—"

"Shut the fuck up, Perry," Flynn said softly, his voice heavy with disgust. He went to his desk and opened the middle drawer, threw a sheet of paper on top of it, perched back on the corner, and said, "Take a look. Go on."

Vic did not move.

"That's a copy of the conversations I had with a Mr. Thomas H. Vail, manager of Household Finance Corporation, three talks in the last month, and all three times I've covered your ass, even made noises about finding things wrong over at the local office, maybe a little background check on his office employees, maybe get a list of all clients owing HFC money out of that office, see if they might have been harassed a little bit, or too early in the morning or late at night, that sort of thing, and I covered for you, asshole. But no more. You're on your own.

"Claire tells me you're two payments behind on your mortgage, and you haven't paid a utility bill in two years until you get a shutoff notice. And you're right, that's none of my business. What *is* my fucking business, though, is your conduct while under my command. This"—he waved at the paper on his desk— "is my copy, to show you. There's another copy in your file, stays there, Vic, in your jacket, as part of my evidence against you. Your wife can testify against you at the departmental hearing, Perry; it's not illegal, like in state or federal courts."

Vic raised a hand shakily, confused. "Evidence? Christ, testimony, what the fuck, Captain, you've got me tried and convicted already, for Christ's sake; can't we talk this thing over, come to an understanding?"

"I understand only one thing: You're an alcoholic. That's all I understand. And I won't have a lush out there on the street working for me. Now you got two plays you can make: You can seek help. Go to a rehab center, or start going to AA meetings; either way you're gonna have to start going to meetings, they'll beat that into your head in whatever rehab center you go into. Or, your second play, Perry—you can deny you've got a problem, keep up the way you're going, and lose all that you have, everything—wife, home, job, bank account, if you have one, not to mention your self-respect, your sanity, and then maybe your life. The choice seems pretty clear-cut to me."

Vic was astonished. "Hold on, back up a minute, Captain, will you, please? Why can't you just tell me to quit, I can do that. Hell, until today I figured you just wanted to save my soul or something, I didn't know the job was on the line, that you felt that way. Or maybe just let me put in for a transfer, hell, there's a lot of precincts need detectives where the captains aren't hard-line against a man having a drink once in a while."

Captain Flynn sighed softly. "You think I'd just give you away to another precinct and let you fuck up over there? Forget about it. As for your quitting alone, it can't be done. I've given you your choices. Now decide. I've got the detective's number in my pocket, liaison man for the department, he'll fix you up with a list of meetings in your area, or get you into treatment." He stood now, walked over to Vic, looming over him.

"So?" he said.

Vic looked up, not understanding how his job could suddenly be on the line with one of the few men in the department who he thought understood him. Hell, he'd been in this office a dozen times in the past six months, shooting the breeze, and now the man was trying to fuck him.

He'd take the number, maybe give the man a call, bullshit him a little bit. He couldn't get anywhere with this bastard here, that was for sure. He looked up at the captain contritely.

"Could I have that number, Captain?"

But of course he never called, not yet, give it another day. He spent the evening roaming from one bar to another, staying out of the usual hangouts, the cop bars, where some ass-kissing snitch might be hanging around, would rat him out to Flynn the next day. And he thought about Claire, who had been cutting her own throat by calling the captain on him. See if he'd bring *her* home any more booze, the bitch.

He remembered her trying to hang out with him, and how he'd enjoyed it at first, but God, when she got drunk, what a pain in the ass. So he'd just stopped picking her up before heading out, but shit, he'd brought bottles home for her, why'd she have to call the captain, for Christ's sake?

"Say something, buddy?" the bartender asked. Vic started. He hadn't realized he'd been speaking out loud.

"Shaid, gimme 'nother drink," he stammered.

The bartender shook his head. "You had enough, buddy. Whyn't you go home, sleep it off; it's almost closing time."

Vic was tempted to pull his gun and make this ass-hole give him a drink, on the house, but grabbed his money off the bar top, muttering curses, and bounced from bar to wall, weaving to the door, cursing, wishing the floor would stay still for a minute, until finally he made it outside, held up the wall in the same position he made suspects stand in, and began to vomit. He got most of it in the street, but enough had landed on his pants and shoes. And the next thing he knew he was being spun around and he could not catch his balance, and he went down, right on the back of his head, helped along by the bartender's fist, which had cracked the side of his head on the way down.

"You fucker!" the bartender shouted, "what the fuck you doin'? Couldn't you wait till you got to the curb?" The bartender had his leg back, ready to kick, when he spotted the gun in the shoulder holster. He muttered under his breath, hoping this fucking cop or gangster or whatever he was didn't remember him or his bar in the morning, and helped Vic into his car.

Vic got stopped less than a half mile from the bar, because the bartender had made a phone call, and the two young officers who stopped him checked his license and his badge, and proceeded to follow their desk sergeant's orders and let Vic ride home in the back of the squad car while the other officer drove his car for him. Vic was having none of it.

"Bitch called the fuckin' cap'n today, got me in hot water, damned I'm gonna let a couple of wet-behind-the-ears squaddies take my car!" He reached for his gun, and was subdued violently.

He awakened slowly, putting pieces of it together, not all of it, but enough to make him have to fight back the tears. He was in a cell, he knew that much. He had given a couple of squad-car cops a hard time, they had beat up on him. Shit.

He opened his eyes, seeing the wooden cot that was smashing his nose up close. The back of his head hurt terribly, as did his eyes and his mouth and his nose and his back and his kidneys and his arms and his legs.

When they came for him he went meekly, not even seeming to be bothered by the indignity of being cuffed behind his back. They ushered him into Captain Flynn's office and he stood there, staring at the floor. His union rep was there, explaining that Claire had called when he hadn't arrived home, and they had to tell her that he was under arrest, locked up, and they tried to quash it before the captain found out, but Claire had said, "Good, leave him there, at least he won't kill anyone, the bastard." Because of the gun the two arresting officers wouldn't lighten up, but the guys had kicked in the hundred for bond and he was free to go, after he got through with the captain. The officers had given in enough not to have charged him with resisting, thank God, so he could forget about that, at least. So it was driving while intoxicated. Not too bad, if the captain wanted to be cool, but it didn't look that way because he'd ordered him to his office in cuffs, so the whole crew could see him like that, and then Flynn had left Vic and the union rep alone to try and talk things out before he formally gave him the punishment.

Vic looked up for the first time, noticing that Flynn was indeed out of the office. "He's gonna hang me," he told the black precinct rep, who backed away at the smell of Vic's breath.

"He's hard on drinking, Vic, that's for sure. He chewed your ass out good last night, didn't he?"

Vic ignored the man. He was thinking. "Listen," he

said. "We tell him we went out last night. I showed you I was taking medication, see, and—"

"Uh-uh, Vic," the man said. "No way am I gonna lie for you. The captain and me, we got a good working relationship."

"You'd do it if I was black."

The precinct rep looked hard at Vic, his eyes tight. "What the fuck you mean, Perry?"

"Just what I said. I was a nigger, like you, you'd bend over backward to get me off."

The rep looked at him, hard. "You wasn't in cuffs, you drunked asshole, I'd kick the shit out of you."

"Take the cuffs off," Vic said loudly, but it hurt his head something terrible to raise his voice.

The rep was shaking his head now, silent, and Flynn walked in, shooting Vic a disgusted look, and threw the papers he was carrying down on his desk.

"Sixty days suspended, subject to discharge upon review," he said to the rep, ignoring Vic.

"Captain, I—" Vic began, but was cut off angrily.

"Get out of my office, you fucking drunk," he said to Vic, and the rep, just doing his job, going through the motions, said warningly, "Captain," and Flynn nodded, composing himself, and said to the rep, "Get this fucking drunk outta my office, now."

He picked up his belongings, shamefaced before his brother officers, who tried not to get caught staring when he looked up, which was rarely; then the music from Claire; and finally down into the basement alone, shaking and afraid for the first time, really, since coming home from the war.

Lying on an old Army cot he had bought when Claire had first started acting up, he was staring at the ceiling, trying to remember how many times he had tried to quit drinking alone and had not made it. A hundred? How many times had the pounding, blinding headaches and the rolling guts gotten to him, and he'd sworn to stop, to give it up, and had been back in a gin mill that very night, forgetting about just one, or two, drinking until he was shot, climbing into the car, driving with one eye closed.

How many times?

So maybe he did have a problem, maybe he couldn't stop by himself.

But he knew someone he could call who would give him an unbiased opinion, so he went to the basement wall phone and called Dr. Richland Masterfield, all the way out in California.

Masterfield knew something was wrong right away and ignored Vic's beating around the bush, asking how he liked the Sunshine State, if the hospital was up to his standards, and let Vic talk himself out. At last he got to the root of the problem and Masterfield minced no words.

He told Vic that he had probably been an alcoholic, at least in the early stages of alcoholism, when he worked for him all those years ago in Vietnam, and when Vic asked him when in the hell he had planned on getting around to talking to him about it, Masterfield had asked him one question: "Would you have listened?" And after thinking it over he thanked the doctor and hung up, shaking worse than ever, his worst fear realized.

What had he expected? That Richland would laugh it off?

He got out his wallet, found the number Flynn had given him, and that evening went to his first AA meeting.

And of course Flynn had been a member of AA for several years—how could he have not figured that out? —and the liaison man was a member, too. Flynn had welcomed him at the meeting and had told him afterward that this had nothing to do with the job; if he could make it, he could make it, but he, Flynn, would make no promises about helping him at the hearing and Vic had said that was all right, he wasn't there for his job anyway and Flynn had nodded, knowing what he meant.

The hard part, the painful part, didn't come for a couple of days. But the third night, that terrible, terrible black night, he had called on the phone, sweating, a blanket wrapped around him to keep him from shivering, dialing the numbers the men around the table had given him, and they had told him this was normal, this was what detoxing felt like, that he was not going to die.

And, to a man, they asked him if he wanted them to come over and stay with him for a while. Vic had been amazed. These were working guys, most of them, with families and jobs, and here they were offering to come out in the middle of the night to sit up with somebody who hadn't even had the guts to speak up at one of their meetings.

He had refused each man, but he never forgot the fact that they had *offered*.

He had dried out, walked away from the review board with his job less back pay, beaten the DWI in court, and had proceeded to make sergeant while most men he'd gone through the academy with were just getting their second precincts, still getting their hearings. Lieutenant took five years minimum after that. But why not? He had a rabbi. Flynn became the commander of the citywide Major Crime Unit teams, and when they had been organized he had pushed, naturally, to have his old buddy and AA fellow, Vic Perry, assigned to his unit. But it was a large command, and filled with so much political soothing and shitwork just to get the Old Guard to *allow* the teams to keep operating that Flynn did not have time to keep up with the day-to-day progress of every case. But he knew figures, Flynn did. And he knew that Perry's team had the highest conviction rate of any team in the city.

Vic looked at his friend now. He'd filled Flynn in before and after the meeting. Flynn had been angry that Vic hadn't waited in the office for the call he'd promised to make. Vic had cooled him down, told him about the work they'd been doing.

Their food arrived, and they ate silently. Vic had skipped breakfast and missed lunch because he'd spent so much time with Rebeccah Lesco.

"Good idea, the cancer story," Flynn said at last, not worried about the untruthfulness in it, knowing that the press got it wrong half the time anyhow.

Vic shrugged, sipping his coffee. "I figured it was worth a shot. Earl, you know that cancer patients have the same problem at first as we do?"

"How's that?" Flynn asked, not getting it.

"Denial, Earl. Ask any doctor. Ninety percent of them, cancer patients, when they find out they have it, they respond with denial, like an alcoholic. Not *my* body, they say, it would never betray me. Cancer's for other folks. But here's the odd thing. Ninety-*five* percent of the people who read the paper believe every single word they read."

Flynn appeared puzzled. "So? Wouldn't this psycho just figure, if he *did* read it, and then if he *did* believe it

169

. . . isn't there some chance he'd just start killing more people, as many as he could before he dies?"

Vic shook his head and put catsup on his French fries. "Listen to this, see how this runs down to you. Say you got a kid, severe social and sexual problems, perverted, wants to marry his mother, kill his father, hates all men and all authority figures, say he was raised a devout Catholic. Later on, to suit his own purposes, he plays as if he's a devil worshiper, renounces God, blasphemes before all his friends, keeps them in line with the idea that he's a confirmed satanist and the fact that he spent time in a VA mental ward, section-eighted out, as a matter of fact.

"Now you got this punk, strung out on drugs, drinks like a fish, too, right? For his own reasons, we don't know why yet, he kills a nun and figures there's enough evidence to link him to it somehow, we haven't figured that out yet, either, and he runs; takes off in fear, leaves his room, cleans it out, right?

"Now maybe the dope's wearing off, he's coming down, he wants to know if maybe they got his name, if he has to blow town, and he picks up the papers, and in the *Times*, right here in print for all to see, they write that he's got cancer. No name, no ID, nothing yet. Hell, he's got to think, why should the medical examiner's office lie about it? They're not cops, they're doctors, for Christ's sake.

"Now, Earl"—Vic was getting into it now— "what does this closet Catholic junkie who's been playing games with the devil do when he finds out he's going to die a lot earlier than he planned?"

"He repents?"

"Give the man a cigar!"

Earl shook his head, a skeptical look forming on his face. "Reaching a little, aren't you?"

Vic put his hand down on the table. "A*ha!*" he said, "that's what I thought you'd say. So I saved the best for last."

He told Flynn then about his talk with Avery Russell, who had told him about all the guilt Geere was carrying, not only for wanting to sleep with his mother, which was mostly a subconscious desire, but for crapping out under fire the first time he had ever been tried in Beirut, throwing down his weapon and running away, being saved only because the corpsman happened to be in his way and the medic held him down and shot him full of morphine until he was a walking zombie. He told Flynn how the others in the fire team had wanted to shoot Geere on the spot, how they almost did while he was waiting for his psychological reports to come back so he could get sent to the States, to undergo therapy for his sudden night terror and fear of small places. He told Flynn about Geere's treatment, how the shrinks back then had decided that he was faking, but anyone willing to undergo the peer torment and the lifelong trauma of being section-eighted out of the Marines without a second thought was sick already, deserved to be out of the military, but for the wrong reasons. He told Flynn about Geere's getting the government to foot the bill for years of medical treatment while he lied and tried to con the shrinks and medical men into giving him drugs, and how they had all refused, until Geere had gotten a green card from welfare and conned outside civilian shrinks into being his suppliers and they had written out prescription after prescription for him, gone to court with him, even paying for his legal fees. And feeling righteous in the fervor of helping this mis-

understood victim of a war he had them convinced he
had participated in.

Then he told Flynn about the phone call Dr. Russell
had gotten that afternoon, Geere's asking for help, saying he was losing track of time, trying to convince Russell that he was possessed by demons, and almost,
almost getting talked into coming in for inpatient treatment.

"Now, Earl," Vic said, "this guy picks up a paper
tonight, after already beginning an alibi for the nun's
murder with the VA Hospital, and he finds out he's
dying. Where do you think the first place is that he's
gonna go?"

"To the hospital?"

"Bingo!"

"I still think you're stretching, Vic." Flynn said, not
wanting to hurt Vic's feelings.

"Bet you a dinner we get him tomorrow, when he
goes to Russell for confidential psychiatric help, where
he can mention to the doctor this stomach problem he
just started having when he read the *Times.*"

"It's a bet, Vic," Flynn said ambiguously.

Vic was switching on his beeper. "Hey, Earl, we got
guys out on the street, bluesuits throughout the city,
everybody's got his picture. I got Dooley to plant the
story; I got a door-to-door going on; I got a guy waiting
in the mother's house; I got guys going to anyone who's
ever been busted with Geere, getting them checked out.
I got Masterfield as a last resort, and his guy, Avery
Russell, to help out here. If he calls, fine; if he doesn't,
well, I wasted an hour and a half, and had a pretty good
line. But it's not like all my eggs are in one basket. It's
manhunt time out there, and my guys run a manhunt
better than anyone in this city."

"I've been meaning to talk to you about that, too Vic," Earl said, and Vic knew it was coming, some political bullshit Flynn needed help with. Hell, half of Flynn's hair was gone now, and the deep lines in his face were not from character. He had heavy problems juggling the MCU ball. Vic always hated to give him another one.

"Couple of things," Flynn said, nodding his appreciation for Vic's silence. "First, we got a dirty one in your team, Vic."

"Ray Tomczak?"

"Uh-huh. You knew?"

"Suspected. I couldn't prove a thing. Or else he'd be gone."

"Too bad, because he's giving us a black eye. Friend called today from OPS, he heard they're about to pop him, and the so-called friendly opposition in the City Council are going to be lying like snakes in the weeds, trying to close me down. The argument is going to be that we're all dirty, because one of us is."

"They got anyone else from MCU, at all?"

"Not that I know of. But if Tomczak turns, you know how it is, he's allowed to entrap, for God's sake. He'll take a couple of young, greedy guys down with him. I'm reassigning him tomorrow. And don't give me that look. This thing is bigger than any one man. My moving Tomczak so quickly is going to jeopardize my source inside OPS, so it's a sacrifice for me, too. They're opening up a war here."

Vic thought it over.

"And speaking of OPS," Flynn said, his eyes twinkling, "we got a call from them about you today, too."

"Me?" Vic said, unsettled. "I don't even jaywalk."

"Nuns down at the convent say you had a couple of

guys, watching their place, busted for no reason. Guess who the next call was from?"

"Campo?"

"Great detective you are, Vic. Yeah, Campo's lawyer called, so Tommy's boys are back in place, and they're gonna stay in place, you hear me? What if you have them busted and this wacko comes back and ices another nun? How you figure it'd look in the press if Campo goes to the *Times* saying he's a straight businessman, and this lieutenant with the MCU stops him from protecting those nuns?"

"Campo has that much juice with you?"

"Don't talk like an asshole, Vic. You know how the game's played. Campo ever goes down, it'll have to be by the feds, not by us. He's too insulated. Too high up now."

Vic took a sip of coffee, craving a cigarette, hurting for nicotine. Fuck it. Campo won, but Geere wouldn't.

"So where you got Tomczak now, Vic?"

"His wife lost her baby this afternoon, early. He came in wanting to work, so I sent him on stakeout, over at the Geere woman's house. Let him house-sit, feel important. I know what he's going through."

"You mean Elizabeth?"

Even hearing the name spoken brought a tightness to Vic's chest. "Yes," he said.

"Okay," Flynn said. "Let him sleep over there, where people can't talk to him, it's better for us. Hell, the kid won't go there, he can't be dumb enough to think we won't have his mother's house covered. In the morning, send him to me. I'll get him an office job somewhere until OPS rolls him up, if they haven't already.

"Now, Vic." Flynn leaned over, squeezing Vic's forearm. "I got a *lot* of heat on this one. I don't usually bother you with this kind of shit, but now I got no choice. If my hottest MCU team can't track down one psycho, I'll have a time explaining *that* to the guys who want to cut our throats, and, believe me, there're enough of them out there with the razor ready."

"I don't play politics, Earl."

"Don't kid yourself, Vic. It's more than politics. It's deeper. It starts with politicians, yes, but how many cops do you know who aren't beholden to an alderman, a councilman, someone with political pull? We have to watch the guys over at Eleventh and State like hawks, what with the OPS guys right next door. And you know Jacobs, right? Captain, OPS? His *brother* is an alderman, loyal to the last mayor. He'll listen to anything about us and take the word of a street junkie over ours. Everybody on the force who got hired because of his family's clout, if it isn't Mayor *Konrack's* clout, then they're the enemy. And I mean enemy.

"This isn't the loyal opposition, not different ideologists working toward the same goal. These are guys who will cut your throat, and the throats of the whole MCU, if you give them an inch." He spread his thumb and forefinger apart to show his point. "One inch, Vic. So quit acting above it all. It's *all* politics, and don't you forget it."

Vic felt the soup he'd eaten floating around in his stomach like molten lead. He did not argue with Flynn about any of it, because in his heart he knew it was all true. When his beeper went off, he felt as if he'd been saved by the bell, but the feeling was momentary. When he came back from the phone, his face was lined and pale.

"That was Richland," Vic said. "It seems he has some very interesting news for us about Geere. Russell dug it up out of his active-duty folder. It was buried in the basement of the hospital. Russell figured it might be worth a look, so he went down there."

"What's the problem?"

"Too much to say over the phone, but he says it's juicy, and believe me, Earl, the Marines don't put things in your jacket if they can help it."

Flynn sighed. "You going over to pick it up tonight?"

"Yeah. Let me drop you at your car."

"That's okay, I'll take a ride with you," Flynn said.

Chapter Fourteen

Thom Geere was lying in the corner, wondering what had awakened him. He didn't have to piss, and his body felt exhausted, drained, the drugs gone now, for the most part, leaving him shaken and confused, feeling sorry for himself. A little hung over.

"What the fuck did I *do?*" he whispered, remembering. It had not been the best of lives, but it was at least uncomplicated. Get the check each month, do a little dealing, make a few bucks. Stay high. All gone now, brother. The heat was on.

But they couldn't be on him yet. Maybe it would all work out.

But nothing ever worked out for him, and he lay there sniffling already, without the thoughts even fully formed in his mind yet, but already crying for himself a little bit.

Daddy left home, he thought, divorced Ma, left us alone for another woman, a young bitch who gave him a heart attack a year later. *Good* for him. Only, she got the insurance checks, not them; *never* them.

And he was left alone with a mother who worked all day and went to the Catholic church every night. Until they had the problem at the church, long after her husband had left her, after he had *died,* for Christ's sake, when Father Asshole Campeau had refused to allow her to get married again until some mucky-muck in the Vatican ruled that her first marriage had been annulled. Annulled and voided, he had thought at the time. If the guy was dead, for Christ's sake, then the church didn't recognize the divorce in the first place, did it? he had asked her. And she had shaken her head while he hid his inward joy. She'd have time for him now that that Knights of Columbus usher had dropped her. He couldn't very well marry her without the church's permission, now could he, the spineless asshole? Which was okay with Thom. He hated the guy anyway, and the feeling was just mutual as all hell. They headed their separate ways after that, drifted apart, as if the guy couldn't wait for her, as if she'd be tainted even after being cleared by the Pope. Well, Thom had heard them talking downstairs after he had gone to bed, when they thought he couldn't hear them. He heard all about the bastard's plan to put him in Glenwood School for Boys after the wedding. His mother hadn't done a whole lot of arguing. She was actually caving in under the argument that it would be "for the boy's own good." An orphanage, for Christ's sake, when his mother was alive and well. What was that was supposed to mean?

The tears were flowing freely now as he swam in delicious self-pity, remembering all the unjust blows of childhood. Remembering how not even the way the church had dicked her around had turned his mother off religion. She had joined the Church of the Spiritual Redeemer within the month, and he remembered with glee the night Father Campeau had come to his mother's house, speaking in threatening tones about the mistake she was making, leaving the true Church over a matter of pride, one of the deadliest of sins. And Thomas Geere had done what his mother would not, he had told the Father that if he cared about anything at all, it was about losing the free maid service his mother had given him, the free pew washer, the lady ready to do any chore he wanted done.

Father Campeau had bustled from the house, never to return, and he had tried to convince his mother that she did not need that fool Lesco, she was just trading one evil for another, one slavemaster for another, and she had told him to shut his mouth because the Reverend Lesco was the wisest man in the world. And he'd asked her if she was fucking him and that had been the first time he'd been thrown out of his mother's house, when he'd joined the Marines, where his *real* troubles began.

He remembered someone coming over earlier, ringing the bell, and then knocking. Probably some old geezer friend of his ma's, wanting to shoot the shit. But he knew this wasn't knocking now that had woken him, this was something else. He sensed danger like a rat on the wharf.

Yes, footsteps now, somebody banging their shin or something, because there was a thud, then a loud, half-drunk-sounding shout or curse. God, he wished he could hear better! And he knew it wasn't the man coming into the house that had woken him up, hell, he'd never have heard that. It was Ginny barking, *that* was it.

So why had she stopped?

Ray Tomczak had made a couple of stops before coming to the house. One at a bar, the other at a liquor store. He'd had a bottle of Scotch wrapped in a paper bag when he entered the house, and he'd been seething with resentment because Vic Perry had sent him over here without saying *shit* about a dog. If it hadn't been in Lou Michaels's report, if Lou hadn't promised the Geere woman that the stakeout cop would let the mutt out, why, Ray might have gotten his ass bitten half off. He didn't know if the dog was good or bad, hell, how should *he* know? And he'd have walked in, not knowing squat, and would have tried to run when he heard the thing bark, and that would be it, dogs could smell fear all over a man. But knowing about it, now, that made all the difference in the world. Knowing about it, he could ease the door open, call it softly, and let it out into the fenced yard after it barked a couple of times to show him who was boss.

He took the bottle out of his overcoat pocket and put it on the kitchen table, which he could see from the outside lights, and walked into the living room, feeling for a light switch, and yelled as he banged his shin on a tabletop that she had right inside the door.

He found the light, then the phone. Called and checked in, asked Franky Meadows why they were still in the precinct, instead of out checking on the Petrovich kid, like he'd told him, putting up with some garbage about who's running the unit now, and "Ray, are you drinking and getting mad?" Then Franky hung up the phone on him.

"Uh-huh," Ray said. Then, "Bastard." He got up to let the dog back in, tired of hearing it bark. He got his bottle and found some ice, sat down in the Herculon chair, and used the remote to turn on the TV. He needed to fill the room with sound, take his mind off Tina and the baby.

Franky had hung up on him. Jesus. Hung *up* on him. Well, Ray thought, maybe this wouldn't be too bad an assignment after all. Hang pricks like Franky and Vic, sending him over here knowing full well that Geere wouldn't be coming around. Too bad about Vic, though. He was a good boss. Maybe he should have warned him, given him a hint back there in the office, let him know what was coming down, or given him enough so he could figure it out. But then what? Vic's main man was Flynn, head of all the MCU teams. Flynn gets the word, then he pulls me off the team, I go to the joint. Sounds like a lot of laughs. Screw Vic. And Franky. And all the rest of them. If they're clean, they got nothing to worry about.

Ray took a deep drink, refilled the glass right to the top, scratching the dog's head, letting it lick his hand. Thinking, if they're clean they got nothing to worry about. They only have to worry if they're dirty. Bent cops.

Like me.

Thom had lit his Zippo and set it on the floor next to him so he could see. His hands were shaking and he was filled with fresh terror. What'd I *do-oo-oo*, he thought. Killed a fucking nun? And who was in the house?

He searched through his things until he came to the speeders, dropped a half dozen of them dry, then a couple more. He needed strength now. He was under a lot of stress and had to think straight if he was going to get out of this one.

He heard the guy downstairs using the phone, but didn't make out any of his words, which pissed him off to no great extent. It was a cop, that was for sure, or else his mother had to be entertaining. But if that were so, how come he hadn't heard *her* voice?

From the crack in the ceiling next to the gutter he knew it was dark outside. He had to get moving; hell, the thing at the Spiritual Church of Redemption or whatever the fuck the name of it was started at eight-thirty and ended around ten. He had to be at the bank by then, waiting. How was he supposed to get any of this done with a cop downstairs, if it was a cop?

Into the pocket again, taking the last of the little white pills. Fuck it, he'd be seeing Petey soon and—

Petey. Petey with the ass like a pear, that's why they'd started calling him that. And how he hated being called Petey the Pear. How he'd hated it when that beaner down in Miami had shot them down, told them to come back when they were something. He'd blamed Thom, Petey had. And as soon as he could, he'd trick-babied. Right to the Man. How else would they know where his mother lived? Sure, Petey'd told them, as soon as they'd hung up this morning.

He got his knife out of his pants pocket and opened it, felt the razor-sharp edge.

The speed was starting to kick in, and he felt strong, ready to go to Florida, do it all, if he could just get some financing and get away.

They'd have to have gotten his mother's permission to come into the house, wouldn't they? And so she'd have to pay, too, the bitch.

He crawled over to the steps, lowered them as silently

as he could, wondering why the fuck his mother hadn't ever oiled the hinges on the damn things, and he was climbing down with the knife in his teeth and looking like a pirate, he just knew it. Through the kitchen, running now, getting the knife in his hand, into the living room, *flying* over the coffee table and ramming the blade into the broad muscular back of the man just now beginning to get to his feet, reaching for his shoulder holster. Geere plunged it in, landing hard, pulling the guy down with him, stabbing him again and again, filled with joy because the guy'd had a *gun* and he'd only had a *knife.* He pushed the knife in and out, in and out, until there was nothing there to plunge it into but wet, gooey stuff, then he pulled it out and sat back, out of breath, laughing.

Ginny was there, barking.

"Good dog," he said, getting down on his knees, smiling at her, holding out his bloody hand. Good dog." And there came Ginny, licking at him, the stupid bitch, and he plunged the knife in, man, deep, right inside of her there under her tits, and she howled like a woman, the dummy, and he twisted the knife. Ginny rolled over, not panting or anything now.

"Good," Thom Geere said.

He'd taught the cop a lesson, and he'd taught the dog a lesson. Him, all alone, against an armed man and a seventy-pound dog.

He began to trash the house.

Methodically and carefully, looking for money. He took a shower after he finished with the kitchen, changing clothes from the meager supply still in his closet, in case he had to take off, then he began again.

At last he was in the bedroom. He pulled out and turned over all of the drawers, spilled all of his mother's underwear onto the floor, and now he stripped down slowly, staring at the sensible, plain white cotton caressing his feet. He picked up a slip and stepped into it. . . .

He left behind one smashed and shattered home. The only thing still in one piece was his mother's bed, the pillow arranged so that his seed could be seen clearly the second she entered the room.

The two bodies, the man and the dog, stared sightlessly toward the bedroom, the way he'd positioned them.

Chapter Fifteen

He crept down the alley, back in control, the speed racing through his bloodstream. Petey the Pear's was the fourth house from the corner, upper rear on the left-hand side. Up the steps on sneakered feet, the knife in his right hand feeling like an extension now, growing out of his fingers, while he turned the knob with his left, into the hallway, down to Petey's, stopping, listening.

At Petey's door, he put his ear to the wood. Silence. Probably still asleep. He tried the knob. Locked.

He knocked twice, waited, then twice more, heard a rustling inside and let his breath out in relief. He would not have to bust in and waste time searching for the goods. Petey'd tell him where they were right quick.

The door opened a crack and Thom pushed it wide, stepping in and closing it behind him. He ignored Petey and went quickly through all four rooms, half-expecting one of Petey's little teeny-bopper girlfriends or boy-friends to be lying around, sleeping it off or getting high. But they were alone. Thom took this as a sign.

Petey was standing there in jockey shorts, looking scared but trying to act casual, calm, collected, a friend. "Man, I thought I asked you to not come around until things cooled off."

"Cops was at my mother's, Petey. Now who could have sent them?"

Petey seemed to notice the knife in Thom's hand for the first time. He shrank back, his bony chest heaving with his effort to breathe normally. He lifted his hands in a gesture of *slow down*, and said, "I'd never rat on you, Thom. You *know* I'd never rat on you, Thom; come *on*, man!"

"You're the only one knew I did that hit this morning, Petey." A hit, that sounded good.

"Put the knife down, Thom, we can talk. . . ." Suddenly Petey thought of something. "Hey, man, listen, I ain't got nothing to do with it all right! I can prove it—listen; you was on TV tonight, man, at least the cops was on, saying they had a suspect, and a reporter man, from the *Times*, the TV guys was trying to interview him, about who you were—"

"What?" Thom shouted. "Did they have my *name*?"

Petey put his hands out again. "No, no, man, they ain't said your name, but this cop, this Perry, he got it, Thom, everything *but* your name, man, said the cops expected to find you within forty-eight hours."

Geere relaxed. "They always say that, Petey."

"No, no, Thom, you don't get it; the cop said that evidence at the scene was linked to a suspect with a long history of mental problems." He saw Thom's eyes narrow dangerously and the knife jump in his hand, and he backtracked quickly.

"Hey, come on. You and me, we know it was a scam, with the shrinks and the devil worship and all, man; come *on!*"

Thom feinted with the knife at the mention of devil worship, to get Petey's attention.

"Don't ever think my lord and master Satan is part of my scam, Petey, *ever!*"

"I'm sorry. I'm sorry, Thom; hey, man, you know I don't think you—"

"Shut up, Petey."

"Okay, okay, Thom."

"Where's the stash, Petey?"

"Oh, man, after all this time you're gonna rip me off?"

"Where's the stash, Petey?" Thom asked again, moving in now, the knife making threatening gestures in Petey's direction.

Petey walked to the bathroom hurriedly, saying, "I'll get it, man," and Geere was all over him, hitting him from behind, reaching around with his forearm to cut off the scream he knew Petey would let loose from his fear. He smelled something.

"Petey shit his pa-ants," he sang. Beneath him Petey shivered, the knife at his neck, an arm around his throat.

"I can't breathe, man," he whispered.

Geere let up. "You scream, I'll kill you, Petey."

"I won't scream, honest to God, Thom, I won't scream." He was shaking with terror now. "I'll get the stash. Just don't cut me, all right?"

Snot was dripping down Petey's upper lip, tangled in with the tiny, nearly hairless mustache that looked like a fuzzy insect now. He was crying. He walked slowly into the bathroom, removed a piece of large tile from the shower wall, and stepped back.

"No, you take it out, Petey."

"Okay, Thom, whatever you say, just don't cut me, all right? Just be cool, man!" He reached into the hole and removed five plastic baggies, sealed with strips of tape, each holding maybe an ounce of grass.

"What else is in there, Petey?"

Petey dropped the baggies into the sink and reached back in, got the coke, about six grams of coke, uncut still, dammit, and maybe a hundred white crosses in another baggie. He tried a sly grin. "This what you want, Thom?" he asked, holding up the pills and the coke.

"The rest of it," Thom hissed. "You're pissing me off, man!"

The smile died and Petey reached deep inside the hole, right up against the wallboard, and ripped the baggie away from the tape holding it there. He took the money out, put the tile back, and felt a ripping deep inside his back. Had he pulled something? Then the pain came, sharp and clear, almost sweet in its intensity, his and his alone, and the wetness down his back made him accept that he had indeed been cut. He turned on Thom.

"You *cunt!*" he hollered, "You devil-loving nutcase cock*sucker!*" But then the knife was at his throat, ripping deep, and he found he could no longer breathe. He fell over into the shower and felt the water beat down on his face as Thom turned it on above him, then, blessedly, nothing.

Thom was shaking over the sink, pushing the drugs

and money onto the floor with the tip of his knife, turning the hot water on, washing the blood from his hands.

"God*damn!*" he shouted, then caught himself. The tenants around here would mind their own business, but the walls were thin.

In fascination he watched as the blood from Petey the Pear swirled down the shower drain. Unending, it seemed, coming and coming, pink after it hit the water. Lighter pink, then lighter still, until at last clear water flowed. Petey had been drained. Jesus Christ. Drained.

He picked up the drugs and tried using toilet paper to smear the blood off the baggies, then ripped open the cocaine bag and breathed deeply of it, licking his upper lip, getting all of it, using his fingers to clean the rest of it off his face and touching it to his gums, ahhh. He had to be careful here, he knew. Very, very careful with this shit. Too much would fuck him up beyond help.

Crazy, am I? You fucking Pear, it wasn't for me, you'd still be selling speeders at the penny arcade.

He had an idea then, and smiled, still shaking, grooving madly from the coke on top of the eight pills he had taken earlier.

He tried to put the money in his pockets, a big bundle, larger than his own, maybe two grand there; on top of his thirteen hundred, it'd last awhile. But he saw with horror that his clothes were covered with blood. He dragged Petey from the shower and left the water running hot while he searched for some of Petey's clothes. He found jeans, a sharp blue-and-red lumberjack shirt, and a leather coat he had always admired. That fucking Pear hadn't even said anything about his disguise, he was so scared. But he had told the Pear who he was from outside the door, hadn't he? He showered while he thought that he was washing off somebody's blood for the third time that day. He dried, stepped into his new clothes, admired himself in the bathroom mirror. He tore the loose tile from the wall and searched around with his right arm; it would be just like the Pear to leave something good behind.

And there it was. It took a little fishing around, a little feeling all over the wall, but he found it, another glassine envelope, plastic or something, taped to the inside of the wall. Thom fished it out, glad now that he'd killed Petey. Why let a guy live if you couldn't trust him?

It was a key and a piece of paper.

Thom pulled the key out and put it in his pocket, then unfolded the piece of paper. On it were dates, with numbers written next to it, dollar signs in the front of the numbers. Big numbers, too. The last entry was dated two days before, October 29. Fifteen hundred dollars. The previous amount had been $14,500. Looking up the note, Thom could figure out that the box had been opened just about the time that they had come back from Florida. After their humiliation.

And it was just about that time that Petey the Pear had started to have a lot of trouble turning over the drugs they profited in equally. Geere dug in his pocket for the key. On the front it was stamped: PROP OF SO. CHGO. BANK, DO NOT DUPLICATE. On the back were the numbers 1277.

Box number 1277, in the basement vault over at the bank. Pear, you cock*sucker*.

This! After all Thom had done for him. Set up the kids, brought them around. Hell, they were supposed to be fifty-fifty partners, and all this time, Petey had been ripping him off.

Geere put the key back into his pocket, stuffed the

money and drugs into his coat pocket and zipped them in there safely, then stood over Petey the Pear's body. He removed the cross from around his neck, knelt over Petey, and pushed the base of the cross into Petey's rectum.

He got up, washed his hands, went into the hall, and peered cautiously into the darkness outside the door. Empty. He looked once more into the apartment, at his friend's body. "Crazy, huh?" he said quietly, and drifted into the night.

He dumped the laundry bag with his bloody clothes in an alley trash can several blocks away. What had Petey said about the cop and him being on TV? He had to get to the East Side now, before it was too late. He had come too far to quit now. There was the money, he had to think of that. At least five grand. He'd get that, close up shop in Chicago, then drift for a while, maybe go to Florida or California for the winter. He'd have almost ten grand cash, and plenty of drugs to sell if things got lean; probably, if he took it real easy, enough to last him a couple of years if he played his cards right, lived quietly, lay low. Maybe get to Florida and become a big-time drug dealer. Hell, anybody could make it big in Florida nowadays.

But first he had to get a paper and see what was going on.

He took the bus over the 106th Street bridge, got off on Ewing Avenue, and walked the four blocks to the 7-Eleven. He was three blocks away from the Church of the Spiritual Redeemer.

He entered the store casually, looking around, checking it out. He felt a little bit down when no one recognized him. He realized he was sniffling, trying to get some of that good coke off the hairs in his nose. He stopped, went to the counter, paid for his paper, picked up a pack of cigarettes. The girl behind the counter just looked bored.

He went next door to the Taco Bell, ordered an enchilada and a large Coca-Cola, not feeling at all hungry but needing something in front of him while he sat down at a table to read the paper. He forced himself to eat a little of it while he read.

He was front page. This was really something. His name, naturally, was never mentioned. A Lieutenant Victor Perry was heading the investigation, commanding an MCU team. MCU! Christ, he had hit the big time. There was a picture of the cop there, big guy, it looked like, big fat dago nose, head of wavy guinea hair, broad shoulders. Thom was glad he'd never have to meet him. Said he was anticipating an arrest within twenty-four hours. Well, Geere was anticipating being halfway across the country in twenty-four hours. It was the same thing the cops always said when they had nothing at all.

Reporter's picture on the next page, a little sidebar story, add some color to the meager facts. Said that a very highly placed source within the medical examiner's office stated that the stool samples left at the scene of the crime proved that the killer was suffering from an advanced case of colon cancer.

The word jumped out at him like a bird from a bush, and he jumped to his feet, banging his hip hard on the bolted-down table. Forgetting his desire not to attract attention, Thom walked quickly from the Taco Bell and onto the street, his face ashen.

So he had cancer. No wonder he couldn't shit right these days, why he had the pain in his gut deep and sharp unless he was high, only then feeling relief. And he thought it had been withdrawal.

Tears of self-pity came now, sweet and sharp, and Thom Geere wallowed in it, enjoyed it, staggered into the alley embracing it to him.

He walked down the alleys smoking cigarettes, crying, dropping a white cross every so often, not caring if he OD'd.

He found a gangway leading to an apparently empty house, checked it out, yes, a For Sale sign out front, DABBS REALTY, windows dark, uncurtained, the living room empty of furniture. He broke a basement window, crawled in, and felt his way into a damp corner.

He began to bang his head slowly against the stone wall, crying desperately now, cursing his luck, wondering if praying would do him any good, if God would forgive him for the games he played, pretending to worship the other guy.

A light went on above him and he screamed and leapt to his feet, his back against the cold stone wall, staring at the burning light over the washtub.

A timer. No curtains on the windows, no furniture in the house, but they had the place rigged to a timer, for God's sake, to scare off crooks.

Geere walked over and turned off the light switch, thinking that he'd have to straighten the whole thing out very fast now. It was after eight already. He sat down on the hard cement floor, away from the windows, wondering about the cancer, wondering about life and death, wondering if he should call somebody—hell, old nigger boy Russell had been eager enough to help him this morning.

All right. A half-hour. Make up your mind one way or the other within a half-hour. That's all the time he could spare. Then he'd either go with the original plan, do what he had to do to get enough cake together to take over Florida, or he'd wait here till morning, give Russell a call, see what they could work out. He'd give it a half-hour. No more than that.

Chapter Sixteen

With Vic gone, Lou Michaels was in charge, by virtue of his experience and seniority with the MCU. He watched with impatience as Frank Meadows argued with Ray Tomczak on the phone, wondering how to get rid of Franky for the night. He was getting on Lou's nerves.

Franky hung up the phone, cutting Ray Tomczak off in mid-sentence. "Real fuckin' sweet," he muttered to Lou and Mick. "Guy's out there, supposed to be working, he's drunk as a skunk. Sent Bobby home, we still gotta work."

"You got a date tonight, Franky, do you?" Lou said through a mouthful of Double Whopper with Cheese. "Ta-ta, go on, beat it." Thinking, *that* ought to do it.

Franky looked at him. "You mean it, I can go?"

"Do us a favor," the Mick said. "Go on, get out of here."

"What's that supposed to mean?" Franky said. There was a difference between doing somebody a favor, covering for him, and not wanting him around.

"It means," Mick said, "that your partner lost a child today. And you hang up the phone on him."

"Fellas, fellas," Lou cut in, "we're all tired, let's not get into a situation here." He turned to Franky. "Go ahead on your date, we'll handle the Petrovich kid."

"Thanks, Lou," Frank said, grabbing his jacket and shooting a fierce look at the Mick. "Hope you're off your period tomorrow, Kung-Fu." He went out of the room whistling.

"What'd he call me?" Mick said, and he and Lou laughed, knowing Franky would hear them and not giving a damn.

"I mean, for *years* now," Mick said, "every morning, no matter what we've been working on, I've always managed to get my half-hour meditation, and today I didn't get it. Hell, a half-hour, right now, and I could go another twelve hours, no sweat, but look at me, I'm dragging my ass, I'm jumping on a pussy-hound like Franky Meadows for no reason, hell, what do I care about him and Ray having a lovers' quarrel? I don't, really I don't. But Ray's a scumbag, and Franky has no honor. So it comes out the first time I'm tired, you know?"

Lou decided to pretend he knew what the kid was talking about. It was common knowledge that Mick had studied karate or something for the past ten years or so, since he was in high school. If he was going to freak, Lou didn't want it to be on him.

"You want a quiet half an hour, I'll give you a quiet

half an hour," he told Mick, getting up to put on his coat and gloves. "That Whopper just got me hungry. I'm going down to the Golden Rail, down on Ninety-sixth Street, get some tacos. You want some?"

"You mean it?"

"Yeah. You want some tacos, I'll get you some tacos."

"No, no, about the half-hour, I mean. You'll leave me here alone for a half-hour?"

"Sure, an hour, you want it."

"No, we gotta get to the Petrovich kid tonight. I'll be ready in a half-hour."

Lou left the Mick disconnecting the phones and shutting off lights, and he thanked God as he walked to the street that he was mostly partnered with Vic Perry. He hadn't realized how goofy the rest of the team was. Ray needing a drink was understandable, but man, if the lieutenant found out about it, on the job, ooheee, the shit would hit the fan. And Franky, thinking all the time about nooky. Bobby, rapping about his aching dogs from walking all day, rubbing his bare feet and putting his wet socks on the old steam radiator there in the room. And now the Mick, the supposedly solid one, talking about his half-hour. He wondered fleetingly what Mick *did*, exactly, during that precious half an hour. He had an image of the Mick jerking off, and was chuckling as he got into the green department Plymouth and headed for the Golden Rail.

He didn't envy Bobby or the bluesuits who were doing the door-to-door. As he drove the mile over to the restaurant he noticed that the streets were nearly silent this Halloween night. Gone were the usual packs of children in costumes, their trick-or-treat bags trailing as they ran down the street with bars of soap in their pockets, looking for a house that wouldn't give up some candy. In the houses, the faces would be wary and suspicious, and doors would be double-locked and safety-chained. Already that afternoon there'd been a fire fatal to six less than two blocks from the precinct house. The burglar bars, installed and locked sure and secure before noon this terrible day, what with the murder of the nun right down the street, had been what had kept the six in. They'd stood there and burned, trying desperately to tear down the bars that were supposed to keep the bad guys out. Tonight every third car was a squad, it seemed to Lou. He'd nod, letting them know he was on the job, if they couldn't tell from the stripped-down blackwall-tired piece-of-shit city vehicle he was driving.

One murder would never panic a city, Lou thought, but it could sure mess up one hell of a good neighborhood.

Six tacos and two beers later, he picked the Mick up and was amazed at the change in him. Hell, he looked as if he'd slept ten hours, and showered. Alert, ready to go. Bright-eyed and bushy-tailed. Maybe, Lou figured, he should start jerking off again. Look what it did for the Mick.

They were already in South Chicago, so it was a short ride over to the apartment rented to a man known as Petey the Pear. Mick and Franky and Lou had all gotten his name independently, from junkies, from school kids, from other cops, and heard that this was Geere's friend, his Ace Coom Boom. His bro-ham. So they'd go up cautiously, not expecting Geere to be in there, but not taking any chances, either.

Up the stairs, guns drawn. Knock lightly at the door,

Mick to the right of the doorjamb, Lou to the left of it, guns up, at shoulder height. Reach a hand over lightly, carefully, and rap twice, hard, watching the door swing open and shaking their heads at each other, wondering about a backup, knowing how it'd look if two MCU heroes called in for a backup and this punk had just gone down the street for a pack of smokes. Okay, Lou nodded his head at Mick, telling him silently, I'll go first. Mick crouched down, then, in a burst of speed, Lou was in, jumping to the left, and Mick was turning the corner into the room on his knees, his gun extended, with the hammer back.

Nothing.

Mick was on his feet, the two of them spreading out, making separate targets that way, both converging on the bathroom at the same time, seeing the corpse there, the cross stuck up its ass. The bathroom light caught a reflection off the eyes of the Christ figure, and they blazed at the Mick, who closed his eyes and moved a foot or so to his right, so it wouldn't look so eerie.

Without touching anything, they established that the place was empty, and Lou picked up the phone with his handkerchief wrapped around it, called for the scene boys and the ME, then dialed Vic Perry's beeper number and left his message.

"Jesus," the Mick said, when Lou finished his calls.

"Good thing," Lou said, "that you got your half an hour, Mick. 'Cause it looks like we got a night ahead of us."

"How long you think he's been dead?" Mick asked, panic edging into his voice. "If I hadn't taken that half-hour, could we have maybe *been* here—"

"Get it out of your head, Mick. Shit, he's been dead

awhile. In any case, get it out of your head. We didn't kill him. Okay?"

Mick looked at him. "Okay, Lou."

"Just one thing though, Mick. Don't say nothing about the half-hour to the lieutenant."

Chapter Seventeen

Thomas Geere had whimpered in the corner for a while, unable to sleep, staring sightlessly into the darkness above him, his mind racing, seeking a way out. After a while, one came.

Three, in fact.

Wasn't it he who had told Petey the Pear not to believe everything he read in the papers? Wasn't it he who made fun of the reporters to young kids who bought from him, every time the feds claimed to have confiscated three hundred million dollars' worth of drugs? Just how many times had he held the paper up in ridicule, claiming that if they were *lucky*, they might have scored maybe twenty kilos of low-grade stuff, maybe a million dollars' worth on the street, and multiplied that by three hundred to show the people how diligently they were chasing down the dopers?

He asked himself why the paper would print that he had cancer. Were they stymied? Was it a trick conjured up by this bastard, this Perry who was running the investigation? It had to be. They would have sent messages to every doctor in the city, wanting the names of any male patients who came in thinking maybe they had a problem in their stomachs.

He thought of his options. Continue with his plan, option number one. Do what he planned at the Holy Roller joint, then split.

Or he could call Russell, the shrink, but if Russell turned him over to the law, he knew good and damn well that the cops would drag him off to the County, would have their own shrinks look at him and would pronounce him sane enough for trial, and as bad as the Army nuthouses were, they were heaven, he knew from experience, compared to Cook County Jail. They'd never even get to fry him in the chair for raping a nun, because he'd get shanked while he was waiting for a court date. So option number two was out.

His third option was to fade now, split while the splitting was good. But all of this, the entire thing, had been leading to tonight's work at the church.

What he'd set out to do, all along, was to find out if he had the guts to do something big-time and heavy at a church. He'd been raised Catholic; gone to school and to Mass at Our Lady of Sorrows. If he could bust in there and desecrate a cross, then he could do anything. Wrap the night up with a little armed robbery over at the spiritualist place. Piece of cake, after strapping a cock and titties on the Holy Cross.

But Lord, had he messed up over there!

Thom felt good about it, though, all things considered. And decided that he had killed the nun for nothing if he split now; she had died for no reason. He had set out to do something, and, by God, he would. And *then* he could split the scene.

He giggled. Split more than scenes, before I'm through.

He wouldn't let himself think about it yet, but some part of him knew it was his mother that he wanted. He'd been to the Lesco's house with her, after services, kowtowing and trying to keep his eyes off Rebeccah Lesco's breasts, and he had seen the amounts of money the church collected, had even driven with them over to the bank to drop it in the depository, and when he'd been dreaming this up, this Halloween surprise, he'd dreamed of the money. He'd pretend now that it was the money. But it was the thought of his mother, seeing him with a blade in his hand, backing them all down and taking their money away from them that had really been what it was all about. And maybe her coming with him.

And now there was the problem of Petey the Pear and his key. Fourteen, sixteen grand, just sitting there, waiting. His money. It had been his plan, all along, from the beginning, way back before he'd even aced the nun, to do the number at the Holy Roller joint and then split for a while. Get away from it all. Allow the heat to die down. Planes left every hour for the south, out at O'Hare. There was also a train leaving tonight, Amtrak, that he could be on. He'd checked all this out yesterday, when he was still considering whether to do it or just keep going. He had checked all the possibilities. But that was out for tonight. Maybe tomorrow, if all went well.

He had a shot at major money now, so did he need the hassle at the spiritualist place? He sure didn't need that money, not with the bank and with the horse-choker bundle stuck in his pants pocket right now.

Go tomorrow, get the money and run. The MCU was on to him. They didn't play around. He could forge Petey's name better than Pear could write it, he'd done it before, lots of times, on checks and stuff. Fix his looks again, be on the plane in the morning, get the hell out for a while.

But he was going to be here all night anyway. What was wrong with getting a few more bucks out of it? He was so wired now, with Petey's coke to play with all that he wanted, that he'd never sleep anyway. Stick to plan A. *Then* fade.

He wanted his mother to know.

He allowed himself to think about it now. He could see her in his mind, running away with him.

Loving him.

And he thought about how a cop with good-looking hair and big shoulders thought he was stupid enough to believe what was printed in the paper. He thought about how maybe the cop had the reporter in his pocket. Maybe all the reporters were working with the cops. How often did you see something bad written about cops, unless it was in the *Daily Defender* or some other Black Power scandal sheet. He thought about how cancer never had run in his family. Heart trouble, yes. But not cancer.

He thought about other things. Like maybe having cancer for real. He wondered whether it would beat sitting in a cell.

And he thought about the devil.

It had all been a con, all along. Thom had only put up the upside-down cross and spouted all the talk because it was the only way he could see a guy like him

getting anybody to be afraid of him. But if there was a
heaven and hell, he'd for sure never get to heaven, not
after what he'd done that morning. No sirree.

So what was so bad about hell?

Thinking about it, Thom zipped up the pockets on
his new jacket. He'd had enough dope for now. He'd
wait awhile. He moved through the house like a ghost,
silently, without effort, almost as if he were floating.
Cool. If he *had* cancer, like the paper said, then he was
going to die anyway. If he did *not* have cancer, if it was
all bullshit, as he suspected, then he would show the
cops how brave he was by pulling off the score tonight,
while the cops hoped he was curled up in a ball somewhere, waiting to die of cancer.

He went back to the basement and set the timer to
turn on the light in one hour. Then he strolled over to
the bulb, took out his knife, and carefully tapped the
glass around the bottom of the bulb, until he had a
bunch of cracked and broken fine glass in his hand, the
filament bare and untouched. He reset the timer. Cool.
Upstairs, to the stove. Turn that mother *on,* blow out all
the pilot lights.

Quickly, he zipped his new jacket and left the house,
before the shit hit the fan. He wanted to be far far away
before it happened. Over at the bank there, waiting for
his mother and Rebeccah, the cunt. Get the money,
have some fun, and then split.

In the morning. Get the hell out of town.

He wished he could be there to see it when the gas
filled the house and found its way to the basement.
Then, when the timer clicked on, the filament would
light for a fraction of a second before burning out. He
remembered, years ago, the guy down the block had
had a gas leak, and the asshole, he'd come home late at

EUGENE IZZI

night, and the simple act of putting his key in the lock had sparked enough to light the gas, blew the son of a gun all the way across the street.

Thom giggled. He had another idea. He turned around, jogged back to the house, and stood in front of it, burning the address into his mind. He ran back the way he had come, toward the 7-Eleven and the outside phone mounted on the wall, found a quarter and dropped it into the slot, dialed 911.

"Police Emergency," the operator said.

He was searching his mind, trying to remember the name, then pulled it out of his memory from the paper and from what Petey the Pear had told him.

"I need to talk to Perry, quick, it's about the murder at the church this morning."

"What's your address there?"

"Lady, I need to talk to Perry, with the MCU, this is an emergency."

"Please hold."

There was a series of clicks, and Thom began to wonder if they were tracing the call. He thought it took three minutes to trace a phone call. If he wasn't talking to Perry by then, he'd be out of there.

"MCU, McBride," a voice said, and he sighed with relief.

"I need to talk with Perry. The guy in charge of the murder of the nun this morning."

"Lieutenant Perry isn't here; I'm on call. He's over at the station house in the precinct where the crime took place. If you'd like to give *me* the information, I could forward it to him, or you could try him there, if he isn't out in the field."

"You're not MCU, then?"

206

"Yes, I am, but not in Perry's unit. Now, how can I help you?"

Thom weighed it in his mind for a second. If he tried to call Perry, and he was out, it would be a wasted idea, because there were only about forty-five minutes before the shit hit the fan. On the other hand, if he gave this stroker the lowdown, he'd be able to give it to Perry, call him on the car phone, or something.

Into the phone he said, "Look, I got it from the horse's fucking mouth that Geere is gonna be over at—" He'd forgotten the number of the house already. "It's a gray house, over on 115th and Carandolet, got a big 'Dabbs Realty' sign on the lawn; he's gonna be there in forty-five minutes exactly." And he hung up the phone.

He began walking hurriedly down the street. Now that his mind was made up, he had to hurry to keep to his schedule. This was turning out better than he'd hoped. Shit, he had the MCU after him. No sweat there, they knew who he was. Pear had taken care of that.

Now, in a half an hour or so, he'd be teaching a lesson to that stuck-up cunt, Rebeccah, and his mother.

He was looking forward to it.

Chapter Eighteen

Rebeccah Lesco told herself it was only five blocks to the bank. She told herself that it was after eleven, late at night, but it wasn't late really, when you thought about it. To some people, the night was just beginning. She told herself these things so that she would not worry about being alone in the car taking the money to the bank. Usually, Leona Geere came with her. But she'd left Leona in deep conversation with her father, and could not bring herself to bother either of them about such a routine thing as the offering.

She had, in a green bank bag next to her on the seat, seven thousand, three hundred and sixteen dollars.

Much of that came from people wishing to be healed. They'd make a show out of dropping hundred-dollar bills into the basket, betokening their dedication, as if that would draw her father to them at the next service.

EUGENE IZZI

What a laugh *that* was. He himself never knew who would be cured, healed, at any service. He'd close his eyes and let the power of God come into him, and he'd be *drawn* to the person God had chosen.

What the big spenders, and there were more of them each month, did not know was that none of this money would be used by her father, who had little say, really, in how it was spent. Where did it all go? she'd ask herself when a bunch of bills would come in and she'd find pennies left in the account.

The car was paid off, and the house. But for the most part they lived on the edge, week to week. Eating two meals a day and a big dinner with meat on Sunday. But 95 percent of all the donations taken into the church would go overseas. The San Salvadorans would be getting their share now, as they fought back from the devastating effects of yet another earthquake that had struck, killing thousands. A few years ago, it had been the Mexicans. And always, the Africans. The needy, those who could not afford food, shelter, and clothing. That's where the money went from week to week.

The car doors were locked, the windows rolled all the way up. She could see the bank from here, waiting at the light on the corner a block away, watching the young men on the corner eyeing her over, trying her best to ignore them and act naturally. My God, though, what if one of them pulled a—what was it called—a smash and grab? She reached over and pulled the money bag to her, dropped it down beside her feet, then kicked it under the seat. There. She almost smiled, thinking of herself explaining to a policeman that she'd been the victim of a smash and grab. With seven thousand, three hundred and sixteen dollars in her grabbed bag.

THE EIGHTH VICTIM

The policeman in her imagination was the officer she'd seen that afternoon. Vic Perry.

The light turned green, and Rebeccah stepped gently on the gas pedal, driving slowly, trying to remember the last time she'd felt about a man the way she felt about Vic Perry. There had been an immediate reaction there. An immediate attraction. And it was for reasons other than his obvious good looks. She sensed a gentleness there, a sensitivity she had never guessed a policeman would have. There was a message, too, in the way he'd stopped dead and stared at her. Could he possibly be interested in her, too? After all the times the police had been called to disperse the picketers after services? My God, the policemen in the Fourth Precinct must all think we're insane. Did he have enough to see through to the things that were underneath all that?

And then, there *were* his looks.

That black wavy hair, going straight back, without a part, in little steps, almost. What was it called, fingerwaves? She wondered if he had it done somewhere. She would bet that he didn't. She decided to kid him about it and watch his reaction the next chance she got, if she ever got the chance, if things ever got personal between them.

And those eyes. Deep and clear. And that aura!

Signaling to turn into the empty bank parking lot, waiting for the northbound traffic to pass so she could go in, she had a terrible thought.

What if he was married?

What if he was just another big handsome cop, looking for a clean partner to mess around with behind his wife's back? But no, that couldn't be possible. Not with that aura of his.

She made the turn when all the traffic had cleared,

thinking, where did it all come from, this late on a Monday night, and pulled into the parking lot slowly, her lights on high beam.

The bank's night depository was directly to the left of the huge double doors through which entry was granted to the depositors during regular banking hours. The alcove leading to the depository was well lighted, but naturally deserted at this time of night. Rebeccah still felt a little tense. She was not used to doing this alone. She pulled to the curb directly in front of the steps leading up to the doors and decided to leave the car running. She got the bag out from under her seat and put it on her lap, wondering why she had never noticed how dark it was right to the left there, where they had drive-up windows for customers in a big hurry. She'd been here a thousand times at night and had never noticed it. Six drive-up windows, each serviced by a concrete-based machine that sucked your money upstairs, where the tellers waited. A roof went out over the entire area, cloaking it in blackness when the overhead lights were turned off. The roof ran from the stone wall of the bank on the right to a concrete wall way over on the left, maybe fifty feet away. She could not even see the automatic windows, that's how dark it was.

Rebeccah reached into the bag, searching through the bills, looking past the deposit slip, knowing full well she had rolled up a bag of coins—there they were, six rolls of quarters, sixty dollars' worth. She clenched the small sack in her right hand and held the money bag under her left arm while she unlocked and opened the car door. She transferred everything to her left hand while she walked with quick, purposeful steps up the stairs and right then, to her left, from out of the dark, came a screaming, slight figure.

THE EIGHTH VICTIM

Rebeccah jumped as his scream rent the night, terrified her, and she could not understand what he was screaming just then, as she was backing up, away from him, seeing the leather jacket and the black watch cap on the head, knowing as soon as she saw him that it was Thomas Geere, with some sort of gunk that looked like chocolate smeared above his eyes. Knowing who it was eased her terror a bit, and he was closing in on her now, she had no time to run for the car or to the street, he was blocking the way to the drive-up banking stations anyway, which was the nearest way to the street from where she stood. The stuff over his eyes gave him an amateur theatrical look, but there was nothing pretend about the knife in his hand. He was right there, reaching for her, and Rebeccah acted without thought, seeing his left hand coming across for the bag, his eyes drawn away, though, looking at the car. *Into* the car. My God, he's looking for his mother, she thought, as she hit him as hard as she could, connecting across the bridge of his nose. He ran right into it, really, not looking straight at her, thinking he had her. The blow staggered him, his eyes filled with surprise, and Rebeccah thought *good* and moved forward as he stepped back, stunned. She got the bag of quarters in her left hand, the right hand felt broken, and she hit him with the heavy coins, right on the nose again, and he almost went down. He staggered back, flailing his arms for balance, and Rebeccah took a quick step forward and kicked him between the legs, and now he *did* go down, both hands between his legs, screaming still, but not a curse anymore. There were quarters all around her, she could see them in the light of the bank's lobby, and it was then that she realized that the bag had broken open.

My God, my God, he was going to rob me and kill me, she thought.

She staggered backward, trying to find the money bag —she had dropped it without noticing, there it was— and then to the car. She tripped on the bottom step as she backed up, began falling backward, seeing the money bag on the ground, a foot from her as she stumbled back down the steps, landing hard on her backside, fighting back the tears beginning to form. "No!" she said aloud and turned, reaching for the bag, scrabbling up the steps, angry and hurt, scared again now.

And his foot landed on her hand.

He was standing above her, both hands at his crotch, leaning his weight onto her hand. She tried to pull away, he stumbled, the weight going off the hand, and *there,* she had it, the bag was in her hand, but *dammit,* he was stumbling down the stairs. Falling on her, the knife held between them, and she felt it sear across her chest, right under the breast, and in her terror she pushed out with her legs, getting the bottom step, sliding a little out from under him, smelling his breath, feeling herself getting sick. The money bag was clutched tightly in her right hand, and she watched Geere trying to get back on top of her, and her legs were out from under him now and she looked him right in the face and saw madness. He snarled, trying to fall forward, on his knees now, trying to trap her again, and she lashed out with her left foot, caught him on the thigh, dammit, not far enough to the left. But it toppled him to the sidewalk.

Rebeccah wasted no time now.

She got to her feet, clutching the money bag, watching Geere trying to fight back vomit through clenched teeth. She ran to the car, making little high-pitched noises, she knew, but not thinking about them, not caring about them, all that mattered was getting—into—the—car. And then she was there, pulling the door shut, locking it. She dropped the bag between her legs and put the car in Drive, looking around her, putting her left hand to the horn as she drove with her right, wondering where everybody was; there had been ten cars in her way when she'd wanted to turn, and now there was not even one. And where were the kids on the corner, less than a block away, the ones who had checked her out? Where were the cops when you needed them?

She looked in the rearview mirror and saw Thom Geere standing there, his hands still between his legs but on his feet now. The knife was sticking straight out from his clenched hands, like a sharpened, deadly penis. Even through the closed windows she heard him screaming at her. Heard what he was calling her.

He was calling her a cunt.

He had wanted the money. And his mother, maybe even more than the money. And he'd done something terribly wrong to have two detectives looking for him. He was going to steal from the poor and kill his own mother.

She turned the car around and trained the headlights on him. She saw his eyes go wide and watched him lurch away lamely, as if he were in a potato-sack race for his life, and she steered the car toward him. She braked, not wanting to kill him, just hurt him enough to keep him from getting away, because she'd decided it was up to her to put a stop to this evil.

Ten feet away now, slowing down even more, she did not want to crush his legs, but she was too late. He was behind the concrete column the automatic teller was built into, in the first lane. She steered around it, through the lane, past it, then threw the car into Reverse and backed up, faster this time, and he hopped away, from aisle to aisle, lane to lane, and she felt the back end of the car crumple as she smashed into the concrete. She put the car into Drive and began to turn the wheel hard, coming around, not worrying about his life anymore, just trying to stop him.

She heard him scream over the sound of peeling rubber, a loud scream, terrified. Good for him, she thought, and he was twisting away, around the far wall, toward the street, to *safety*, and his foot, the right one, pulled away a second before she would have crushed it. Her car hit the wall hard, throwing her against the steering wheel. The engine died.

She mouthed a silent prayer as she wrenched the car door open and got out, running behind him where he'd gone, past the wall, and turned the corner in time to see him limping into a driveway across the street.

"Geere!" she shouted. "Come back here!" And she started after him, her ribs on fire where he had cut her, and she fell into the street.

On her hands and knees, she saw the lights coming on, saw maybe a dozen faces looking at her from curtained windows and she felt a moment's great anger, wondering how long they'd been watching. And how long they'd been doing nothing. And if any of them had given up watching the show to call the cops.

Somebody must have, because as she tried to get to her feet there it was, the squad car, lights flashing, pulling up in front of her.

The policeman helped her to her feet, walked her to

the car asking her simple questions she could not under-stand. He sat her in the back seat and she took deep breaths, coming down.

She started to say something. But she couldn't finish it, because now she was sobbing.

Chapter Nineteen

Vic was beeped as he drove to the VA Hospital, and he'd changed course, and headed south. When Vic had first seen the body of Petey the Pear, he'd almost choked at the sight of the holiest of Catholic symbols, Christ on the cross, used in such a way, and had backed out of the room. Flynn looked in, turned away, and took Vic by the arm and led him down the hallway, out in the vestibule, away from the other cops swarming around the apartment. The hallways around them were no longer silent; now that the cops were here, it was safe, and curious heads stuck out through doorways. It would be no better on the street out front, Vic knew, as did Flynn, so they walked together, silent conspirators, past the know-nothing faces to the stairwell, to the roof; up the last cramped flight of steps. Flynn unlocked the bolt, and they stepped out into a biting wind that was not impeded by any taller buildings. Flynn left the door open so some wiseass wouldn't lock them out. He turned to Vic. "Time to take the news gag off," he said, and Vic's eyes widened with shock. The wind forced tears from their corners, and he wiped his sleeve across his face.

"Earl, this is my case, I know how to run it. We take the gloves off, this guy's gone, underground, and we'll never get him."

Flynn spoke calmly now, logically, which was a bad sign. "The kid knows we're on to him, Vic. Or he wouldn't have killed his drug buddy. He's tying up loose ends, maybe this guy downstairs knew about the nun's death, maybe not. But if he didn't already know he was a suspect, this probably wouldn't have happened. There's another thing, too. Geere knows he was busted here before, and that as soon as we found Petrovich's body we'd start in on everybody who knew him. Now, why else would he kill off a guy, knowing we'd be on to him as soon as the guy started to smell?

"This punk, he *got* no friends anymore; from what your people are saying, he just killed his only buddy. There's no underground for him to disappear into. We put his face on the front page of the *Times,* on the television, we got him. Someone will either see him or remember him doing something."

Vic had been looking away while Flynn spoke. Now he turned around.

"I got it figured now, Earl," he said. "I know damn well why you're pulling the gag off. You're afraid of the mayor finding out we knew the name before the second killing, you're afraid he'll look bad, with his pet unit, the MCU, not giving the public everything they think they need to know. You're afraid that the papers will get on the mayor and the unit, maybe you'll lose your fucking hotshot position, head of the—"

"That's it." Flynn cut him off. "You're off the case. If it was anyone else, you goof, I'd slap hell out of you for talking to me like that." When Earl Flynn spoke now, it was as a commander to a subordinate, as if the ten years had never passed, as if they were in his office, ten years ago, and Vic were hung over and sorrowful. Beneath pity.

"That's all, Perry; you're off the case, and if you make a move on me, you're off the *force*. Now go on home; I'll put Michaels in charge for the time being." He turned and began walking toward the door, saying over his shoulder, "Report to my office, nine sharp, tomorrow morning. We'll talk about reassignment."

Before he could get to the door Mick Muldoon's bulk filled it, his face relaying his urgent message before he spoke.

"Sir," Mick said. "Lieutenant, we just got a phone call from—"

"Downstairs, Sergeant," Flynn commanded. "The lieutenant is no longer in charge of this investigation."

The Mick's face showed his shock, and he looked longingly at Vic, as if he would like nothing more than to express his condolences. "Yes, sir," he said, and went back down the steps, with Flynn right behind him, leaving Vic Perry staring off into the freezing wind.

Flynn enjoyed being back in the saddle. He'd had too many years behind a desk to his liking, he'd forgotten how it felt to be the man in charge of a murder investigation instead of just reading the reports in the morning, trying to see ways to beef up his budget and manpower in what was written there. He'd deal with

Vic in the morning, give the kid a chance to calm down. Put him back at the helm if he'd apologize, although even thinking of Vic's words made him want to go back up the steps and slap hell out of him. Of course he was worried about the mayor, that was his job, couldn't Vic see that? He'd straighten him out tomorrow. In the meantime, he had a murderer to catch.

He had Lou Michaels and Mick outside the police line now, away from the gore-seeking crowd, in the safety of his car, away from the reporters, who would put it together without their help anyway by morning. Couldn't Vic see that, either? They'd get the man's name on their own and be unmerciful toward the police for holding it back.

"I got to make a statement to the press, Lou. You and Mick here, go over to the house the dispatcher described, take a couple of squads with you. Don't take any chances; for all we know, this punk got a gun outta the house here." He thought for a second. "Where's Frank?"

"Well, sir, Ray's over to the mother's house, Bobby was relieved, and—"

"I said, where's Frank?"

"He had a date, sir," Lou said.

"Man worries about his personal life, we're about to collar a killer?" He nodded his head, filing Frank Meadows away for the future. There wasn't much he could do now, a man was entitled to time off, but when it came time for advancement, well, Flynn carried a big stick, and didn't always use it to help people advance.

"All right, Ray wants to work, we'll put him to work. This is still unit two, and you can do the job without outside help. Get ahold of Bobby, have him relieve Ray, tell Ray to meet us at the house."

"Uh, sir," Lou said, taking a deep breath, "I don't think we should let Ray in on this tonight. Me and Mick can handle it. We'll get backup from the bluesuits."

"Why not?"

"I'd rather not say, sir," Lou said. "But he's had quite a shock today, and maybe it wouldn't be the best idea to put him with us, on the street. Might be dangerous, sir."

Flynn sighed, getting it now. He wouldn't push Michaels, because he knew the closeness of a unit from firsthand experience. Lou'd take a suspension before he ratted on a brother cop. Good. Flynn liked a man with balls. But something was up, and he would find out before the night was over, if he had to go over to the Geere house himself and find out.

"Okay, you guys get moving. I'll make a statement and be right behind you. Michaels, you're in charge for the rest of the night."

"Sir?" Lou began.

Flynn turned to him. "You got a problem, Sergeant?"

Lou looked back at him for a full five seconds before shaking his head, getting out of the car and holding the door open for Mick. Flynn watched them walk back to their city Plymouth, stood out like a sore thumb, goddammit, before getting out and going to meet the press.

He passed Vic Perry on his way to his own car, and they walked by each other as if there were nothing more to say to one another, ever. And maybe, Flynn thought, there wasn't.

"Christ," Lou said to Mick, driving the three miles to the house on 115th Street, "I thought he was gonna nail me about Ray. Thank God, he let it go."

"Whaddaya think about Vic?" Mick said, looking at his crumpled notes, trying to remember what he had written down about the house.

"I don't know," Lou said, "but I'll tell you, I'd feel a lot better about this whole thing with Vic here. Nothing feels right, you know?"

Mick turned on the dome light, surprised that it worked, wishing the heater worked better instead. "Says here, the caller gave Geere up by name. What do you think that means? It was either Geere himself, setting us up, or it was this Petrovich character, giving him up; maybe that's why Geere aced him."

Lou turned the corner onto 115th Street, drove slowly until he came to the gray house with the sign. He pulled to the curb and cut the engine. "You want to call for backup?"

"Fuck no."

"Neither do I. I didn't spend eleven years of my life, working for a promotion, to need a patrolman to do my job for me." He took out his pistol and Mick followed suit, both of them opening their doors at the same time and getting quickly from the car, moving toward the house, shivering a little from the excitement and the chill in the air. Lou nodded his head for Mick to go around back from the right and he himself moved to the left, around the side of the house, softly, slowly, his pistol held up at shoulder height, moving his feet forward without lifting them, sliding them along and feeling for objects in the way.

He saw the broken window and quickly made his way to the back of the house, meeting Mick at the back door. "Window's busted," he whispered.

"Probable cause to go in, don't need the realtor or the owner."

"Or a warrant."

Mick smiled in the dark, feeling the fear begin to creep up his spine, into his bowels. This was what it was all about, for him, why he'd joined the force in the first place. With a trusted partner, there in a silent backyard, closing in on a killer, maybe, in a house surrounded by the good populace of the city sleeping soundly. This was it.

"How you want to go in?"

"Fuck the window. If he's in there, he's probably guarding it. I'll take the front, you take the back."

"I'll give you a ten count."

And Lou was gone, running around front, counting silently under his breath, his eyes used to the dark now, unafraid of tripping over something, giving his position away to the enemy, past the broken window, a rotten-egg smell catching up to him, wondering what was going bad in the basement of an empty house, but too fired up to let that stop him, to take the time to put it all together. And now he was rounding the corner, hitting seven in his mind, up the steps, opening the screen door, now raising his foot, hitting ten, then kicking, hard, at the doorjamb right under the lock and it was in-like-Flynn time, the door flying open, and he was inside, seeing the door fly open in back, Mick, right after it, weapon in two hands, spraying it around the room, his mouth opening, shouting, "Gas!" And they were both at the windows now, busting them out, shouting, letting the neighbors know to get the fuck out, *now,* thanking God that the locks on the door were probably brass, because if they'd been the old-fashioned iron type . . .

Getting the thought out of his mind, not wanting even to *think* about it anymore, Lou hung out the kitchen window, gasping for air, screaming on top of his lungs for the neighbors to get away. Mick was doing the same at the opposite window. Lou leaned back in and, heading back to the door, saw the knobs on the old-fashioned white stove turned all the way to the right. Lou stopped, holding his breath, and turned all the dials left again, shutting the hissing sound off, and turned to follow Mick out the door, seeing him standing against the fence, leaning hard, his head over into the alley, puking. Lou concentrated on getting over to the doorway, the air bursting from his straining lungs as he tried not to breathe. Get out first, get out, you don't want a lungful of *that* stuff. And a brilliant white light went off, brighter than the sun, it seemed, and Lou Michaels was dead before the blockbusting explosion rent the night in two.

Victor Perry was down. As down as he could remember being, including when he'd been drinking. His big mouth, goddammit, had done him in. He couldn't wait, couldn't keep his mouth shut until he'd thought it out. He was driving aimlessly, cursing himself, through South Chicago and now onto the East Side, past the Church of the Spiritual Redeemer, his mind pulling him onto the territory of the beautiful young redhead with the Mona Lisa smile, remembering her giving him her phone number, her address, which he had written down very slowly and clearly into his notebook.

She'd probably be asleep now, he thought, then decided to drive by anyway, take a look at the house, see if there were any lights on.

And lights there were, along with the revolving blue dome lights of two city squads, an officer hanging out of one of them, looking at Vic with astonishment as he rolled to a stop.

"Sir," the bluesuit said, "I was just trying to raise you. Lady inside, she was assaulted by your stop-and-detain about half an hour ago—"

And Vic was racing up the steps, into the house, thinking, Fuck Flynn, he didn't take my gun and badge, didn't make it an official suspension, he was still a *cop*, goddammit, and his job was to protect the public, and Rebeccah Lesco was a member of it.

She was sitting there, the report all taken, the three other bluesuits standing around nervously, trying to steal a look at her breasts without getting caught. She had a rip in her coat, and her eyes were red and puffy, as if she'd been crying, but she looked up as he entered and he was heartened by the look that passed across her face. She half-rose from the chair, reaching for him, and he helped her up, held him to her, and he knew that it was going to be all right.

The cops were clearing their throats now, looking even more nervous than before, wanting nothing more than to get to their respective squad cars and debate the matter of the lieutenant of the MCU team running in and hugging the daughter of the psycho Lesco, who had to be protected from picketers in front of his church at least once a month.

Vic seemed to notice what he was doing and let Rebeccah go now, a stricken look on his face, and he stepped back, shocked at what he had done in front of the officers. They were standing there, all four of them now, and he wondered how far his authority went, now that he was off the case. He was still a lieutenant, though. A guardian of the public good. The hell with Flynn. There was a murderer loose.

"The perp's our suspect in the nun's slaying," he said, seeing their eyebrows raise. The stop-and-detain order he'd put out that morning had only been for questioning in a murder. Vic knew that Flynn was making a statement to the press right now, so why shouldn't their own men know about it first?

"Get going, he can't be too far." Vic was already scanning the report, smiling when he read that Rebeccah had kicked Geere in the nuts. Good for her. "He's within a mile of the bank, count on it. Call for more units, check with Flynn if the watch commander gives you a problem, manpower or anything." He handed the report back to the officer. "Get this guy, tonight."

The officer he had first spoken to outside spoke up. "You want some guys around the house, Lieutenant? In case he comes back?"

Vic could have reached out and slapped him. He heard Rebeccah's sharp intake of breath and saw the look of terror pass across her face before she got it under control.

"I'll take care of that. Get moving." He turned to Rebeccah. "Can I use your phone?"

He called the precinct, talked to the watch commander, and requested a squad in the alley throughout the night. And got the reaction he'd expected. Manpower shortage. If a witness in a murder case was afraid for his life, he could come in, get protective custody; he was having a hard enough time tonight, he told Vic, without baby-sitting any witnesses. Vic told him he'd take care of it, then repeated what he'd told the uniforms. The commander said he'd check with Flynn if there was a request for additional units.

Vic hung up, knowing why the commander was giving him such a hard time. His last sentence had been the giveaway. Flynn had called him. Told him Vic was no longer in charge of the case.

Vic turned, and standing before him was one of the tallest and handsomest men he had ever seen. Piercing cobalt eyes stared warmly into Vic's but looked shocked, also, as if there were something behind Vic's head. So, this was the good Reverend. Staring off into space with a vacant look. Maybe the local cops were right. Maybe the guy is nuts.

"Reverend Lesco?" Vic said, walking to him, holding out his hand. The man just stood there, staring at Vic, a slight smile twitching at his lips. Give the citizen the benefit of the doubt. He'd been through a lot today.

Finally Vic broke the spell. "Reverend Lesco?"

Rebeccah touched her father's arm, and this seemed to return him to reality. He muttered an apology, but kept staring.

Once more Vic extended his hand. Lesco gripped it firmly, and Vic felt a reassuring warmth in the fingers. He no longer had the urge for a drink, as he'd had all day. He no longer craved a damned cigarette, as he'd craved for the last five days, since smoking his last one. He felt calm, hypnotized, almost. And suddenly, he believed.

"I'll be damned," Lesco said.

"Papa?" Rebeccah said.

Lesco turned to her, as if just remembering that she was in the room. "Hmmm?"

"Is—is everything, well, okay?"

And the Reverend Lesco, in spite of the gravity of the situation, began to laugh. "Okay," he managed, "okay? Well, I would guess that would be up to you, now wouldn't it?"

Vic and Rebeccah stared at him, a dawning in her eyes, Vic with no idea what was going on.

"Mrs. Geere has somehow managed to sleep through

all this confusion," Lesco said, slyly smiling still, his voice light, his manner hearty. "I do believe I'll try and sleep myself, now that everything seems under control. You *are* all right, darling?"

"I'm fine, Papa, and yes, of course, please try to sleep; you did perform a healing tonight, after all."

"Yes, I did," the Reverend replied, turning his bemused attention to Vic now. "Are you a believer, Mr. Perry?"

Vic didn't remember introducing himself. No, he hadn't. Maybe one of the bluesuits had called him by name. Maybe.

"Uh, excuse me, Reverend Lesco, but I don't know enough about it to say if I am or not."

"Good answer," Lesco boomed. "Safe answer." He turned then, nodding his head to them, saying an off-hand good-night over his shoulder, shaking his head. He stopped at the bottom of the stairs and looked back at them, just as Vic called his name.

Their eyes met for just a second, locked, and Vic felt the sense of warmth and comfort he'd felt when they touched hands. In the back of his mind, things began to fall into place, he was beginning to understand where he was going wrong, why he was feeling the powerful urge to drink after ten years, why he'd been dying for a smoke.

"When I came here tonight, sir, no disrespect intended, but you looked at me, *stared* at me for the longest time. Is . . . I mean, I'm familiar with who you are and all, well. . . ." He decided just to blurt it out. "Were you seeing anything *wrong,* sir?"

The Reverend Lesco laughed. "Wrong? Like perhaps some sort of tragedy coming into your life? No, no great tragedy, Victor."

He had the first name, too, Vic thought. Maybe the girl had told her father about him?

"As a matter of fact, Victor, I believe your tragedies are all behind you, if I may say so."

"Sir?"

Lesco sighed softly. "You've a fatal disease, have you not? One that has just recently been recognized as a disease?"

Vic nodded.

"And there have been more than enough tragedies otherwise? You know what I mean."

Again Vic nodded, thinking of Claire, and the nun.

"Why did you change your name?" Lesco asked.

Vic shrugged. "My father thought it would be easier for me with a name that didn't sound like a gangster's. He changed it, not me. After his death, I respected his beliefs and let it stay as it was. Besides, by that time I was so used to Perry that Perrino would have sounded like a stranger's name."

"I was seeing that in the doorway, Victor," Lesco said, "that, and also one of the most beautiful auras I have ever had the pleasure of seeing." And he was gone now, as if that explained everything.

Chapter Twenty

"So you don't believe him?" she asked, hoping she wouldn't offend Victor Perry but feeling a little bit defensive; they might as well get the air clear right now about where they stood about her father.

"As a matter of fact," Vic said, "he was dead on target, on both counts. So I have no doubt that what he said about the aura was true. Also, he seemed to know my first name. Did you mention it to him?"

She waved it off with a flip of her hand. "Oh, he knows everyone's first name. It comes naturally." She giggled. "And what he said about your aura is true. I've never seen one quite like it before."

Looking embarrassed now, Vic said, "Rebeccah, those cops that were here? Did they give you any advice about taking on assailants with knives barehanded?"

"Oh God, did they ever! What was I supposed to do,

let the man rob me, or worse? You should have seen him, Vic, he was like something out of a nightmare, screaming about Satan, his knife in his hand, it was just —just second nature to stop him."

"And your wound?"

"It ripped my dress, and I thought, with those officers here, fighting to keep their eyes off me as it was . . ."

"I see," he stammered. "When I came in, I—I didn't mean to be so forward, Rebeccah, I was just so relieved that you were okay."

"Don't be sorry, Vic, I enjoyed it."

"Really?"

She nodded her head, her hair falling slowly around her face.

"I'd better be going," he said shyly.

Rebeccah couldn't think of a way to keep him there without seeming forward, and so she walked him to the door, a step behind him, holding the coat over her ripped dress and the bandaged scrape, thinking that he'd be back, this didn't seem like a game to him, a con, a little ego thing.

He stopped at the door. "Why'd you do it?" he asked.

"It wasn't his," she said.

"As simple as that?"

"As simple as that."

"Good night, Miss Lesco."

"Good night, Vic," she said, and then he was gone and she closed and locked the door behind him and leaned against it, closing her eyes, feeling happy because he *hadn't* hit on her. He was a cop and interested and he hadn't hit on her. She knew cops, she knew them all right, especially big-city cops; how about the way those goons of his had ogled her before he arrived, how about all the uniformed guys playing Mr. Chivalry every time they ran across her, trying to hit on her without letting on that they were.

I was just so relieved that you were okay. His words rang in her ears while she went through the house, checking doors and windows, as she did every night, smiling, thinking of him, wondering how long it would take him to come back.

Chapter Twenty-one

Psychos in a big city always think that they can get away with murder. Often, they are right.

It wasn't just the MCU, the special squads, who caught big headline-grabbing cases. Every detective, every cop, for that matter, in any big city, sees people who thought they could get away with a crime.

In a South Side suburb a young man was stopped for swerving in and out of lanes late at night, and in the backseat of the car the arresting officers found the frozen corpse of his mother. He'd killed her and put her in the freezer until the weekend, when he was out of school and had the time to drive her away from their fashionable North Side home. The officers learned that he had been planning to take her to an Indiana cornfield and bury her. He was driving erratically because he did not yet have his driver's license. He was fifteen years old.

In Uptown, where the Native Americans fought the Appalachian whites for bunks in two-dollars-a-night flophouses, two patrol officers had watched a suspect in fourteen murders carry three separate bags of bloody garbage out of his apartment and dump them at the curb, not even taking the time to carry them around to the alley. They'd spotted him a block away, and sat and watched, calling a backup unit when they noticed the blood. Inside the bag were the remains of three pre-teen youths, their bodies cut into packageable hunks with a hacksaw. The suspect, when apprehended, claimed that he had killed them in self-defense, then had panicked.

More times than most cops cared to remember, they had been summoned to a hospital to check into an "accidental scalding" and had been shown the cooked corpse of an infant, skin nearly off, and when the offending parent had finally broken down they would say something about punishing the child, doing it for the child's own good.

In the previous year there had been over fifty cases of infant murder, where a neighbor or passerby or sanitation worker had found the body of an infant not yet a day old, abandoned in alleys, hallways, garbage cans, in the backseats of cars in parking lots. The child had almost always died of exposure, or starvation. But ten percent of the time the baby's head was crushed in.

A South Side father had murdered his son for using all the hot water during his shower, then tried to pass it off as suicide.

Also on the South Side, a mother and son had been playing a card game called Three Card Gimmy, a variation of rummy. The mother, betting with her welfare check, cleaned her son out of his unemployment compensation, and as she walked away, going out to have a little party with the unexpected windfall, her beloved son came up from behind and stabbed her in the back seventy-three times. When the police found him in the bar on the corner, he expressed first surprise, and then shock, at the news of his mother's death. And his clothes had been bloodstained, his knife was still in his pocket, and his mother's welfare money was on the bar in front of him.

Three times that year already, officers had found the naked, brutalized torsos of blond-haired men in their twenties. Across the border a short way, over in Calumet City, five heads were found in a forest preserve during the full moon for five successive months. The rest of the bodies were never found, nor was the case ever cracked.

Chicago had its fair share of devil-worshipers, serious ones, not losers like Thomas Geere who used the practice to instill fear into his few friends. There were witchcraft practitioners, too. And there were more than enough cases of necromancy, child molestation, and homosexual rape to keep things interesting.

In the city of Chicago there are over four million people.

In the city of Chicago there are twelve thousand cops.

That means one cop to every 333 people. If even one percent of these citizens happen to have homicidal tendencies, there will be at least three psychos for every cop.

The good guys are outnumbered.

And of those forty thousand people, the one percent, maybe ten percent of *them* will snap and commit a murder.

Which accounts for four thousand murders. The trouble is, the psycho rarely stops at one. Any cop in the city would lay serious odds that not one of these killers ever expected to get caught.

Psychos roam the streets, plotting, planning, looking pretty much like the rest of us, seeming to mind their own business, but the second no one is looking, they go to work.

Every one of them believes himself or herself to be invincible. Uncatchable. Beyond the law. They have grandiose dreams and plans, schemes to get them through the night while they lie twitching in their beds, seething with resentment, hating the world that has done them terrible wrong so many times. They outline their revenge, plotting, thinking about where they will go and what they will do when their ship comes in.

For Thomas Geere, that dream was Florida, to play Scarface and to sell dope, be a big-time enforcer and show them all.

The fact of the matter was, you couldn't get Thomas Geere out of Chicago with a stick of dynamite, not after the kick in the balls.

He, of course, was not aware of it, but it would not have surprised Vic Perry or any other working cop to learn that killing the nun had pushed Geere over an edge he had been teetering on for fifteen years, since the first time he'd touched himself and found sexual satisfaction by thinking of his mother.

A working cop would never try to psychoanalyze him, though. A working cop's job was to stop these people. That's all. Not to go out on the brink themselves, looking.

But a psychoanalyst would tell you that Geere had

been conjuring up the waters like a sorcerer for years, and had now gotten in over his head.

Thom Geere, though, would be the last to see that he was drowning.

It had crossed his mind that what he was doing was wrong. But he did not care. The nun had been the turning point, when the water had washed over him, and all he could see now was what his visions showed him. The only place he could go was where they took him, and he would wash ashore wherever they dropped him.

Without even knowing it, Thomas Geere had gone to war.

To war with the church, where he had been humiliated and belittled all his life. He had killed the nun, setting things in motion, then ridden the wave, hitting top end, hanging ten, winding it all the way out, enjoying power, tasting it for the first time in his life.

Petey the Pear hadn't ratted on him, and maybe, if he'd given it any thought, he would have figured it out. But Petey the Pear had a telephone. Geere had never had a telephone. Petey the Pear had girlfriends. Geere bought his sex, or convinced one of the teeny-boppers stoned out of her head at Petey's house that he was hot stuff, all right, and he sometimes got them to have sex with him. It wasn't like having a girlfriend. Not at all. And Petey the Pear was good-looking. Thomas Geere had been cursed with frizzy black hair and more than his quota of ugly.

Which was why, when he'd seen the newspaper and seen the picture of Victor Perry, Geere went to war with him, too. Good-looking, tall, handsome head of black hair but not frizzy, not steel wool, wavy and slick-looking. So he was on the list.

His mother had to go, that was all. He'd been at war with her his entire life.

Thomas Geere was enjoying being at war. Had forgotten, for the moment, Florida, the Big Fade. It would have to wait a little while, because now there was a witness. He'd been stopped, stymied. And this woman was now talking to his enemy, his archenemy, in her house, and it was getting, for Thomas Geere, very personal. He would stop the witness. Had to shut her up, and all the people she might tell. The four uniforms over there, who had already left, did not count. He had watched them from his vantage point, lying in a grassy gangway across the street, several houses down. Had seen the second squad arrive. He hadn't been there when the first car arrived, the squad car that had brought Rebeccah home; Thomas Geere had taken a little longer to make his way the five blocks to the Lesco house. But the four uniformed officers were working stiffs, spear carriers. They did not know him, and never would. He was nothing but a name on a sheet of paper to them.

He was more than that to Perry.

He was more than that to Rebeccah, and her father.

He was more than that to his mother. Far more, he hoped.

They would have to die, all of them. A man with a gun had been in his mother's house, a policeman. Only she could have told him, he knew now. Asked for protection. Well, now she was probably sitting in that house with the Lescos. There was simply no other place that she could be.

He had to get in there. With something more than a knife.

There was a place he could go, he knew, and get what

he needed. And then he could come back and settle all the scores. Get it all over with, ride the wave till it peaked, and then glide to shore, landing on his feet and ready to see when the next wave was coming.

In Florida. The wave would get him there. And he'd have enough money. That is, after he got Petey's money from the box at the bank. But the money now would have to wait. Until he got rid of all the witnesses. The witnesses to his shame.

Rebeccah and her father.

His mother.

And Victor Perry.

The cunts.

Chapter Twenty-two

It all started coming down on Vic as he walked down the front steps of the Lesco home. The run-in with Flynn, being relieved of command, why he'd picked the fight in the first place. What had begun earlier, in the Lescos' house, thinking about what was wrong with his life, continued to fall into place as he walked to his car.

Geere had wrecked his fantasy. Simple as that. Geere had done the unthinkable, broken the last taboo. He'd raped and murdered a nun. And this, coupled with Vic's guilt over his relationship with Claire, had put him into a dry drunk to outshine all dry drunks, had made him weary, irritable, hateful, and angry. And had damn near sent him back to the bottle.

He wasn't worried about the city or its reaction to the murders. That was Flynn's job, to worry about public relations and politicians and voters. Vic's job was to get the bad guys.

And the city was used to it. They'd been there before. It would take a hell of a lot more than this to bend its uncaring facade.

There was no major panic. In a city grown hard, there usually never was. Son of Sam hadn't kept many people indoors at night. Girls tittered and changed their hairstyles, young men strutted and put on the act, telling their girlfriends how they just *wished* that psycho would try and mess with them.

Chicago had seen Speck, Gacy. Murder was no big thing. Murder was always for somebody else.

The morning editions hit the street well before dawn —picture, name, story, the whole shot. People shook their heads, then turned to the sports section. The moves necessary for public safety were already made, community plans submitted, discussed, and reluctantly approved.

For the first time in recent memory, old St. Mary's Church on Van Buren canceled its morning and evening services. Masses would be said in the daylight hours only, and members of the Knights of Columbus would be placed strategically in the building, worshiping, but watching as they prayed.

Bingo nights had been canceled, particularly on the South Side, and the weekly players were calling and complaining, while the pastors and the assistants called the archdiocese with their own complaints and threatened to start keeping all of the offerings to make up for the loss of revenue.

Despite Vic Perry's threat to Tommy Campo, the nuns at the church were being watched, protected, day and night. They had allowed cots to be placed in the basement. The swarthy men who stayed with them, saying little, gave them quiet reassurance and cooked them rich Italian dishes in their kitchen to pay for room and board.

Churches throughout the South Side had locked their doors at dusk on the first night, Halloween, and some would be closed and padlocked throughout the day so as to discourage the inevitable copycats who might get into a church and perform a blasphemy for the fun of it.

Parishioners would complain to their priests, the priests would complain to their pastors, who in turn would respectfully inform *their* pastors, who in turn would speak in hushed but urgent tones to their monsignors. The monsignors would speak to someone at the archdiocese, and word would filter up to the archbishop, who had already had one quiet meeting on Halloween afternoon with his dear friend, the mayor. The mayor would be on the horn to his commissioner, who would bring the heat down on the chief, who in turn would have words with the inspector in charge of the MCU. And then Vic Perry would get the word.

The city never panicked. The wheels of the machine just started spinning faster.

Aldermen were in front of the television cameras demanding an immediate resolution of the case. Reporters were already tracking down leads, trying to establish whether the killer's name had been known, and if so, why hadn't they been informed to warn the public? Precinct captains were unplugging their telephones as the churchgoers called over and over, demanding a police escort to their church in the morning, threatening to vote Republican in the next election if they didn't get more than a new garbage can from now on.

The South Side was moving the quickest, as it was on

their turf that the unspeakable had happened. Street gangs were shooting for a little free and favorable publicity, putting the word on the street that they would personally escort anyone who wished to get to church, anywhere, anytime they desired to worship. Synagogues, churches, Catholic, Lutheran, it made no difference. No nutcake would be allowed to frighten the good citizens of their own neighborhoods away.

As daylight was breaking, squad cars were stopping and searching the gang members, having spotted them walking boldly down the street ahead and next to and behind a little old lady in black, who seemed painfully aware of their attention. Arguments ensued as the young men told the cops that, if the law couldn't keep their streets safe, then they themselves would. And the little old ladies would call, later that morning, the Office of Professional Standards and demand to know why in heaven's name these poor children who were only trying to help her were being brutalized and arrested by the local policemen, who had refused to help them themselves?

The heat was on, that was all. A few new doors were triple-locked and bolted, a few shades drawn, but no hiding in closets and under beds. No more than usual, that is.

The heat was on, and if the officers in charge did not come up with something really quick, then heads would roll, sacrifices made to the gods of media and public opinion, with little thought given to whether the rolling head might be one that could have solved the puzzle.

Vic Perry had had the heat on him before—more than once. He ignored it as best he could, because he knew that what the politicians and the media and the public wanted was impossible. There was no way the police force of any big city in America could keep its streets safe. It was an impossibility, the result of well-meaning laws, terribly tight budgets, and the Constitution of the United States itself. Vic did not allow himself to be frustrated by worrying about Supreme Court justices who didn't live in the ghettos or changing neighborhoods, rarely had to be concerned about muggings or break-ins, and had bodyguards paid by the taxpayers to keep what went on in the streets as far removed from themselves as possible.

What Vic Perry did was simple.

Vic carried his badge proudly and his gun always, and did the very best he could to help the largest amount of people he could. One family at a time, one person at a time, if need be, which was what he was planning to do this night, ignoring the heat, ignoring the spinning wheels. There was a single individual he could help, two, really, and protect them he would, to the best of his ability.

And Vic Perry's worst was a hell of a lot better than a lot of cops' best.

And so, to Vic, it was first things first. He couldn't stand guard outside every single church, couldn't even post guards there, not enough manpower.

But there was a family he could watch over, and a very likely possibility that they might need guarding. The Lescos he would see to, himself.

Chapter Twenty-three

*B*ecause it wasn't his, she had told him, and he had felt like an eighteen-year-old kid again, the simplicity of that statement carrying him back nearly twenty years, when things really were simple. He got into his car, thinking of Thomas Geere, and of this young woman taking him on, knife and all, without a second's thought, hell, without thought at all. The money wasn't his. She was willing to die for that simple truism. Well, then, the least he could do was lose a little sleep. He was getting to know Geere now.

Vic drove over to the 7-Eleven and bought a thermos, filled it with three cups of hot black coffee, paid for it and a carton of Camels unfiltered, along with a half dozen chocolate doughnuts, and was back outside of the Lesco house within a half-hour.

He got out of the car and walked quietly around the neighborhood with his pistol inside his overcoat. On both sides of the block, he looked into each house, every shadowed driveway, every grassy side lot and backyard, stopping and checking anything that looked at all out of place. And there it was, four houses down, across the street, a damn gangway, the grassy, muddy area between the driveway and the house, the grass matted down, in the shape of a man lying on his belly, a short man, about the size of Thomas Geere.

Vic smiled and moved quickly into the alley behind the house, jogging north, in the direction of Geere's old room, just for the hell of it, but after three blocks of running in the dark he gave it up as a lost cause. Nothing moved, no shadows shifted.

Back to the car. He knew he was on the right track, reading this punk the right way. He was covering the Lesco house himself. Was there anything he was forgetting, anyone he hadn't covered that this punk might conceivably have a hard-on for?

He laughed aloud. It would be a long time before Geere got another hard-on. Even with all that coke in his system.

He poured a cup of coffee, opened a pack of Camels, and settled in for the night, feeling safe that all his bases were covered.

At fifteen minutes before five the lights went on in the Lescos' living room. Vic started awake fully from the half-sleep he'd been enjoying and was out of the car and on the bottom step racing for the door before he stopped himself.

He had checked the back. No way the punk could get

in there without breaking glass, which he would have heard out in the car. And certainly no one had come up the front steps.

Then the door opened and Rebeccah Lesco came bouncing down the stairs in an orange jogging suit, jumping a couple of inches into the air at the sight of him.

She stopped in her tracks, her face registering first fear, then recognition, and with that, relief. "Up a little early, aren't we, Vic?"

"Uh, sorry, Rebeccah," he managed, then turned and trudged back to his car.

She had followed him, though, and as he opened the car door she saw the thermos on the front seat and the mike disconnected from the dashboard and caught the smell of too many cigarettes, and she touched his arm lightly.

"You've been out here all *night*, Vic?"

"I decided after leaving that he might come back, Rebeccah," he said, the authority back in his voice, a cop once more. "To avenge his dishonor," he added.

"How thoughtful!" She closed the car door before he could get in and said, "My goodness, you could have stayed in the living room. The least I can do is offer you a good breakfast."

"I didn't want to alarm you or your father, naturally, so I stayed outside, but thanks anyway; now that you're awake I'll be leaving shortly, thanks anyway," telling himself, Shut *up*, you sound like an idiot.

She was thanking him again, giving his arm a squeeze now, telling him she'd see him at the station when she went to file her complaint against Geere, and then she was off, jogging, down the street, her red hair swaying back and forth. He wondered if he should follow her, then cursed his paranoia, blaming it on lack of sleep.

Even Geere had to sleep sometime. He wouldn't very likely hide somewhere, watch Vic watching the house all night, then run after Rebeccah. It wasn't possible. Especially after she'd nutted him one.

A squad car turned the corner slowly, cruising, Vic guessed, but it swerved to the curb behind his car. He walked to it. There was a single officer in the car, a face Vic didn't recognize.

"Lieutenant Perry?" the officer asked. Vic nodded. "Watch Commander sent me, on orders from Commander Flynn. Says he wants you at the station, *now.* I'll watch the house."

"How'd you know I'd be here?"

The officer shrugged. "Flynn said you would be."

Vic grunted and got back into his car, thinking, screw Flynn, I'll see him after I get some sleep. He knew I was here all night, wouldn't send even a cup of coffee. To hell with him.

Then he thought of Rebeccah.

He'd have to get some rest, see Flynn, then maybe, in the afternoon, see a lawyer. Something was happening here, with this woman, and he wanted his freedom now. Not that he thought she would ever be interested in getting something going with him. What reason would she have to get involved with a divorced alcoholic cop? Still, he found himself thinking of the way she had squeezed his arm beside his car, the intelligent smile that almost always was on her lips, the simple righteousness of her decision to resist the robbery.

He parked his car and went into the house, his pride and joy.

When he had gotten rid of his drinking problem he

had found himself with an immediate raise in pay. Twenty to thirty dollars a night not spent in bars added up to a tidy sum. Within six months he had his bills straightened out and for the first time had cash in the bank. He had also found energy and drive he had never had when he had been drinking. So he had taken a long look at himself in the mirror one morning and seen the roll around his middle, not much, but getting there, and had decided to do something about it.

He had turned the basement into a gym, with the iron blackweights and the abdomen machine and the thousand-pound-capacity bench and the speed bag and the heavy bag and just about everything he could get at a health club except a sauna.

When he had finished he had gone to work on the other parts of the house, until now it was a showpiece in the relatively newer Avalon Trails section of Hegewisch on the far South Side.

But it was the gym that meant most to him. He had lost fifteen pounds, gotten to his present 195, and tightened up. Now he could press three hundred pounds several times and go fifteen rounds on the heavy bag and do sit-ups for an hour straight. Dressed, he looked fit and trim, a little slender even, because his shoulders were wide and his waist small, but undressed his body looked like tempered steel, every single muscle tight and ready to go, not an obvious ounce of fat on his six-foot-two-inch frame.

He stood in the basement now, wondering if he had the strength to work out. He cursed the cigarettes in his pocket. He shook his head and went back up the stairs. He'd sleep first. Then, when he was rested, he'd run a couple of miles around the park directly across the street, come back and pump some steel, then maybe whack the bag for an hour or so. When he was rested.

But he couldn't get the Lesco woman out of his mind, and he sat down at the kitchen table, drinking a Pepsi out of the bottle, chain-smoking, gazing out at Mann Park across the street, across 130th Street, looking at the sun porch where the kids hung out until the middle of the night and remembering one drunken night taking careful aim through his kitchen window thinking the piece was unloaded and squeezing off five rounds *click click click click click,* then *BAM* on the sixth and the window shattering and Jesus Christ, the kids were running, on their feet, taking off even though they were a couple of hundred feet away and had no chance of getting hurt. But one of them had *sworn,* the little bullshitter, that he'd heard the window shatter and a bullet whiz past his ear before he'd heard the gun's report, and man, did Vic have to do some fast talking to get himself out of *that* one.

Why remember that stuff? Why not be grateful? How about because he knew it was better than thinking about Geere. A lot better to remember a painful past than a frightening future.

There was no doubt in Vic's mind that when it got dark, Geere would be coming back. For Rebeccah. He'd seen hundreds of young punks in his career. He knew.

He rubbed his face in his hands and rose from the table, finished his Pepsi, and took a hot shower, letting it wash away all the dirt and grime he'd felt settle upon him in the past twenty-eight hours.

He dried himself and dressed in a pair of shorts and a T-shirt, ready for bed. One more thing to do. He went to his closet and got down his other piece, his Police Chief Smith and Wesson .38, the twin brother to the one he carried on the job. Slowly, he loaded it, checked it out, made sure it was ready for action. He slid it into the well-oiled clip-on holster and put it on the nightstand next to his other weapon. The squad would stay with Rebeccah until his shift changed. Three o'clock. By that time Vic would be well rested, and would have talked to Flynn. But he would not tell Flynn of his suspicion that Geere would return to the Lesco home. That was out. That was his secret. He'd be there when the uniform split, a little earlier, maybe to make sure. Then wait in the car or find a reason to visit for a while. Stick around again all night if he had to. Wait for Geere.

He'd be coming.

And then, Vic would kill him.

He slipped into bed and the phone rang. It would be Flynn. Telling him he was suspended, probably—two weeks, insubordination. Let it ring. The hell with it.

But maybe it was someone calling to tell him that Geere had been busted. Wouldn't *that* be something.

Wearily, Vic reached for the phone and lifted it to his ear, and was surprised when it was another voice he knew well.

Chapter Twenty-four

They'd be looking for him now. The cow had probably given them a description, so he'd have to be careful, use his alleys, his gangways, the backside of the city in which he was so comfortable. No one could catch him in the alleys. So he kept to them, all the way back home, crossing streets at a normal pace when he had to, but ready to bolt at the sound of a car, let alone the sight of one.

And at last he was there, walking up the back sidewalk past Mrs. Calloway's garage and quickly up the front steps. The outside door was locked, as always after ten at night, so he used his spare key, slammed the door shut, ran up three steps and down three steps, then flattened himself against the wall so she couldn't see him through the large glass window on the useless apartment door. He heard her now, coming slowly to the door, wondering who was coming in after midnight with him gone.

The hall light came on, and he could feel her next to him, staring through the door, her face full of fear, eyes searching. He heard the sound of the chain, useless piece of hardware, sliding away from its metal holder, the bolt being thrown, the key turning, then the door was opening toward him and he grabbed it, yanked it out of her hands and was on her, falling to the floor with her, his hand over his mouth before they landed on the carpet even.

He had the knife at her throat. "Don't make a sound, you hear me, you old bitch?" And her nodding head was like a little brown dog in the back window of a beaner's car, up and down, as if her head were floating there, on springs.

He got them both to their feet, closed and locked the door, pulled the little lace curtain over the window and dragged her roughly through the kitchen, shoving her into a chair, listening to her say her prayers, realizing that she figured he was gonna kill her and wondering, why would I do that?

And an answer came to him. "You should never have called the cops, you old bitch," he said.

"I didn't, I didn't, I swear to God, Thomas I didn't tell them or call them, they came here looking for you. I swear to God that's the truth, and they made me and Mrs. Postalik give a statement—*Help!* . . ." He hit her before the second shout could come and she was down, out, on the kitchen floor.

He tore the cord out of the coffeepot and tied her hands behind her, cursing the other one who had kicked him in the nuts, because this was turning him on but the pain was too much to get a hard-on, he couldn't handle it, so he left her there, on the floor, dripping blood from her ears onto the tile. Maybe he'd hit her too hard, or maybe she'd smacked her head on the floor too hard. Jesus, too bad. He'd always liked Mrs. Calloway.

In the bedroom he found her husband's Army .45 right where it had always been, in her bedside drawer, the nightstand next to the tiny single bed, more like a cot than a bed; another just like it made up as if the old man were planning on coming back soon.

Let's see if he remembered the piece from the Marines. Slide the safety off, push the button, the clip drops, okay, fully loaded. Ready to go. Geere smiled and stuffed the gun down his belt, making sure the safety was back on, he hurt enough down there already, for Christ's sake.

Back in the kitchen, Mrs. Calloway on the floor still, her mouth moving without sound, eyes open. He returned to the bedroom and got a handkerchief out of one of the drawers, found a clean shirt and a pair of the old man's pants in the closet, threw them on the couch while he went to gag Mrs. Calloway in case she decided to scream some more.

As he was dressing in the slightly baggy clothing, he remembered what she had said. She and Mrs. Postalik had been taken down to make statements. Uh-huh. And so, if she and Mrs. Postalik should have accidents, maybe, it would have to look like accidents, wouldn't it, then all they'd have would be nothing, nothing at all, not that they had anything now. Hell, if they caught him tonight there wouldn't be a fucking thing they could do except ask him questions, and he wouldn't say shit until Bertram, the lawyer, got there, anyhow; so, without them, without the two old bitches, they had even less of a case than they had now. So, how to get rid of old Mrs. Postalik?

He'd think about that later.

He couldn't make coffee without the cord, so he took the quart of milk out of the fridge and drank right out of the carton, enjoying the coldness hitting his empty stomach. He forced himself to eat some cheese as he searched the house, finding eighteen hundred dollars hidden in the mattress, all *right,* a box of shells for the pistol, which he dumped loose into the right-hand pocket of the leather jacket, then zipped them in tight, and a copy of the *Red Streak,* the early edition of the *Times,* the same paper he had read earlier in the beaner restaurant.

She had the regular edition delivered each morning, so she must have gone out and walked seven blocks to the newsstand to get this, hoping, probably, that his picture would be in it, maybe her own picture on the front page, the heroine who had broken the case with a phone call, the dime-dropping old bitch. He read the article again, the name Victor Perry leaping out at him, the cop. The same cop Petey the Pear had told him would be catching up with him, the one Petey had seen on TV that night, promising an arrest within forty-eight hours.

He had another idea. The cops weren't the only ones who knew how to hunt.

He found the phone book, finishing the cheese, trying not to throw it back up; he needed some nourishment. There were two pages of Perrys there, for Christ's sake. Well, he had all night, and sleep was out of the question.

He set the phone up on the arm of the couch, found a pen, and began making calls. On the seventy-third try, he got lucky.

"Hello, this is Officer Gentry at the Fourth Precinct, it's an emergency, I have to talk to Lieutenant Perry right away," he said, expecting the usual assorted curses and arguments he had been getting in the past two hours; it was getting to be as boring as it was fun, waking these stiffs up. Hell, there had been thirteen Victor Perrys in the book, so he'd called them first, had struck out, then started at the beginning, with Alva Perry, and he was about to hang up on the tenth one, a fuzzy woman's voice, slurring her words, drunk, he figured, when he started to understand what she was saying.

"That fucker doesn't live here, goddammit," the woman was saying, "getting a goddamn divorce, the bastard, you better try *his* house, not my fault he's not home, probably with some whore from AA or something—"

"Mrs. Perry, this is an emergency, ma'am, or I wouldn't trouble you, but could you give me the number, please?" And she did, clear as a bell, and he wrote in the margin of the phone book, wrote in clear letters, so he wouldn't mess up calling the fucker, then he said, "And the address?" And she started getting wise.

"This the which precinct?" she asked.

"Fourth, ma'am," he said, feeling it begin to go downhill now, he was losing her; drunk as she was, she wasn't that dumb.

"Vic worked outta the Fourth for seven years, pal, they all know him, where he lives, his phone number . . . now who *is* this?"

He fought the urge to hang up. She might call and warn her husband off, and he did not want that, not yet, anyway.

"Ma'am, I'm new on the desk here, and the sergeant told me to call Lieutenant Perry and get him down here fast, we got a suspect in custody on the nun's murder, and he'd kill me if I didn't get ahold of him. All I got's a number he ain't at, and your number in case of emergency. I don't want to get in trouble with the sergeant. So I was gonna send a car out to the lieutenant's house, have them wait till he got home; please, don't make it any worse for me than it's gonna be, you don't wanna give me the address, all right, I unnerstand, but, Christ, don't call the station and the sergeant, please." He held his breath.

"You sound like a good boy," Claire said. "You a rookie?"

"Yes, ma'am."

"Make you a deal, kid, you cross off my number from your list there, and I won't call the station, all right? I got other things to do the middle of the night than take calls for that holier-than-thou asshole."

"It's a deal, ma'am," he said, then hung up without saying thank you.

So, a divorce. Geere wondered how close the two of them were, still, and why they'd broken up. Perry would still have to have some feelings for her, wouldn't he? So he'd call Perry later, after. After.

He checked where he had crossed off the last name he'd dialed, then the one under it. "C. Perry, E. 95th St.," the 7300-block. Piece of cake, less than two miles away.

Oh, the night was still young, and was he going to have himself some fun before he slept the sleep of the dead. If he ever slept again. Because he felt strong, in control. He could do whatever he felt like doing, and there wasn't a damn thing they could do about it, he was the devil himself, no longer one of his messenger boys, he was the top dog.

He'd wrap it up here, go take care of the Postalik bitch, then get over to C. Perry's apartment before dawn, then take care of the lieutenant himself, the bastard. Forty-eight hours, huh? Cancer, huh? He didn't give a rat's ass.

He found Mrs. Postalik's number in Mrs. Calloway's phone book, written in beautifully legible Palmer method. He dialed, let it ring until she answered. Hung up, dialed again. Let her wake up, let her get nervous. Just uneasy enough to call Mrs. Calloway, five doors up, her old buddy. Not scared enough to call the cops. Just enough to call here, which she did after his third call.

He let it ring five times, while he put on his jacket and took the gag and the cord off Mrs. Calloway, who'd ceased living while he was on the phone. Then he picked up the receiver, laid it on the couch, and ran out the back door, into the alley and down the block, to Mrs. Postalik's. Let her try calling the cops now, there was an open line at Mrs. Calloway's, and she could not get a dial tone for a minute or two, and that was all the time he'd need.

He was up the steps, looking at her through the window in her front door, her back to him, holding the receiver to her ear, jiggling the disconnect button. Thom chuckled and knocked hard on the door. She jumped at the sound. This was going to be a piece of cake. He waved frantically at her, mouthing *help* soundlessly, over and over, hoping she'd connect the problem with calling Mrs. Calloway to the sight of one of Mrs. Calloway's boarders, Thom Geere, waving and yelling help; that she'd be thinking, Did Mrs. Calloway have an angina attack or something, maybe a stroke?

Mrs. Postalik looked out at the frightened expression

he had on his face. The police had never mentioned his name, that would be prompting; they had just asked that she tell them what had happened with Mrs. Calloway over coffee the morning of the murder. And so she went and held the door open, and he was inside, grabbing ahold of her arms, saying, "Mrs. Calloway, my God, she's . . . she's . . ." He was staring at her, shocked and terrified, and she stammered, "What is it, Thomas, my goodness, what is it?" And he closed the door, walked toward her, as she backed up automatically, fear beginning to clutch her heart with an ice-cold hand, and he said, "She's dead." And he pulled out the pistol.

Christ, he thought, these old broads die easy. Lots easier than the nun did.

He had just put the tip of the pistol in the woman's mouth and ordered her to suck on it when she gave a little gasp and clutched at her chest with both hands. He had thought it a trick, a chance for her to trick him into thinking she was sick, then booting him in the nuts like the redheaded cow had, and he had backed off, but the blood was draining from her face and it was stark-white, whiter than he had ever seen a face before, and he'd seen three dead ones already this day, so he helped her stay on her feet, forced her to walk around the room, running now, shouting encouragement, while she gasped and tried to fall. But he had her now, helping her, laughing at her, and she began to gasp and wheeze, and then, boy, it was all over for poor old Mrs. Postalik.

He dropped her on the couch, searched her purse for her keys, then went to the door. "I'll be back," he said to her corpse, "don't go away." Then, giggling, he walked out to the garage.

He had wanted to write things on their walls, but

then it wouldn't look like an accident. They'd figure out, the law, that it had been done by him, or by *some-one*. So he couldn't mark anything up. But he'd take good care of things when he got to the redheaded cow. He'd make sure they knew good and damn well that she was no accident, but let them try and prove anything, the fuckers.

He'd realized earlier, lying in the grass by the Lesco house, that the redheaded cow would have to die. Not only for the humiliation she had caused him, but because now she was the only one who could identify him and link him to a crime. The Perry bitch might not have to die. She sounded like a drunk, and what jury'd believe a drunk? He'd have to see about that when the time came, if he was feeling generous or not.

He pulled out of the garage, got out of the car in the middle of the alley, and closed the garage door by hand, then got in and drove down the alley to the corner. He turned right, going over to Ninety-fifth Street. From there it was less than a mile to the 7300-block, and, if he remembered correctly, two or three blocks up to C. Perry's apartment.

It was a three-story house. Once, when the Jews owned South Chicago, it had probably been a mansion, but Jesus, the beaners and the niggers fouled up a neighborhood if you let them get a foot in the door. The outside door was busted, naturally, probably from the shines putting stones inside the damn thing to keep it open when they forgot their keys or didn't want to carry them because they'd show through the pocket of their five-hundred-dollar slacks.

He was inside, staring at the mailboxes. C. Perry, second floor, middle apartment. Up the steps, quietly, as if it mattered. In this neighborhood, no one ever stuck his nose into other people's business. Especially if it was trouble. Which made it easy for guys like him to make a good living.

It was almost too easy, in the end. He had been ready with a story, him being Officer Gentry again, sent over by her husband to bring her to his house, the nun killer having escaped, the lieutenant was afraid for her to be alone. But he was saved the acting job because the crazy old drunken bitch had been dumb enough in this neighborhood to leave her door unlocked, not only unlocked, but with her keys still stuck in the lock on the outside, an open *invitation* to rape and murder, for God's sake.

He took the keys out silently and brought them in with him, making sure the door was locked, the house secure. He didn't need any street gangs walking in on him.

Empty bottles were all over the kitchen table, cheap ones, vodka, wine, a couple of whiskey bottles. Under the sink, the cabinet was full of cheap bottles, still full. Must have got her welfare check, he figured. He took one of the full bottles and cracked the lid, took a deep long drink, enjoying the warmth as it exploded in his belly, going to immediate war with the milk and cheese down there.

And she was in the bedroom, in an old dressing gown, her face down in the pillow. The gown had slid up her thigh, giving him a good beaver shot and a full shot of the left half of her ass, firm and soft, white, too, no line where she might have gotten a tan that summer. He walked to her and sat down on the bed, looking at the half of her ass that was visible, then lifted the gown to see the other half. Not bad at all. Hmm. Maybe he'd need a warm-up before taking on the redheaded cow. Yeah, sure, that's what he needed, a warm-up. Like the fighters. Always take a fight with a bum before going at the champ, see how you're feeling.

He felt his prick stiffening as he undressed, leaving his clothes in a pile on the floor, and by the time he stood naked with only the knife in his left hand it hung there at a 45-degree angle to his thighs, throbbing with his heartbeat.

He picked up the bottle of whiskey in his right hand and took a swig, then got into bed and began softly stroking the woman's ass, stroking it lightly with the knife. Nothing. He put the bottle and the knife beside the bed and slapped her hard with his right hand, his cock jumping as he looked at the red handprint on the white ass. She jumped. That got her attention.

Then she was sitting up, pulling around her neck, her back against the wall. There was no headboard, and as she cowered against the wall, the bed began to inch out into the room. He reached down, lifted the bottle, held it out to her.

"Care for a drink, there, Mrs. Perry?"

She reached for the bottle quickly, grabbed it and took a long, thirsty pull. She coughed some, put the bottle down, and let the sheet slide down to her waist. "Got a cigarette?" she asked.

He gave her one.

"You the fella was up here last night?" she asked. "No, I remember a young guy, good-looking, like you, left a couple fifths on the table this morning when he took off."

"No, you never met me before, lady."

She tried a sexy smile. "You heard about me then, huh?"

He was disgusted now. "You're a whore?" he said. "A lieutenant's wife and you're a *whore?*"

"The hell with *you!*" she said loudly, and he rocked her with the back of his hand across her mouth, and again, before she screamed and lay back, terror in her eyes now as she stared at him, wondering how he'd gotten in, what he wanted, what he was going to do.

"You're a slut, you know that?" he asked indignantly. "Man comes into your house when you're sleeping, whacks you on the ass in your bed, and inside of two minutes you're putting the make on him. Slut." Then he got an idea. "Say it, slut."

She sucked on the cigarette, hoping she was dreaming, trying to block him out—he wasn't there, this wasn't happening, it was the d.t.'s, but he slapped her again and she knew, this was no dream, this was for real; okay, so get through it.

"C'n I have a drink?"

He held the bottle out to her, smiling, and when she reached for it he pulled it back.

"*After* you say it," he said, teasing now, enjoying himself.

"Say *what?*" she shouted and he hit her again.

"Keep quiet, baby, keep quiet," he said and she nodded, beginning to sniffle now, self-pity filling her; why did this have to happen to *her?*

"Say what?" she asked softly and he smiled now.

"Say, 'I'm a slut.' " And he held the bottle out.

Claire Perry wiped at a tear. "I'm a slut."

"I can't hear you." She lifted her head then, and he held the bottle out invitingly and repeated, "I can't hear you."

"I'm a slut," she said, louder now, and he gave her the bottle and she tried to kill it, to finish it off so she'd pass out but he saw that coming and he took it away after a few good belts and held it out, away from her.

"And you want to be punished, right, slut?"

Claire was sucking on the filter now, trying to get smoke into her lungs, and all he had to do was raise his hand and she cried out, "And I want to be punished." He handed her the bottle.

"Well, let's clear your soul of its sins right here, baby," he said, removing the bottle from her hands.

He had had enough coke and enough booze to last him a week instead of one night, and his nuts were still sore, and the combination made him last right up till dawn, using his belt, his hands, whipping her, making her beg for more, giving her drinks with his prick still inside her, her sobbing making him stiffer yet. And when he finally exploded in her she was covered with sweat and welts and pinch marks and burns from his cigarettes and he rolled off the bed as soon as he was done coming so she couldn't make a play for the knife. He smiled at her.

Never had it been so good, not even when one of the young sluts he played with let him spank her, not even *close* to this. Knowing that he was in charge, that it was not a game but for real, that he held her very life in his hands, had total and complete control over her existence, this made him feel as he had never felt before, and he smiled down at her as if he were a god.

"One more thing, slut, and I'll let you go," he said, dressed now, searching through his back pocket for the slip of paper.

Claire did not answer him, just stared at the ceiling with her eyes squeezed shut, sobbing silently, out of it, all tears exhausted long before, ducts dry, but humiliation forcing her to try.

He slapped her until her eyes cracked open a bit, then he asked, "You want another go-around, bitch?" She shook her head violently, then began to beg him, please, please, no more, she'd do anything, just please let her go. And he said, "Sure, just call this number, and let's tell him what happened here tonight," and she reached eagerly for the phone, ready to do or say anything as long as he'd *leave* her *alone*.

The phone rang and rang and rang, and Claire began to think that Vic wasn't home, and terror mounted in her, wondering what this crazy man would do to her if Vic wasn't home. Oh God, please, please, let him answer the phone.

"Give it five more rings, bitch," the madman said, and she began to pray to a God long ago forgotten that Vic would wake up before the five rings ended.

Chapter Twenty-five

At first he felt anger at hearing Claire's voice, and he was ready to give her hell when her words filtered through his fog telling him she was a slut, crying, begging forgiveness. And there was a male voice in the background, urging her on in a sick soft voice, singsonging at her, and she was sobbing and telling him of an inhuman punishment she deserved and had gotten. He was on his feet, the phone on the bed, searching for clothes, praying, keep talking, Claire, keep talking. And dressed now in jeans and T-shirt and jacket, he grabbed his holster and raced from the house, into the early morning light, into the car, and was speeding down to Torrence, the quickest way from here, on the radio now calling for backup units at Claire's house—murder suspect armed and dangerous there.

And cursing himself for not thinking that she'd be a

target. He had begged her to get an unlisted phone, but no, this was cheaper, two bucks a month, maybe, and she had refused to allow him to pay it out of spite, would take her two hundred a month separate maintenance and throw it in his face that she was paying twenty a week for the room and—oh shit, he'd disembowel that little fucker with his bare hands if he'd harmed Claire. Please, God, let her be all right.

In front of the house now, screeching to a halt, he saw two squads already there with lights spinning, and he was out and pinning his badge to his jacket. His weapon was in his right hand as he raced up the steps and burst through the door hoping the uniforms had him, had him cuffed and ready to go so he'd be able to put the gun in the little prick's mouth and pull the trigger.

Claire was there, in shock, one of the uniforms covering her naked shivering body with a blanket, elevating her feet. Vic was on his knees next to her, saying softly, "Claire?" but when she recognized him she began screaming and wailing and he had to leave her alone. He went into the hallway and lit a cigarette with trembling fingers.

He watched in a daze as the ambulance attendants came and he stepped into the dark shadows as they carried the inert form out quickly and down the stairs. Then he went in and demanded a report.

He was still in the neighborhood, that was sure and certain. The two squads had arrived together and heard someone running out the back way as they pounded up the steps and had checked the house in a minute. The three other uniforms had given chase while he had stayed behind, calling for the ambulance and trying to assist the woman.

THE EIGHTH VICTIM

Vic raced down the steps and into his car, stuck the portable revolving light on the roof and proceeded to race down the alleys and through the side streets, searching, vowing to do a better job than Rebeccah had done the night before. He'd run the little prick down, only he'd just crush his legs, then get out and put bullets into his groin and his elbows slowly, hearing the little bastard scream for help and not getting any.

He shut down the siren and pulled to the curb, removed the flasher. He drove a few blocks until he was out of the neighborhood, on a quiet street of warehouses with nobody around, then pulled to the curb and began to sob.

Chapter Twenty-six

Vic had made it into Flynn's office at nine, needing coffee desperately, a fresh package of cigarettes in his shirt pocket, and he avoided the sympathetic eyes of the other MCU guys on the fifth floor of Headquarters, over at Eleventh and State, nearly downtown.

It was a problem that was always in the back of all of their minds, every working cop in every city in the nation: Some deranged psycho will go after my family. But it had happened to Vic, not to any of them, and they couldn't know how he was feeling.

Flynn shook his hand, like a man, forgetting their foolish squabble of the night before.

"The Chief's on his way," he told Vic, getting up and personally pouring Vic a cup from the coffee maker on the table against his office wall. "Wants to express his condolences personally." Vic nodded his head.

"And Claire?" he asked Flynn.

"At her own request, she entered an alcohol rehab after they checked her out at the ER. She's at South Suburban Council on Alcoholism; they're the best, Vic, they'll dry her out, put her back on her feet, get her a shrink to work her through this shit. Vic?"

And Vic looked up at the pain in Flynn's voice. What could be worse than this, what could Flynn say to him now? Was he going to fire him?

"Vic, she doesn't want to see you." And he was coming around the desk as Vic buried his face in his hands, dropping his coffee to the carpet.

"Hey, she'll get over it, Vic, goddammit, it wasn't your fault!"

"Oh, Earl, oh, shit, I spent the night outside the Lescos' house, keeping an eye on Geere's mother and Lesco's daughter, in case he came back; oh, Jesus, why wasn't I there for Claire, why didn't I think of my own wife?"

"Shut the fuck up," Flynn said, and the harshness of his words shocked Vic into looking up.

"Who do you think you are, God? She left, pal. *She* left *you*. And she turned into a lush. Bad things happen to lushes, Vic, we both know that. Now, she's alive, and I can't have you cracking up on me, feeling sorry for yourself. Claire doesn't need that either." He took a deep breath, then blew it out. There was no other way to do it than to put it right out on the wind.

"Lou Michaels is dead, and Ray Tomczak. Mick is in SSCH, burned up pretty bad. That's what I wanted to tell you earlier—"

"WHAT? *How?*"

And Flynn told him.

Vic listened without comment, his pain for Claire

lessening with each word Earl Flynn spoke. About finding Ray Tomczak and the dog at Leona Geere's house. About the explosion and fire in the empty house on Carandolet. It was fifty-fifty whether Mick would get his hearing back. A cold anger took the pain's place, filling him with the impulse to find this Geere punk, now, today, and have him get his ass shot resisting. He knew guys who had gotten away with it. Why not him?

"And Bobby," Flynn said, and Vic wiped the tears from his eyes—half his crew gone, Jesus *Christ,* now what had happened to Bobby? "Bobby went back to Mrs. Calloway's boardinghouse this morning, to try and figure if she had any idea where Geere might have gone. They struck out last night, even with six squads, a picture, and a door-to-door. Found the woman in the kitchen, dead, wounds on her wrists and mouth and neck, from being bound and gagged. A milk carton with Geere's fingerprints on it was next to the telephone, on a cocktail table.

"Down the street, after they got a line on who she might have been calling for help—the phone was off the hook, by the way, prints all over it, Geere's, again— they found Mrs. Postalik, her neighbor friend. Dead, and the body had been sexually molested after death."

It was too much for Vic. He stood up.

"Where are you going?"

"Going? I'm going out and *find* this animal, Earl, and I'm gonna put two thirty-eights in the back of his fucking *head,* that's where I'm going."

"Sit down, the Chief's coming here to talk to you."

Vic sat, angry, staring up at Flynn, letting his displeasure be known.

Two cups later, the Chief came in with his bodyguard, waddling over to Vic, taking his hand. Vic did not bother to get out of the chair.

The Chief overlooked the snub and went to Flynn, shook his hand gravely and they muttered something about the quality of the criminals they had to deal with these days. Finally the Chief turned to Vic.

"Of course you're off the case, Vic. Too much personal involvement. Can't have it, it'd cloud your judgment. Hurt the case more than help it."

The Chief was looking down as he spoke, trying to avoid the glare Vic was leveling at him, and Vic watched Flynn raise a warning finger at him behind the Chief's back. He fought to compose himself and began to explain his position.

"Chief, this is my case. If you take me off of it, you'll be telling every scumbag in the city all they have to do is declare open season on an officer's family and he'll be off their backs. I can handle it, Chief. This guy killed two of my men and raped my wife. I want him."

"This is just the sort of thing I was talking about," the Chief said. "No objectivity. No, Vic, I'm sorry, you're off the case, and that's that." He turned to Flynn. "Give him some time off, to get his shit together, or assign him to a desk, if he wants to work." Without another word the Chief was out the door, his bodyguard right behind him.

"Take a couple weeks, Vic," Flynn told him, after they'd gone. "You'll still get the collar, MCU will, we did our job, identified this guy, and the deaths, they'll get us some public sympathy. Take a couple of weeks, maybe, say, until the week after Thanksgiving."

"That's a month, Earl," Vic said, his voice emotionless.

"Whatever. Look, you'll land on your feet, you always have."

Vic stood and walked over to the desk.

"Yesterday, Ray Tomczak was a piece of shit to you, you were going to bounce him. Get him out of the unit. Today he's a public-relations asset, to get some sympathy from people who were trying yesterday to cut our throats. Don't deny it! You don't give a fuck about the public! You want to throw these deaths in the faces of the Old Guard in the city council, asking them how can they disband the MCU when two brave officers just gave their lives in its service." He started for the door.

"Leave the badge and gun, Perry," Flynn said. "We'll call it a medical leave. Okay, give you a month. That's it. Or resign."

Vic turned and walked stiffly back to the desk. He threw his badge on the desk and put his weapon down gently.

Flynn stared after him a long time after he was gone.

Driving away, Vic was consumed with guilt and pain. Lou and Ray, gone. Mick burned up, Claire raped and beaten. And the real reason for his anger at Flynn, he knew, was that the man was *right,* one hundred percent. Vic would have charged out into the street and gunned Geere down on sight, and what if, Jesus, what if he'd missed? The animal would have a civil-rights beef a mile long prepared before Vic emptied his gun, and he'd beat the case if Vic violated his rights. His *rights.*

He'd never had so much trouble with a case, and now, suddenly, he knew why. He'd taken it personally. From the moment he'd seen the nun, his old teacher, lying there, he'd been on a crusade. And he didn't even have to ask himself why, because as soon as he hit upon it, he had the answer.

Pride and ego. The killers. Right after resentment, there were pride and ego, bringing alcoholics down right and left, chewing them up and spitting them into the gutter, getting them to pour that demon rum back into their bellies before they knew what hit them.

Did he think he was safe? Did he think that because he had ten years without a drink that he was never going to pick up another one?

He entered his house like a dreamwalker, his mind a million miles away. They'd get Geere without him. Let the pros handle it now. He was too close to this one, he'd been acting irrationally. He knew now what he had to do, the calls he had to make, the apologies.

And so he stripped down and put on a pair of shorts, some Adidas, and the bag gloves, and went to work on the heavy bag for awhile. For a long while. Letting his mind go, concentrating on the punches, fast and hard, working up a sweat, feeling everything pumping as it was supposed to, taking all the pain away, all the anger, taking it somewhere else, deep inside him, where it belonged. At last, aching, sore, and smiling, he walked to the shower.

Drinking coffee now, staring forlornly across the street at the park, smoking, feeling good, chin in his hand, he wondered why he couldn't just pick up the phone and do what he had to do.

He put his coffee mug down on the table and got his other gun. He grabbed a light fall jacket and was out the door and into the car, driving without thinking. He'd done enough thinking since this all began.

And then he was in front of the old two-story brick

house, walking up the steps, and she was opening the door, holding it open for him, her smile still on her lips.

Thank God.

What made him think that it wasn't a mistake, his coming over like this, was when she opened the door wide and invited him in. She sure *seemed* glad to see him. She was offering him coffee. An angel from heaven, if there were such things. Vic didn't know what to believe in these days.

They were silent as he added cream and sugar to his coffee, but it was an all-right silence. Not the kind where you sat, mind racing for something witty. It was the nice kind of silence that happily married people felt after years together. When Rebeccah broke in, it was with a concerned question.

"Are you tired, Vic?"

"Very. It shows?"

She wasn't smiling now, but seemed to be looking around him instead of at him. "Not really. But your aura is just the slightest bit dull today. Not much, though."

"My aura?" Vic said. Trying not to smile. He *was* tired.

"Can I ask you a question?"

"Sure." And Vic thought, here we go, ask me what I know about auras, or maybe astral projection.

"Where do you get your hair cut?"

"What?"

"I want to know who does your hair."

"Uh, Ken's Silver Shears. It's in Sauk Village."

"Is Ken a stylist?"

"No, just a regular old everyday barber, is all."

Rebeccah nodded, as if a point had been proved to her.

"Rebeccah?"

"Yes, Vic?"

"Why?"

"Why what, Vic?"

Vic said, "Forget about it, okay?"

It came out slowly, with Rebeccah doing a lot of prompting. But sooner than he'd ever thought possible, Vic was telling her about it. All of it. Elizabeth and Claire. This case. The seven other victims. Earl and Ray and Mick and Lou, his team cut in half, just like that. And now a suspension. Close to half his life a cop, and now this.

Talking rationally—confessing, really—made him feel better. And she seemed to be a good listener, nodding at the right times, making the right sounds of encouragement.

So far so good.

Having a friend was all right. Having a female friend was even better. A lot better, now that he thought of it. Getting it off his chest with this afternoon's talking was making him see things more clearly.

From time to time the Reverend Lesco would walk by the room, looking at Vic beatifically. Mrs. Geere went past, too, probably wondering what he was doing here instead of being out after her son.

Chapter Twenty-seven

Geere had terrible dreams: Mrs. Calloway and Mrs. Postalik coming at him, Mrs. Calloway's ears dripping blood, her eyes up deep in their sockets, looking like something out of that movie *Night of the Living Dead*, and Mrs. Postalik no pin-up girl either, her bloodless face upturned to him as if begging him to give her life back to her. And then the nun, oh God, the nun was coming at him, now, naked, her hand upraised, and he shot up straight in the bed, Mrs. Postalik's bed, breathing heavily.

Daylight outside. Mrs. Postalik next to him, oh shit, what had he done during the night? He couldn't have . . . no, God, he *couldn't* have . . . but knowing in his heart that he had indeed—but wait a minute, not during any night, no, it was coming back to him now.

He'd heard feet pounding up the steps to the cop's wife's place, and he'd run like a madman down the back steps two blocks to the car with the law somewhere behind him until he ditched through a gangway, into the car, and away with a screech of rubber and a sickening moment as he skidded around the corner thinking he was not going to make the turn, but the ass end swiveled around okay and the car was running straight and smooth down the street and he was away. He'd driven slowly back down side streets until he was three blocks from home. Knowing enough not even to think about taking the car into the alley during the day, he took the chance and walked through the alley, bold as could be, to Mrs. Postalik's house, entering with her keys, and dragging the old dead body up into bed and laughing like a madman, laughing, laughing, like a madman.

Oh, goddammit, he was nuts after all, they had all been right all along, every one of them. . . .

He found the bag of coke in his jacket pocket and just bent his nose down to it. He had gone a week once, when he and Petey had ripped off the dago who had ripped off his bosses, and then a day later the dago had been found in the trunk of his car at the airport—he and Petey had gone without any sleep at all, snorting and getting higher and higher. But then he had crashed and stayed in bed for two days, unable to move, unable to eat, unable even to get out of bed to go to the bathroom.

He could feel that euphoria building within him now, and he knew he could go at least another day or two, but then he'd have to rest, have to go somewhere and crash out, and it couldn't be around here. The heat would really be on now that he'd done Perry's old lady. And someone would find Mrs. Calloway and come sniffing down the block, and then where would he be? Not here.

He got up and carefully inched back the draperies. There were two squad cars in front of Mrs. Calloway's house. He dropped the curtain as if it were on fire. Paranoia rose up in him swiftly, and he ran around the house in a panic, dressing, taking more coke, trying to remember where he had fucked up at Mrs. Calloway's, then remembering the open carton of milk he had swilled and left half-full on the table, and the plate of cheese he had munched on, and, *Jesus Christ,* the telephone book opened to the Perry bitch's address, and he realized that in spite of his careful planning he had blown it.

There was no time to search the place now for the money all of these old women kept somewhere in the house. They remembered the Depression and didn't trust banks. They all had a nice stash around.

Thom flew out the back door and down the alley to the car. The heat was on too heavy now. He'd have to go. He'd have to come back for his mother and Rebeccah after things cooled down. Six months, a year, they'd never remember him. Or at least, they wouldn't be out looking for him. He was hot, on fire, burning up. They were that close to him.

But the farther from the house he got, the better he felt.

Okay, one last thing, then. Get the money from Petey the Pear's box. That would be it. He'd get the cash, then disappear. It helped to have a plan. The closer he got to the bank, the better he felt.

* * *

An old guy with an admiral's uniform on waved him into a parking lot. Thom got out, took the half a ticket the old guy gave him, and walked down the sidewalk, through the big glass double doors, into the bank. Left, to the stairs, down to the vault. This would be the tricky part. If the guy was a real dickhead, he'd ask for identification. If he did, Thom would be in trouble. He couldn't pull his piece, put it in the guy's mouth, and demand he open the box. Or could he?

"Morning," he said brightly, and the guy in the suit looked up from his desk, bored. Thom showed him the key and said, "I want something out of my box." The guy didn't give him another glance. Not even a look at his face. He stood up, as if he were doing Thom a great favor, and held his hand out. Thom handed him the key.

The guy led him into the vault and inserted Thom's key in a box, took out his master and put it in the other hole, and pulled the box out of the wall. He led Thom to a small cubbyhole, dropped the box on a desk inside, and pulled the curtain on his way out.

"Call me when you're done."

Thom had filled his pockets the moment the curtain closed, and he waited, looking through the curtains, waiting, letting the guy get almost to his desk. There, the guy was pulling out his chair. Thom said, "Hey, pal, I'm done."

Thom smiled because the guy looked so pissed.

Outside, he sailed the geezer in the uniform a fiver with his ticket and told him to keep the change.

It shouldn't have been so easy. He'd had to work for everything else. This *couldn't* have been this easy. But it was. Driving now, smiling, nodding his head, wanting to pull over and sniff him a gram at least, he beat his hand against the steering wheel in time to the music on the radio. AM only. Cheap old Mrs. Postalik. Look what it got her, being cheap.

"Yeah!" he shouted, driving along, knowing the expressway entrance was close. Somewhere along Commercial Avenue there would be a blue-and-white sign, directing him to the expressway, and he'd go west, catch up to the tollway, 294; from there right to O'Hare.

And then to Florida.

With his money and dope, he figured to be holding about twenty-five grand in his pockets right this second. More money than he had ever hoped to have at one time. Enough to last him a good long time. The rest of his life, maybe, if he parlayed it into something big.

And there was the sign, hanging off a lightpole, big as day. His road sign to freedom. Amen. A couple of blocks and he'd be on his way. Gone. El gone-o, as the beaners say.

One thing bothered him. He'd taken care of the Perry bitch, shown her and her old man who the boss was. But Perry was a wop, he could tell by the way the guy looked. He had to be. And everybody knew how dagos were about their women, divorced or not. Would Perry just let it go? Be scared off? Or would he be a jerk about it, hunt Thom down? Hmm.

He was feeling real good now, cruising along, thinking things over. The incident at the bank had put him back on top, in control. Maybe he should take a ride by the guy's house. The wife, she'd been so accommodating, she'd told him the house was on the corner of 130th

Street and Carandolet. Right across from the park. Corner house. See if the guy was home. There was an expressway entrance right on 130th Street, for God's sake. Just see if the guy was home. Maybe shoot him. Ace him out. Give the rest of them something to think about. After all, he might not even have been in this bad a bind if it weren't for the MCU. Regular cops, they would never have come as close as these guys had. He got on the expressway heading east, whistling.

He drove down 130th Street, eyeing the guy getting into his car wearing a light sport coat, no topcoat, and knowing, just *knowing* that it was a sign, an omen that he'd made the right move, his problem now being whether to ace the guy at a stoplight or wait and see where he was going. Follow him a little bit, see what happens. He felt good, like James Bond, following this guy who was supposed to be hunting him, getting a bang out of it. The gun in his waistband, his pockets filled with money and cocaine and speeders. What more could he ask for?

Vic Perry's head, with a dripping hole in it, that's what.

And he knew it was adding up in his favor, a banner day, because Vic Perry was parking in front of the Lesco house, so he pulled to the curb a block away and ducked down in the seat. He watched Perry say something to the cop in a squad car, laughing and joking around, as if he had nothing to worry about, and the guy took off.

Oh, sweet Jesus.

Give it a while. See if they came out. The car was idling, ready; he was in a hurry. Give them time to get into bed or something.

Maybe, though, he was pushing it. Maybe he should just take off.

But Perry didn't look as if he were on a dago vendetta or anything. He'd been smiling, laughing with the cop. Maybe it all should wait a few weeks, then he'd come back with some boys. Some of his boys after he'd made it.

Toss a coin. Either way.

On the one hand, he had a fortune in his pockets and a car and a way out. On the other hand, he had his birds lined up in front of him, and he'd been given a sign, for Chrissakes, the guy had gone right into the house. He'd bet everything he had that his mother was in there, too. They were all sitting around, shooting the shit, laughing at him.

All right. The car wasn't going anywhere, and he'd wasted a couple of hours staring at the house. He could be on a plane already, in the air. And he was running low on gas.

Tell you what, if my luck is running, it's running. Go up to the front door, big as day. If the guy's in bed, he won't see you anyway.

Flip a coin.

If the door's unlocked, go right in. Get it done. Once and for all. Tie up all loose ends. Never have to come back.

If it's locked, take off. Come back when you're old. Your luck's run out for the day.

Thom got out of the car and walked in the middle of the sidewalk all the way down the block to the Lesco house. He mounted the steps quietly, his hand inside his coat.

Thinking, flip a coin, try your luck, he reached for the doorknob.

Chapter Twenty-eight

Vic said, "Does it bother you that I'm married?"

Rebeccah looked at him for a long time, until he thought she wasn't going to answer the question. At last she blew out a long, slow breath.

"Vic, things have been moving awfully fast, don't you think?"

Vic rushed to reassure her. "I'm sorry—"

"No, no, don't say it. Don't say something you don't mean, all right? You haven't lied to me yet." She waited a moment, then spoke slowly, seeming to weigh everything in her mind as she said it.

"This is kind of spooky, you know? My father tells me, thirty hours ago or so, that I'm in danger from within. And that a diseased but good man will save me.

Suddenly Geere pops up, trying to do God knows what. Now you tell me he's killed a nun, his only friend, and a couple of good police officers. And two innocent old women he hardly knew. Vic, I mean, my heart is crying out, can you understand that? It wants to grab hold of yours and never let go, but this thing is still going *on,* Geere is still out there, somewhere. . . ." There was a single tear building up in her left eye, and Vic wanted to reach over and wipe it away. She let it roll down her cheek and drop softly onto her lap.

"My father made it pretty clear last night, embarrassingly clear, that you were the white knight I told you about. I believe him, Vic, if for no other reason than he's been right so many times in his visions. You can believe what you want, but they're written in stone as far as I'm concerned.

"But he also talked about evil," she said. "There's evil, and you were supposed to neutralize it, and Vic, oh honey, it hasn't been neutralized, has it?" And as she spoke her eyes looked above his head, over him, and they widened just before she screamed. . . .

. . . and Vic looked behind him and saw the face of evil, the face of Thomas Geere, which to Vic had been, for the past two days, the elusive face of death, and he'd left his gun and goddamn badge on Flynn's desk. He didn't care about tin, Flynn could stick it in his ass sideways, but Jesus, was he glad he had his backup piece, because this guy was pointing a gigantic automatic, standing there holding it one-handed, and as Vic stood he saw the hand shaking. Thomas Geere standing there with four and a half pounds of weapon in one hand, and the hand was shaking from the effort. Vic turned slowly, never taking his eyes away from Geere's.

"How's this feel, handsome?" Thomas Geere said.

Vic smiled, trying to look confused. "Sir?" he said. "Excuse me?" But Geere was pissed off now, damn it, he played it wrong, said the wrong thing. Still, the gun was sagging in Geere's hand, just a little bit, from the weight. Vic tried not to look at it. He struggled to keep his face blank and nonthreatening.

"Don't 'sir' me, Perry. I know you. I know what games you and this cunt here been playing all afternoon while I been outside waiting for you."

Vic watched only his eyes. But he could see the hand wavering.

"You didn't know I was on to you, I can see it. I'm a lot smarter than you gave me credit for."

Vic heard Rebeccah whimper once, in her chair still, too scared to move, but he stayed impassive. Let Geere think he had them under control. Because no matter where in the house the good Reverend was, he must have heard that scream. Vic tightened up, ready, and when he heard the pounding on the steps, Lesco jumping down them two at a time, probably, he charged straight across the room. He heard Geere scream, felt something whistle past his ear and another something prick his neck, just a pinprick, that's all, but only one *BOOM* because the second explosion fell into the deafness made by the first. Maybe there was a third, but it was too late, he was on Geere now, had him.

They crashed together against the wall, in the foyer, Vic's head in Thom's belly, Thom's head crashing back against the wooden door of the hall closet. Then something was crashing down on the back of Vic's head; then again, before he could reach around, try to pull his piece out of the back of his pants; and one more time, stars swimming in his eyes, and he fell down, fighting not to vomit, shaking with fear and tension and the adrenaline rush.

Thom had them now, pretty maids all in a row. He had the gun two-fisted now, too, grinning at the Reverend, and oh, sweet God in heaven, there was his mother, coming down the steps now, her hand to her mouth. She stifled a scream when he pointed the gun at her. And Rebeccah, still in her chair, not so tough now, she hadn't moved since she'd seen him. He watched as Perry rolled over onto his back.

"Help him up," he told Lesco, and Lesco did, staring back at him. Thom wanted to shoot him now, right in the pupil. His mind was racing, he was feeling better than ever before in his *life*. He had cornered this big, tough MCU cop, and he had the great faith-healer Lesco doing his bidding, being his slave. He wouldn't shoot him. Not yet. He had better plans for him. And Perry. And, naturally, for the two cunts.

"Get in the closet, both of you." He watched Perry, saw the battered, well-worn left side of his belt hanging down from years of carrying a gun on it. No gun there now. Probably left it in the bedroom when he was fucking the cow, thinking he was safe here. Too bad.

The old houses around here, Thom loved them. Heavy wood doors with privacy locks on them. He turned the lock after Perry and Lesco were in the closet, then grabbed a chair from the dining room set and propped it against the knob, just in case.

His mother was standing there, looking at him with loathing. Rebeccah was in her chair still, the chicken-shit, holding both hands to her mouth, looking at the closet door as if it were the magic mirror or something.

THE EIGHTH VICTIM

"Strip," he said to them. "The both of you." And Jesus Christ, was he getting a boner now.

It certainly was his lucky day.

He hollered at the closet door, "Hey, you hear that? Hey in there, guess what? I'm gonna fuck both of these bitches, and *there's nothing you can do about it.*" It was so good, so rich, so funny that he almost lost control, standing there in the living room looking at two terrified women, with two guys, had to be five hundred pounds between them, cowering on the closet floor.

"Hey, Perry, your old lady, she got a *good* pussy on her." And he turned to the women. "I said *Strip,*" he said, and he raised the gun.

The first thing Lesco whispered was "You're bleeding," and Vic had been amazed. He'd pulled the gun from behind him and said, "Get ready; on three, we kick the door," but he knew it hadn't sounded right, not even to him, and he was feeling light-headed.

Lesco put a hand to his neck and bowed his head, and Vic was damned if he didn't feel warmth spreading outward from the slight pain in his neck and down, into his chest, and up into his head. Better too. Less spaced out. He heard Geere shouting his intentions and took a couple of deep breaths, then said, "Ready?" but Lesco still had him by the neck, touching him. What in the fuck was he doing? Geere was shouting something now about Claire, about *Claire,* and he tried to push away, but did not have the strength.

He saw for the first time that there was a low-wattage bulb burning above his head. He hadn't even noticed the Reverend turning it on. He looked down. His sports coat was covered with blood, and his T-shirt looked as if it had been dyed red. Lesco removed his hand and Vic

297

felt the strange warmth still spreading. He lifted his hand to his neck, shakily, fighting nausea. He had to get out there, dammit, but there was a furrow on his neck about an inch wide and a good six inches long, still seeping, he could feel it, but not spurting dark arterial blood as he knew it should be. He met the Reverend's eyes and saw relief in them.

He heard Geere shouting to the women, *"Strip,* you cunts, or I'll kill you." Vic leaned back against the wall, compressing a row of winter coats hanging there. "On three," he whispered, and the Reverend put his back against the wall, too, and lifted a long, powerful right foot. Vic began to count.

The door shattered on three. The chair went flying and Thom turned around. Vic could see the terror on his face, and in a blink of an eye he saw Mrs. Lesco, half-naked, and Rebeccah, standing now, but fully clothed, looking defiant. Geere, as he turned, oh Lord, Geere had his prick in his hand, was milking it while he watched his mother strip, but Geere had the gun in his other hand. It would be no contest, though, because Vic had already been pointing the gun when he'd burst through the closet, and he fired, once, saw the red fly out of the back of Geere's body. Rebeccah screamed loudly, and Geere was around now, falling back, the pistol went off and Vic felt a searing heat in his hip. He knew that the bullet had gone right through, clean through, because he'd felt the exit wound on his ass, but as he was falling, he didn't know how much damage had been caused, inside there, banging around, nor had he put it together yet that Geere was hit near the heart and was going out, so he fired three times at the falling body, as he fell himself.

He began to crawl toward Geere.

Reached him, put the barrel of the gun into Geere's mouth.

He saw the surprise, the terrified shock in Geere's eyes. Blood spilled from his mouth and he lay on his back, staring at Vic. Good, Vic thought, and forced himself to smile.

"Get out of the room," he said, hearing the women behind him, Mrs. Geere screaming.

"Vic, don't," he heard Rebeccah say, and then she was next to him, not touching the gun, just looking at him.

He heard Lesco on the phone, shouting for an ambulance. He looked into Rebeccah's eyes and rolled away, not wanting to see Geere anymore, keeping his gun in his hand, though.

"You're the one, Vic," Rebeccah said now, over him, loosening his pants, pulling them down to get a look at the wound.

Damn right I'm the one, Vic thought. "It wasn't his," he said, wondering if his voice sounded as far away to her as it did to him. He was losing it now, going a little dark in there.

Chapter Twenty-nine

She went in the ambulance with him, ignoring the attendants who told her it was against policy.

Vic knew how deep still waters ran. And was grateful; he wouldn't have wanted to make that trip alone, not with his mind racing, and things getting dark, and knowing that if he didn't make it he would be remembered for dying from a bullet in the ass.

She finally let him go in the emergency room at South Chicago Community Hospital, but she stayed in the waiting room.

"That's not possible," the doctor had said. Bullet wounds to the neck and hip just did not stop bleeding by themselves. The doctor had attributed Vic's being alive to hand pressure applied promptly at the scene by emergency medical technicians. Vic hadn't argued with him.

EUGENE IZZI

He had plenty of time to think about this in the hospital, healing. His hip was busted up pretty good. But he hadn't bled to death. It was amazing. As soon as he had the strength, he asked for a hand mirror and saw for himself the size of the scar on his neck. Unbelievable. Utterly. It just wasn't possible. But there it was.

And so he'd called the *Times* and told Dooley all about it, what had happened, what he thought had happened, and Dooley had got the exclusive. He'd read the paper the first few days, read everything Dooley wrote, to make sure he kept it accurate and gave Lesco his due. Vic refused to talk to other reporters. Dooley had done a good job, given it a real human-interest angle; he'd really worked hard on his scoop.

And now Dooley owed Vic a big one.

Two days after the shooting, when he felt able to think and speak rationally, the first thing he'd done was call Ray Tomczak's widow and express his sorrow. Naturally, having died a hero, Ray's problems with the OPS hadn't been made public. His death had been a public-relations boost for the MCU. Flynn was really happy about *that*.

Tina told him that her children were bearing up, better than she was, actually. Their father was a fallen hero to them. The phone call had depressed him. But it had been for the best. Tina would get full insurance benefits, a lifelong pension as the widow of a slain officer. She'd never know that her husband's death had been the only thing that had saved them all from disgrace.

But Vic knew. Flynn had made it clear to him. Vic knew now what had happened to Ray Tomczak the afternoon before Ray had come to see him. Flynn encouraged Vic to reflect on the fact that even if Ray had been able to save his hide by rolling over for OPS, he probably would have wound up in an alley with his throat slit, maybe his tongue cut out. Not all the psychos in the city were roaming out of control. Some of them wore badges. And so, for a while, Vic hoped that the news Flynn brought would make him feel better about Ray's death. But it didn't.

Alone now in the hospital room, he felt almost good enough to try and make it to the bathroom on his own. The dope inside him was making him feel slightly depressed, but at least without much pain. Vic stared over at the nightstand. His badge and his regulation gun were inside the top drawer. Where Flynn had left them.

He didn't know if he ever wanted to see them again.

Two of his men dead, another of them in the I.C. burn unit of this same hospital, his hearing fifty-fifty, all his body hair burned off—Vic figured the Mick was lucky. He wondered if Mick would see things that way. He probably would, Vic guessed, he'd figure himself lucky that he hadn't been blinded, at least.

There hadn't been enough left of Lou to put in a casket, but at least he was single. There were no children to grow up without a daddy, as with Ray. It had been only this morning that Vic had been able to call Lou's father and try and express his feelings. He'd been met with a stony silence, and had awkwardly cut the call short. There'd be a dress service for Lou, and one for Ray, and they'd be buried with full department honors. But Vic would not be able to make it. He'd still be here, getting his steel back, recovering from the loss of blood and the banged-up bones and tendons and fibulas and tibias or whatever they were that the bullet had rearranged as it passed through him.

The gun and the badge. Over there in the drawer.

It was Flynn's way of saying all is forgiven. Flynn hadn't mentioned it, but Vic knew the Chief must have worked like hell with him to put the suspension under wraps so that Vic would have a good, solid reason to be carrying an off-duty piece. He knew Flynn had pulled it off, and the apprehension and justifiable killing of Thom Geere would carry the MCU a long way indeed. Shut up a hell of a lot of the MCU's critics. At least for a while. Until the next Ray Tomczak turned up.

South Chicago would be sleeping better.

Bingo could continue, the churches could unlock their doors again, and Tommy Campo's enforcers could go back to overseeing gambling, extortion, and the more traditional kinds of murder that the city could accept.

There was a knock on the door. It was Richland Masterfield, carrying a large yellow folder.

Masterfield came around to shake Vic's hand. He looked down at the bandaged wound on Vic's side. "How you feeling?"

"Can't kick," Vic said.

"Oh, cute, shot up, you lost a couple of quarts of blood, and you got to be Milton Berle." Masterfield pulled the molded plastic chair over to the side of the bed.

"I read in the paper this morning where the Lesco church is getting besieged by the faithful coming from all around the country, looking for miracles. A cop getting healed carries a lot of weight with them, huh?"

"It was the least I could do, Rich. Hell, I had a nicked artery, I was bleeding to death there in the closet, and here I am. You're a doctor, you figure it out."

Masterfield shrugged, enigmatically. "You up for some serious conversation?" he said.

304

"Shoot."

"I just left Claire . . ."

Vic said, "Rich, please—" but Masterfield held up his hand.

"My friend, that is one very sick woman. Her drinking kicked hell out of her these past couple of years, and she would not have lasted much longer. But she's concerned about you, Vic. At first she was withdrawn, as if I were seeing her on Skid Row or something, even though she agreed to see me. Shy, afraid, a little bit. She knew about it, of course, they have papers and television there, and she knew pretty quick that you were going to pull through. She said to tell you she wishes you luck."

"Rich, why did you have to go see her?"

Masterfield seemed surprised at the question. "She's my friend too, you know. Right now she's in even worse shape than you are. At least we know you're going to make it."

That made Vic feel a lot better. Claire *would* make it, this time.

And so, by God, would he. But they wouldn't do it together. It was finally over, and it was time for both of them to start living again.

He waved his hand at the folder in Masterfield's hand. "Geere's service record?"

Masterfield laughed. "Yeah, and Vic, you wouldn't believe what Russell went through trying to find this thing. When we get guys with service-related injuries, we're sent their entire record, from whatever branch they served in. If we kept it in our regular files, we'd have room for nothing else, but there is a huge basement under the hospital. These things are supposed to be in alphabetical order, but you can imagine what it looks like down there, crates and boxes full of records and rat shit. Russell felt so guilty after you left, he had to go down there and find Geere's whole jacket. He thinks he should have seen this all coming when Geere called, made the connection with the nun's murder sooner than he did.

"So he's down there, digging this stuff up, and here comes a rat at him, not afraid, not backing off, out of the box and right at him, and Russell, he, Russell jumps back, screaming, he nearly shat himself." And Masterfield laughed.

So did Vic. And boy, did *that* feel good.

"So what we have here, Vic, is something maybe we should have known about earlier. But we archive the medical records and keep nothing else, so how could we?" Masterfield opened the folder and flipped through it, way in the back, near the records of Geere's last days in the Marine Corps.

"Ah, here it is, Vic, listen to this. Before the fighting, before Geere freaked, he was under house arrest for his suspected part in four rapes in Lebanon. Now, the Lebanese, they were ready to castrate *all* of the Marines behind this, this is not a simple thing over there. The thing is, before any action could be taken, a formal charge brought, the fight happened." Masterfield leaned forward.

"There were three other men suspected of complicity in the rapes. All three of them were shot, killed during the fight. Before the rapes were fully investigated and charges brought."

Vic closed his eyes tightly. When he opened them Masterfield was sitting back in his chair, the file closed.

Vic said, "And as soon as they were shot, Geere

throws down his weapon, pulls the psycho act, and is shipped to a VA ward."

"Oh, sweet Jesus," Vic said.

"He'd done it before."

"Knew how easy it was to kill."

"And get away with it." Masterfield said, "You want me to leave the file?"

Vic shook his head.

"It has occurred to you," Masterfield said, "that Geere was a war veteran, addicted to controlled substances and alcohol, and came home to a world that wanted no part of him, what he represented?"

"What, I'm supposed to feel sorry for him?"

"No, that's not the point."

"What *is* the point?"

"That Geere was just like you." He stood up now and touched Vic gently on the cheek, his farewell. "The difference is, you're good and he was bad. Simple as that." And he started walking to the door.

"Rich?" Vic said, and Masterfield turned, his eyebrows raised.

Vic said, "Whatever you do, don't let Dooley hear you talking like that, or else he'll do a series on 'The Psycho and the Lawman: Differences and Similarities.' " Masterfield left, laughing.

But this time Vic didn't join him.

He stared at the ceiling for a long while. Not angry, not happy or sad. Just thoughtful. Reflecting on what Masterfield had said.

He reached across and pulled open the drawer of the nightstand, wincing, because he had to put a little weight on his backside and suddenly his wound ached like hell, but he made it, grabbed his badge and ID card, and fell back on the bed with a grunt.

EUGENE IZZI

He looked at the badge, the symbols on it. Rich always could make you think. Rich always seemed to know you better than you knew yourself.

Bobby and Franky Meadows would be given a few days off, then be put at a desk for a while, the way any officer pulls desk duty when a partner gets killed. Then they'd be given some time to decide what to do—whether they wanted another MCU assignment, or something else. Something safe and secure, like burglary or regular homicide. Or something. Vic chuckled in spite of his pain, until a thought stopped him.

There were still seven victims out there, their souls waiting for justice—or revenge, depending on what you believed. A lot more would join them, too. More each day. Too many.

There were too few cops.

And here was one, lying on a hospital bed with his ass bandaged up.

Vic put the badge under the pillow and let his head fall back on it, feeling better than he had in a long while, his decision made, when another knock sounded on the door. He looked over at the plastic chair, wondering if Masterfield had forgotten something. But it was Rebeccah.

She stepped into the room, smiling at him, looking as he remembered her from that first time in the church.

Victor Perry smiled back.

She came to the head of the bed and kissed him on the lips, her hand on his chin, holding him there, as if he could get away, or would ever want to. Then she sat down and put her purse on the floor.

Vic met her eyes with his own, no words needed just yet. They both knew what was happening between them.

308

THE EIGHTH VICTIM

After a while, Vic said, "How did I get so lucky?" thinking, it is time to get on with it, start living again.

Rebecca Lesco said, "Maybe it's karma," and took his hand.